THE WOUNDED HEART

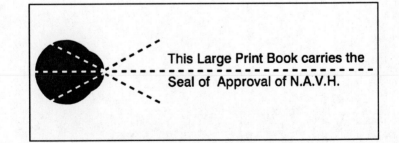

This Large Print Book carries the
Seal of Approval of N.A.V.H.

AN AMISH QUILT NOVEL

THE WOUNDED HEART

ADINA SENFT

KENNEBEC LARGE PRINT
A part of Gale, Cengage Learning

Detroit • New York • San Francisco • New Haven, Conn • Waterville, Maine • London

GALE
CENGAGE Learning·

LIBRARY OF CONGRESS CATALOGING-IN-PUBLICATION DATA

Senft, Adina.
   The wounded heart : an Amish quilt novel / by Adina Senft.
      p. cm. — (Kennebec Large Print superior collection)
   ISBN-13: 978-1-4104-4269-7 (softcover)
   ISBN-10: 1-4104-4269-1 (softcover)
   1. Amish—Fiction. 2. Large type books. I. Title.
PS3619.E6595W68 2012
813'.6—dc23   2011038502

Published in 2012 by arrangement with Faith Words, a division of Hachette Book Group, Inc.

Printed in the United States of America
1 2 3 4 5   15 14 13 12 11

FD350

A 12006 152503

For Karolyn Hudson,
who inspired this book,
and for Marge Burke,
who gave it feet

ACKNOWLEDGMENTS

This book would not have come into being without the help of so many people. My editor, Christina Boys, embraced it before it was even born, and her enthusiasm gave it life. My agent, Jennifer Jackson, championed it when it was just an idea. Marge Burke opened doors for me into the Amish community, while her Aunt Joan helped with facts and encouragement. My best friend, Heather Graham, and my sister-in-law Cindy Bates gave me medical knowledge about their experience with MS, including the T-cell treatment using bovine myelin, and fellow writer Karolyn Hudson was the catalyst of the idea when she told me about her struggle with mercury poisoning.

Thank you to Isobel Carr for her knowledge of what it takes to get a quilt pattern into a novel, and to Cathleen Armstrong and Elaine Goldstone for beta-testing the instructions. To my mother, Carol Douglas, for reading the first draft in one sitting and liking it. And to Timons Esaias of Seton Hill University's M.F.A. in Writing Popular Fiction program, who patiently read many more pages than a mentor should have to, with humor, gravitas, and majestic scorn for the humble colon.

I owe the Amish women of Lancaster County and Smicksburg, Pennsylvania, a huge debt for allowing me into their lives and homes, sometimes only for a moment, so that I could get the details right.

And last but never least, thanks go to my husband, Jeff, who is never without a bookmark in his pocket so he can talk to people about my books. I love you.

But do thou for me, O God the Lord, for thy name's sake: because thy mercy is good, deliver thou me. For I am poor and needy, and my heart is wounded within me.

Psalm 109:21–22 (KJV)

CHAPTER 1

Every piece of fabric held a memory.

Amelia Beiler paused in her sorting of scraps to finger a piece of purple cotton. Sometime last spring in a moment of resolution, she'd cut it up into squares, but she knew every mark. This piece had lain under Enoch's suspenders — the cotton was worn down to the weft threads and half the dye had rubbed away. It had been his favorite shirt — the one she'd made for him in the weeks before their wedding ten years ago. The collar had never sat properly around his neck, so he couldn't wear it to church, and the side seams had a maddening way of twisting to his left. But every time he put it on he'd kissed her and said, "You've wrapped me in love, *Liewi*," and worn it to work in the pallet shop.

She'd learned a thing or two about sewing since then. And about love.

Her lips wobbled and, swallowing hard,

she set the scrap aside. It was really only good for the rag bag. But maybe she'd make a quilt just for herself out of such pieces. After all, the things in the rag bag tended to be what you loved the most and wore out, didn't they? Then she could be wrapped in love, too.

It had been eleven months since the buggy accident had taken him away, but the tears still lived close to the surface where the silliest things would make them well up. The song of the wrens in the trees that woke them on summer mornings. The way his drinking glass still sat next to the kitchen sink, unused, because she always used the glass in the bathroom. His straw hat on the spindle of the rocking chair, as though he'd just hung it there. The wrens still sang and woke her up, and the boys used the glass and the hat, but the fact that Enoch was missing from all of them was enough to make the mourning begin all over again.

Genunk.

She could stand here feeling sorry for herself all day, or she could get all these scraps and squares into her basket and get over to Carrie's. Because it was Tuesday afternoon, and she, Emma, and Carrie would have two blessed hours all to themselves to plan the next quilt. The boys were in school, the pallet shop would run itself without her — she always left David in charge on Tuesdays, never Aaron — and Emma's sister-in-law was probably already at the *Daadi Haus* to spell Emma and give her a bit of a rest from caring for her parents.

Two hours. In that amount of time, you could plan a square, visit and catch up, and remind yourself that you were a woman with a soul that needed feeding.

Amelia laced up her sturdy oxfords — no sneakers on this blustery day on the bare end of October — and wrapped her knitted shawl over her chest, tucking the ends into her black belt apron. She checked that her hair was tucked neatly into her *Kapp* by habit and that its three straight pins — one on the top and one on each side — were in order by feel. A pan of cinnamon buns and two jars of applesauce went into her carry basket, wrapped in plastic and towels. Then she left the house and let herself out the back gate into the fallow field that separated the last of the five- and ten-acre places on the edge of town from the big farms that spread themselves along Edgeware Road.

The air smelled of wood smoke and crab apples, spiced with the tang of frost. Amelia breathed deeply and set her thoughts on

Carrie and Emma and their two hours. If they saw her tear up, they got distressed and fussed with cups of coffee and worried voices. That wasn't what she wanted for their time together. It was sacred to everything light and good, and she wouldn't bring a rain shower in with her if she could possibly help it.

Enoch would understand. He had loved a good laugh and the small moments that God gave a person to appreciate His gifts.

Five minutes' fast walk across the field and a hop across the creek that formed the east boundary of the Stolzfus farm brought her within sight of Emma, who waved from the front porch of the sturdy little *Daadi Haus* as if she were on a train leaving for Philadelphia. She disappeared inside and a moment later ran out the back as Amelia passed the big farmhouse where Emma's sister Karen lived with her husband, John, and their young family. Like Amelia, Emma had a shawl wrapped tightly around her and a big bag suspiciously weighted at the bottom with the rounded shapes of canning jars.

"Hallo," she said as she joined Amelia. "Do you have all your squares ready? I tell you, I've been looking forward to this for days. Our quilting frolics are the only good thing about this time of year."

Amelia opened the access gate between the Stolzfus place and Moses Yoder's pasture and closed it behind the two of them so they wouldn't accidentally let his cows out. "The only good thing? I'd think that finishing up a winter's worth of canned fruit, pickles, and vegetables would be a wonderful *gut* thing. It took me twice as long this year because of having to run the pallet shop. I had to get the boys to help me wash jars and cut beets and apples — otherwise I'd be standing in front of that stove yet."

"All right, two good things."

"And what's wrong with fall? It's my favorite season, with all the colors and things slowing down a bit. Well, except for the —" She stopped. "Oh."

"Ja." Emma kicked a stone out of their path. "Wedding season."

The remains of the Yoder cornfield brushed at Amelia's ankles, sad and brown. "You shouldn't let it bother you, dear."

Emma hauled the strap of her tote bag up onto her shoulder. "That's like telling our creek it shouldn't run downhill. I am what I am, and I get tired of hearing about it, is all."

"You make it sound like you're some kind of strange creature with five legs. There are worse things than staying *leddich*." Like being a husbandless mother with two energetic boys and a business to run. Mothering wasn't the problem — she loved her boys and loved making a home for them. The problem was having to do a man's work on top of it — work for which she had little training and less talent.

"You haven't had Bishop Daniel introduce you as 'the senior single' lately, then, or you wouldn't say so."

Amelia squelched the urge to giggle. She would never hurt Emma by so much as a smile, but — *senior single?* Daniel Lapp had a gift for saying exactly the wrong thing. This wasn't the first time she'd wondered if, by letting the lot fall where it had, the Lord was testing him . . . or the rest of the church.

"You're right," she said at last. "That would be a trial. What did you do?"

"What could I do but smile and hope the woman won't remember me?"

"You might want her to remember you if she has a brother or son in his thirties, with a nice farm."

"Any man in his thirties with a nice farm was snapped up long ago by some *schee Meedel* a foot shorter and fifty pounds lighter than me." Emma walked faster, her

16

eyes on the ground.

"Looks don't matter, and you know it," Amelia reminded her. "The Lord gives everyone different gifts. Yours are a loving spirit and giving hands — and a brain that puts mine to shame."

Emma slowed down enough to slip an arm around Amelia's shoulders in an awkward hug as they crossed the county road and climbed the last slope. They could just see the green roof of the Miller farmhouse through bare branches.

If only there were a way to make Emma see that neither her looks nor anything else about her had to do with her being single at twenty-nine. She was warm, funny, and brave. Amelia could no more write articles for *Family Life* or *Die Botschaft* than sprout wings and fly like a barn swallow, yet Emma picked up her pen and did it. The fact that she signed them "E.S." didn't detract from the nerve it took to speak out on everything from the best way to keep cucumber pickles crisp to why dingle-dangles shouldn't be allowed to hang across the storm fronts of the young men's buggies.

Carrie must have been watching from the window, because she stepped out onto the porch as they walked into the yard, her face glowing with as much happiness as if she hadn't just seen them at church at Moses Yoder's place two days ago. *"Willkumm!"* she called. "I've been waiting for hours, you two."

"So have we." Amelia climbed the steps and hugged her. "There's a lot of hours in a whole summer."

"Come in, come in." Carrie showed them into the front room, where she would set up the quilt frame when they had the top pieced. "Help me move the dining table closer to the window. The sun comes in farther now than it does in June."

"Isn't Melvin here?" Emma picked up one end and Amelia and Carrie took a corner each.

"No. He had to go to Harrisburg to see about winter work, now that the harvest is in." She looked away.

Amelia and Emma exchanged a glance and said nothing. No one ever admitted out loud that Melvin's talents did not include farming. Some men, as Amelia's *Daed* said, were born with dirt under their fingernails. And some, like Melvin, just weren't. Enoch used to casually happen upon Melvin in his fields and offer a helping hand, especially during spring, when equipment inevitably would break down because he'd forgotten to fix it during the winter, or the seed he'd laid in would be moldy, or the horses would get sick and the vet would have to be called out at huge expense.

As a result, he and Carrie were perpetually in debt, and in the slow months he had to go out among the *Englisch* to find work. Sometimes it would take him from home for a week. Once it had even been a month, when he'd taken the train to his cousin's away out there in Shipshewana to work at the RV factory installing upholstery. Amelia wondered how Carrie could bear sleeping alone in the house — why she didn't have one or two of her sisters come and stay with her when Melvin was gone. At least Amelia had the boys to give her home that lived-in feeling. Otherwise the rooms would echo with Enoch's absence and reduce her to hiding under a quilt in his reading chair, rocking and rocking as she prayed for strength.

Carrie adjusted the hand-me-down table until it lay in a square of sunlight, then clasped her hands with sheer pleasure, like a girl. "There. Now we can get started." One thing about Carrie — she might not have much, but at least she had the gift of joy. Their fields might be seas of mud, her washing machine on the fritz, and her cupboards bare of nearly everything for *Kaffi* save for what Amelia and Emma had brought, but her happiness at their mere presence was enough to fill the room.

"So," Emma said, laying out two-and-a-half-inch squares in neat stacks, ordered by color, "have we decided on the piecing? Should we do a twenty-five-square Irish Chain again, like last year? That one was fun."

Amelia pulled out the pile of squares she'd been cutting and hoarding all year and reached over to put them next to Emma's. Without warning, her hand went numb and she dropped the whole thing, squares fluttering to the floor like a drift of leaves after a blast of wind.

She made a rude noise with her tongue and rubbed the circulation back into her wrist. Then she bent to gather the fabric. "Do we have enough shades of lights and darks?" she said from under the table. "We could do a Crosses and Losses, with wide borders. I'd like to try that new style of feathers, where they have them winding around a column in the middle. It's so pretty."

She surfaced to see Carrie looking a little doubtful. "It wouldn't be too *grossmeenich* of us to do that, would it? I wouldn't want anyone saying we were showing off."

"It's not like we're entering it in the county fair to try to win a ribbon," Amelia pointed out. "That *would* be showing off. This is just for us." She lifted her eyebrows, just a fraction.

Carrie said hastily, "Of course. Or maybe we could send it in to the quilt auction in Strasburg next September when they do the big fund-raiser. I like Crosses and Losses. It reminds me of flocks of butterflies."

Emma nodded, unaware that Amelia had nearly given the game away. What Emma didn't know was that she and Carrie had decided on Sunday after church that this winter's quilt would be a wedding present for Emma, should that happy day ever come. Quilting the beautiful feathered borders in the new style would be the perfect way to celebrate the beauty of their friendship as well as whatever skill God had put in the fingers of the three of them. Emma would take their friendship into her new life, covering her when times got hard and nights were cold.

Now if only the good *Gott* would put His infinite mind to providing her with a husband.

While Emma and Carrie nattered about whether the bigger pieces should be darker and the small triangles out of multicolored scraps, or the other way around, Amelia rubbed her hand. Had she pinched a nerve somehow with all that canning? Her middle and fourth fingers were still prickling as if they had pins and needles, but at least now they would bend.

Maybe she should check with Mamm about a remedy for circulation. She'd better do it in the evening, though, and take the boys with her. If she went over on a morning, Mamm would be so delighted that she was actually consulting her about something, she was likely to keep her there all day.

By the end of the first hour, they'd managed to come to some decisions. "I like a quilt that means something," Emma said firmly. "The quilt should say something about the crosses with its lights and darks."

Since it was to be her quilt, Carrie and Amelia nodded. "There are so many choices, though," Carrie said. "What can we say with the colors we have?"

Did *Englisch* women think about these things when they pieced their quilts? Surely they must. The messages in the patterns were half the fun, even if the recipient never knew. The quilter kept her counsel and let her fabric speak for her. Tradition said, for instance, that the center square in a Log

Cabin should be red, to signify the fire in the cabin's hearth. With a Sunshine and Shadow, you started with light colors in the middle, to signify the light of God in the center of life. And the —

Fire. Light. Wait. "*Meine Freundin,* what if we . . . hmm . . ."

Carrie grinned at Emma. "Uh-oh. Amelia's had a brain wave."

Amelia began to lay out squares on the table, folding most of them in half to model the triangles of the pattern. Her heart picked up its pace, like a horse sensing that it was close to home. "What if we shaded the colors from bottom to top? Look." The quilt block grew, and she began another. "In each block we can shade the colors from dark to light, which would shade each row from dark to light. The whole pattern would look like a gradual sunrise, you see?"

Emma snatched up the colorful pile of squares. "You mean like this?"

Amelia could hardly contain herself as Emma's quick eye took in the lay of her squares and triangles and began duplicating it from the other side of the table. This was the part of quilting she loved most — the creation of patterns, the realizing of order from the chaos of bits of memory, all coalescing into a single object of beauty that spoke louder than its individual parts. Something that was utterly practical and yet as unique and lovely as the women who created it.

Carrie fetched a piece of paper and a pencil and sketched the layout as it formed. One time they'd made a new design and tried to rely on memory as they pieced it. That hadn't turned out so well — especially when Amelia brought in her squares and discovered she'd put the whole thing together backward. After that, Carrie usually made a sketch to guide them later, when the thrill of the initial creation had worn off.

"There." Carrie ran a critical eye between sketch and table, then handed the paper to Amelia. "Why don't I make coffee while you look this over? Then if you want to change anything, you can."

Emma got up and rooted in her bag and Amelia's basket, unobtrusively putting jars on the counter as if she meant to open every one and serve up a feast. Then, in the fuss of leaving, she would accidentally on purpose forget to put them back in, and Carrie would have some beautiful golden peaches to offer her husband when he came home from Harrisburg. By the time the coffee had perked and Carrie had served the cinnamon rolls, applesauce, and Emma's chocolate whoopie pies, Amelia had made a few tiny changes to the design and added its borders.

"This will be a good one," she said, tucking it into her basket. "The whole quilt will show the sunrise of our hope in the cross, won't it?" She caught Carrie's eye, and she nodded in satisfaction at a good afternoon's work. "I'll draw copies and get them to you after the Council Meeting on Sunday. Oh, speaking of patterns, I got a circle letter from Katie Yoder up in Lebanon."

"And how is she?" Emma wanted to know. "Does she have any news for us? She said in her last that she was making a baby quilt. If that wasn't a hint, I don't know what would be."

Amelia pulled the bundle of letters from all the girls in their old buddy bunch who were avid quilters. At this time of year, the circle letters went around at twice their usual speed as the women shared what they were working on or traded patterns. "You can read it. I brought them to save a stamp. Mine's already in there."

Emma retrieved Katie's letter and read it in less than a minute. Amelia didn't see how she could do that. It took her nearly a week to read a packet of letters. When Emma got them, she probably read every one of them, wrote hers, and sent the packet on, all in the same day.

"I knew it!" Emma exclaimed. "She had a boy. I hope she went with green borders instead of yellow." She looked up at a sound like the mew of a newborn kitten. "Carrie? Are you all right?"

"I'd be happy with any kind of border," Carrie said quietly. Her cheeks had gone bright red, which made her blond hair look even paler. She blinked, the long lashes that Amelia had often envied becoming slightly wet and spiky with tears.

Emma looked as though she wanted to slap herself. "Oh, dear heart, I'm so sorry. I'm a thoughtless idiot. Of all things to bring up. I didn't mean to hurt you, honest I didn't." She reached across and covered Carrie's hand with her own.

Carrie turned her palm over and returned the squeeze. "I know," she whispered. "Most of the time, I have enough to do that I don't think about it. But when Melvin is gone and it's so silent in the house . . ." She took a deep breath and let it out with only a little bit of a hitch. "That's when it gets to me. At least if I had babies, they'd keep me busy. I'd even welcome crying and fussing, because then I couldn't hear the silence."

"Don't be too quick to wish for that,"

Amelia said wryly. But deep inside, Carrie's words lodged in her heart. Hadn't she just been thinking that very thing?

"But I do. A crying baby would give me someone to hold, you see."

Amelia swallowed. "Babies take clothes and diapers and immunizations. Maybe it's God's will to keep that blessing to Himself for now, until you and Melvin can afford it."

Carrie bent her head as though there were something fascinating in her coffee cup, and she nodded. No one said it, but Amelia knew perfectly well Carrie would give up what little she had if she could only have a baby. When a woman was twenty-eight and had been married for ten years, the fact that babies didn't come only looked stranger with every passing month.

"My mother-in-law was here yesterday," Carrie said in a tone so low that Amelia was glad for the silence in the house — otherwise she would not have heard her.

"All that way and back in one day?" Emma asked in amazement. "Doesn't she live in Intercourse?"

Carrie nodded. "She didn't go back. She's visiting the Daniel Lapps. Mary Lapp is her sister, you know."

"Right. And Mandy's getting married next

week. The first Tuesday in November." Emma sounded perfectly calm. You'd never know what it cost her to say it — seeing that Mandy Lapp was barely nineteen.

"Did you have a nice visit?" Amelia didn't know Aleta Miller very well, except to nod hello to in church when she came down. "I imagine she's coming to help with the wedding."

"She wasn't here about the wedding," Carrie said. "Or not entirely. She had time for a . . . very personal visit."

"How personal, exactly?" Amelia said slowly. This didn't sound good.

"She wanted to know if . . . if everything was all right between Melvin and me. If we were . . . having marital . . . relations."

The clock in the kitchen ticked five times while Emma and Amelia tried to think of something more helpful to say than, *That nosy old biddy — what business is it of hers?*

"What did you say?" Amelia finally managed. She could sort of understand one's own mother asking such a question. Hers had had plenty to say about Matthew's leisurely arrival — as though a two-year wait to see a grandchild was more than a woman should have to endure. But to have your mother-in-law, whom you saw only a handful of times a year, come from twenty miles

28

away to ask such a thing?

When Carrie looked up, the tears had dried, leaving tracks on her cheeks. "I'll have to write her a letter asking forgiveness."

"Oh, my," Emma said. "As bad as that?"

Carrie nodded. "You know how you take it and smile and take some more?" Emma shifted in her ladder-back chair, but Carrie went on without pausing, as if she'd waited so long for this chance to talk that she couldn't wait another moment to get it out. "You walk past your *Mamm*'s buddies and they put their heads together when you're out of earshot, and you just ignore it? Well, by the time Aleta got to our door, I was about full up, and when she opened her mouth and said it straight out, not even trying to put it gently or work around to the subject over coffee, it all came pouring out of me. Like she'd lanced a big, ugly boil and neither of us had a bandage ready."

Amelia could count on the fingers of one hand the number of times she'd seen Carrie angry. Aleta must have hurt her deeply to put this white, strained expression on her pretty face.

"I guess she won't be staying here while she's helping with the wedding, then?"

"Melvin would never understand if she didn't. Which is why I have to write this afternoon, or hitch up the buggy and go over there to invite her back. Not only that, I wouldn't be at peace in Council Meeting on Sunday. You know they're going to talk about forgiveness."

At least she would have peaches to eat with her humble pie tonight. Poor Carrie.

"She wouldn't tell Melvin what you said to each other, would she?"

"I hope not. I have to smooth it over before he comes home Friday. If she's here and still offended at me, then I'll have to tell him what I said to cause it. And I just can't bring myself to do that. He loves his mother, and it would hurt him to know I spoke to her that way."

"*She* spoke to *you* that way," Emma pointed out.

"I know, but I shouldn't have given it back. Most of the time we get on fairly well, but children are a sore spot with both of us."

"Doesn't Melvin have brothers and sisters with lots of babies for her?"

Melvin and Carrie had met at a band hop when they were both on *Rumspringe,* when kids came from as far as fifty miles away to dance and drink and watch each other do what was forbidden at home. It wasn't as though he'd grown up in Whinburg and they'd known his family all their lives. He'd moved here and bought this farm so Carrie would be close to her family. Melvin probably thought he was making a sacrifice for the woman he loved, but in Amelia's mind God knew what He was doing separating Carrie from her mother-in-law.

Except there were separations of distance and separations of emotion. If Carrie didn't close the gap in the latter, it would widen until she'd need more than a trip of twenty miles to heal it. And then how would she be able to take part in Communion next month with a good conscience?

"He does — four brothers and two sisters, and all but the youngest boy are married and having families." Carrie reached over to collect Amelia's empty dessert plate. "That's why I don't understand why she cares so much."

"Maybe he's her favorite," Emma suggested. "My sister Karen is Pap's favorite, and all of us know it."

"I wish Karen would come visit your folks more often." Carrie changed the subject so smoothly and sympathetically that Amelia almost missed it. "She's only on the other side of the lane. It would give you a break."

"I do, too," Emma admitted, making the conversational sacrifice for Carrie. It was

31

clear the latter didn't want to talk anymore about her differences with Aleta, and if that meant that Emma now had to bear the burden of talking about what hurt her, she would do it. "But you know . . . she's busy with her own family and running our place."

"What about Katherine? She could come for a week and let you get away," Carrie said. "She only has the three girls, and the oldest must be ten. Old enough to help with her grandmother."

Amelia buttoned her lip. Only a childless woman would think that three kids under ten would be any help at all in the sickroom after the first hour's novelty had worn off. Not that Emma's father was in a sickroom. But if he got much farther than the barn, he would forget where he was and Emma and her mother would have to go out looking along the roads to fetch him back.

"Mamm would love to see them," Emma went on calmly, "but it's not so easy to get away, I guess."

Carrie was a born organizer, especially when she was organizing other people. "But if each family came for a week out of a month, or took your parents into their homes for a month at a time, you'd have only a few months when you were left to do it completely alone."

Emma shook her head and put a kettle of water on to boil for the dishes. "It wouldn't be fair to Mamm and Pap to be ferried all around the country. Pap has a hard enough time remembering where he is on a place he's lived all his life. How would he manage over in Strasburg with Katherine, or way out in New Hope with Jonas? He'd be upset every minute, and he'd set off down the road to come home not even knowing what direction he was going. It would just be too hard."

"Hmm." Carrie took the dishcloth from Emma's hand and gave her a towel instead. "I'll wash, you dry. It just doesn't seem fair, that's all, you stuck in the *Daadi Haus* caring for your folks with no relief."

"I like how you said that. Caring." Emma's voice held the gentlest of reproaches. "I love them. It's not a burden, not really. Karen comes on Tuesdays so the three of us can have our frolic, and she and John help on Sundays at church, so someone's sitting with Pap on the men's side. And everyone helps clean when church is at our place, so that's no burden either."

She made it sound so reasonable. So straightforward. And maybe she needed it to sound that way, so she could go home again and stay for love, not because God, for reasons of His own, had put rocks in any other path that might be open to her.

Amelia suspected that it wasn't only God who expected Emma to stay home and care for her parents. Everyone did. She was the last remaining unmarried daughter, and had been for enough years that people took it for granted there would be no more courting buggies pulling up in the Stolzfus lane. To everything there was a season, and in the minds of most people in the district Emma's season was past.

There had to be more to a woman's life than that. As she and Emma walked home the way they had come, Amelia pulled up a long stalk of dried grass, its head heavy with seed, and used it as a switch.

There just had to be.

CHAPTER 2

On Wednesday morning the pallet shop opened at nine o'clock. This meant that Amelia got up at six to cook breakfast for the boys. After they ate together, she made their lunches — sausage rolls, fruit, a small jar of homemade apple juice, and a whoopie pie apiece — and packed them in the roomy outer pocket of their backpacks.

"Mamm, I can't find my geography book, and we have to know the capitals of all the states today," eight-year-old Matthew wailed.

"Don't you know them without the book?" Amelia sounded as exasperated as she felt.

"I wanted to look at the map again." Matthew's lower lip trembled. "Miss Hannah said if we got them all right, we could have double recess."

A mad search through the house found the book on the back porch, acting as the roof of a barn for six-year-old Elam's carved animals. Thank goodness it had not rained in the night.

She walked the boys, pushing and shoving each other, to the end of their lane and saw them off on their walk to the schoolhouse half a mile away in the company of the other children from neighboring places. Matthew quit fussing with his brother about the book when they got onto the road, the mantle of responsibility falling on his shoulders like Elijah's cloak. He would see little Elam safely into the school yard no matter what, even if he pushed him into a group of pinafore-clad little girls the second he was inside the gate. And then, after school, they would walk to Daadi and Mammi's and stay there until Amelia came to collect them after work.

How proud she was of Matthew, she thought, turning back down the lane. He was like Enoch that way — serious one minute and pulling a prank on someone the next. Fortunately for both of them, the pranks were never serious or harmful. Short-sheeting some poor newlyweds' new bed had been more along Enoch's line. Nothing like the things she heard went on up north, where a couple had come out of their house the day after their wedding to find their brand-new gas-powered washing machine up on the roof of the barn. It had taken a team of six men and an arrangement of ropes and pulleys to get it down again.

Amelia packed her own lunch pail just the way she'd once packed Enoch's. In fact, it *was* Enoch's. Years ago she'd read articles in *Family Life* deploring the necessity for the lunch pail — which to everyone was the symbol of men leaving the farm to go to work. Their family farms had been split among sons until they couldn't be split any further and still yield enough to live on. Enoch had been one of those. The third son, he'd known that the farm wouldn't come to him. So he'd started up the pallet shop in part of his father's barn. When it had become successful, he'd moved it to a shed on the edge of town, and when he'd earned enough to buy this place, he'd asked her to marry him. They'd been talking about building a shed right here, close to the road, and moving the shop into it when the accident had taken away their future.

Now she walked the two miles into town. Sometimes, if she timed it just right, she could get on the bus when it stopped near the phone shanty on Edgeware Road. And sometimes someone would give her a lift, especially in the winter. But mostly she walked.

She closed the lunch pail and reached for the latches. Her fingers fumbled, going numb and wobbly.

"Not again." For a few seconds, she rubbed her arms briskly, up and down. It had worked yesterday. This time her forefinger decided to behave, and she flipped the latch into place, locking it down with her thumb. Again the third and fourth fingers refused to do anything but prickle. "Well, goodness me." She didn't have time to worry about such nonsense. After shaking her hand as though to dry it, she draped her shawl over her coat and headed off down the lane, walking briskly to ward off the autumn chill.

At the shop she found Aaron King already there, lounging against the door in his *Englisch* clothes.

"Morning, Amelia."

"*Guder Mariye,* Aaron." Hoping to make a point, she didn't return his greeting in English. He slouched into the front office after she unlocked the door, and instead of picking up the small landslide of mail the door had pushed along the linoleum or going straight into the back to start work, he hung around the desk, tapping a stack of business cards until all their edges lined up.

Amelia slid her lunch pail into the cubbyhole under the desk and picked up the mail herself. "Is there something you wanted?" She sat at the desk to fan through it. Bill, bill, order, bill.

"My dad needs me to go up to Bird-in-Hand with him. So I thought I should tell you before we left."

She looked up from the mail in slow motion. "When are you going?"

"Today. Soon as I can get home, probably."

"Today? Did you finish the order of a hundred for that seed company yesterday?"

"No, there's still some left to go."

She would not let him leave her in the lurch again. "Then I suggest you get back there and finish them."

"But —"

"In the time you've stood here working up the nerve to tell me about it, you could have had one made."

"But my dad said —"

"Your dad doesn't sign your paycheck. So if you want one of those, you'll finish the order." She'd never seen him look so flummoxed, his eyes wide under his dishwater-blond brush of hair. "Now, Aaron."

With a mumble that she was just as glad

not to have heard clearly, he fled into the back. Soon she heard the sound of the air nailer going at about three times the rate it usually did.

That would take care of the seed company's order, but it didn't do a thing for the rest of today's work. Building pallets didn't exactly tax the mind, but it was hard labor — and it looked like today she'd be using that nailer herself if she wanted to put a dent in the orders hanging in their metal pockets on the other side of the wall.

Be thankful you have them. Imagine how much worse it would be if there were no orders at all. How would she put food on the table for the boys? Or pay the mortgage? She'd have to move back to the farm with Mamm and Daed. . . . No, no. Better to build pallets with her own hands and have a home of her own, even if it did echo when she was alone in it.

Absorbed in sorting receivables and payables, and wishing she'd paid more attention in mathematics back in her days as a scholar, it took a while for her to realize that the pneumatic whacks of the air nailer had stopped. She stepped into the back and looked around. Lumber, stacks of finished pallets, the hoist, the pallet jack. Tools, neatly replaced on the wall. The air nailer, lying abandoned on the concrete floor next to a trio of studs, its hose snaking over to the gas-powered compressor.

"Aaron?"

Hands on hips, she blew out a long breath, then turned to count the pallets in the stack. Eighty-one. The order had been for an even hundred, so she could assume that number eighty-two consisted of those studs. And the truck was supposed to come today.

"Oh, you are in so much trouble, young man."

She yanked the size-small gloves out of the basket nailed on the wall by the office door and grabbed a set of planks — rough wood that they got from the mill cheap — laying them out in their simple grid. Grasping the air nailer with both hands, she nailed the planks on the studs, then another layer, and, with a grunt, flipped the thing over and nailed down the second side. Though she was supposed to work exclusively in the front office, Enoch had taught her well, and she had it down to a science. One pallet went together every couple of minutes until the remaining nineteen were done. While she wrestled the last finished pallet onto the top of the stack, she heard the roar of a diesel engine as a truck pulled in to the parking area close to the back door.

41

Ach. She'd finished in the nick of time. She yanked off the gloves, checked that her *Kapp* hadn't slid off to hang down her back as a result of her exertions, and dusted grit and splinters from the front of her black apron. The back door was heavy — so heavy that it took both hands and her full weight on it before it began to roll aside.

A set of thick, hairy fingers grasped the outside and gave a mighty heave, and the door rolled all the way open, as meek as a lamb. She stumbled back a few steps, her heart pounding. A man to match the fingers peered into the shop and blinked in surprise when he saw her. "Ma'am?"

Deep breath. He is Englisch, he is a scary one, but he is also a customer. "Thank you. That door is heavy." He was as big as a mountain, but for all his size he seemed even more apprehensive than she as he removed his cap with the seed company's logo on the front. "Are you here to pick up the order for the Lincoln Seed Company?"

"Yes, ma'am. But I didn't know — I mean, I thought y'all were — What I mean to say is, I spoke yesterday to a guy name of David Yoder."

"He works for me," she said briskly, "but he has Wednesdays off. My other helper had to leave, so I finished up the order myself just now. I'm afraid it's still on the floor. Do you have a forklift in the truck? Because if not, we'll have to lift them in the back together."

The man nodded. She was halfway across the shop before she realized he wasn't following her, and she retraced her steps. "Is everything all right? Did I forget something?"

He shook his head, still turning his cap in his hands as though he were trying to reshape it. "I guess I'm a little surprised. I never seen an Amish lady in this part of town before, never mind in here. We been getting our pallets from Whinburg for years. Don't Enoch Beiler own the shop anymore?"

Oh, dear. Oh, dear. "No. Enoch died eleven months ago. I am his widow, Amelia." The man's face paled, and the corners of his mouth turned down in an inverted U. Amelia drew in a sharp breath as she realized how much the blunt truth had upset him. This was different — to be in the position of offering comfort instead of receiving it. "Forgive me," she said. If it had been an Amish man, she might have laid an understanding hand on his arm, but this man was *Englisch,* and she had no idea what he might do. "I didn't realize you hadn't heard."

43

"I'm sorry, ma'am. I'm in — Well, it's a shock." Then she realized that his emotion was not for himself — it was for her. The poor, dear mountain of a man. Any lingering fear she might have been trying to squelch faded away at the sadness in his eyes. "I'm very sorry for your loss. Was he sick?"

She shook her head. "If he had been, we might have been able to prepare ourselves a little. No, it was a buggy accident. A drunk driver crested the hill and didn't see Enoch in the pickup wagon." For the hundredth time, the picture flashed in her head. The headlights, the car, the overturned buggy, the vegetables from her garden scattered all over a neighboring field. She shuddered, trying to block it out. "The other man — boy, really — was killed, too, when his car rolled and threw him out."

If it were possible, the driver's mouth drooped even more. "I'm sorry to make you think about it again, ma'am. Please. Forget I asked."

He was a complete stranger. He was *Englisch.* But in spite of both, his sorrow called to hers — and there was nothing more honest than sorrow. "It's hard not to think of it," she said slowly, surprised at herself for saying such personal things to a stranger. "I don't like working in the shop here, but it does a fine job of keeping my mind occupied."

"You, uh . . . Amish ladies, you don't come out of your houses much, do you? I mean, to work. Of course, I see you driving your buggies all around."

"The shop was Enoch's world, and the house is mine, and there was a time when neither of us knew what to do in the other's," she said. "I like keeping house. We have two boys, you know, and they're a job in themselves." Again his mouth drooped, and she said hastily, "But I've learned to keep the books as well as a home, and I've gotten pretty handy with the air nailer. Your pallets are ready."

Strangely enough, this return to business seemed to reassure him that she was all right. "Just give me a minute to drop the gate and drive the forklift off it."

He was very skilled with the little vehicle, maneuvering in the cramped space as if he'd been working there all his life. Within half an hour, he was signing off on the invoice and helping her roll the door shut.

"You got a nice operation here." He looked the building up and down, with the tidy stack of lumber waiting outside until it was needed. On the other side of the fence was the Steiner family's cabinetmaking shop, and on the far side another branch of the Lehmans who were no relation to her parents kept a freezer place, where families could bring their meat after slaughter and rent a freezer to store it.

His gaze got back around to her. "Ever think of selling?"

Caught off guard, Amelia flailed for an answer and couldn't find a single one.

He went on, "You could get a fair price for it, I bet. Whinburg's a nice town, with good house prices. A man wanted a neat little business to retire on, he could do a lot worse."

"Are . . . are you speaking of yourself?" Only the *Englisch* retired. An Amish man handed the farm's main responsibility over to his sons and kept on helping them. Only when he was too old to work did he watch the proceedings from his front porch, and even then, more often than not, his boys would come to him of an evening for advice and counsel on their decisions. Stewardship of the land didn't just go away when you were sixty-five.

"Maybe," the man said. "If you didn't want to go on with it, I'd make you a fair offer."

And then, money in hand, what would she

do? "I don't know. I never thought of such a thing."

"No hurry. I used to be in this area a lot, but not so much lately. Even Whinburg is growing and changing." He dug in his pocket and handed her a dog-eared card with the seed company's logo and BERNARD BURKE, OPERATIONS MANAGER printed on it, along with a telephone number and a Hershey address. "If you come to a decision, just give me a call." He stopped. "You have a phone here, don't you?"

"We do here. Just not at home."

"Right. You have to get permission for that?"

She nodded. "But it's a fact of life that a business nowadays needs a phone. We don't have them in our homes, though. It's too intrusive, and it would be too easy to spend all day talking and not working."

"I s'pose. I hate the phone myself. I'm a lot better over e-mail. Do you have that?"

"No computer. I do the books in . . . books."

He grinned at her. "I guess it worked for our grandparents, didn't it? Well, you have a nice day, now. And I'm sorry about Enoch. He was a fine man. About the only one hereabouts who appreciated my jokes."

She smiled, and he climbed into his truck.

47

With a last wave out the driver's window, he pulled away and rumbled off up the road toward the highway. She let herself in through the back door next to the big rolla-way doors. In the office she dropped his card in the top left drawer with a bunch of others from salesmen and customers.

A fair offer.

She should have asked him how much "fair" was.

No. There was no point. She had to live on something, and even if she got a good price for the shop, eventually that would run out. And then what would she do? Buy another shop?

Dear Father Gott, is this really Your will for me? Getting blisters through my gloves from wrestling that nailer day after day? What is Your plan for me, Lord? I once thought my life was in Your hands, laid out from beginning to end, with nothing but happiness and good, satisfying work for my family and Your glory in store. Now I feel as if I'm drifting, and I don't know what direction is right anymore. Help me, Father.

Amelia opened her eyes and found herself gazing straight down into the drawer.

Then she took the card off the top of the pile and shoved it into the pocket of her black dress.

■ ■ ■ ■

"A fair offer?" Ruth Lehman, Amelia's mother, dug into the baking pan of apple crumble a little harder than she had to and dropped a large helping into young Matthew's bowl. "What a forward, presumptuous man."

She put a helping only a little smaller into a second bowl, then poured cream over both, jabbed spoons into them, and set them in front of the boys. Matthew and Elam shoveled in their dessert with much more enthusiasm than they'd shown over their cabbage slaw and pork chops and emptied their bowls in seconds.

Amelia took hers and enjoyed the first bite, rich with fresh cream, while her mother chased the boys outside and dished up a second helping for Daed.

"Don't be so quick to judge the man, Ruth," he said in his slow, thoughtful way. "You can't fault him for being interested in a good opportunity."

"I can fault him for not minding his own business. He already has a job with this seed company, while there's men like Melvin Miller having to travel days on the train just to find work."

"Melvin doesn't have the money to buy the shop." Amelia only said what everyone already knew. "Not unless he sells his farm, and if he did that, he and Carrie would have to live in the office and sleep on the desk." She already regretted opening her mouth, but she really did want Daed's opinion on what to do.

Mamm had lots of opinions, but they were rarely useful and sometimes irrelevant to the problem at hand. If she gave two seconds' thought to anything but herbs and physicks, or the running of her house, Amelia would be surprised. Daed was the thoughtful one. She was glad she'd taken after him. If she were like her mother, she'd probably have lost the shop long ago.

"What do you think is a fair price, Daed?"

He lifted a shoulder, clearly enjoying the second bowl of crumble as much as the first. "You might have asked him. But I can see why you didn't. A man is likely to make a woman a low offer just to see if she knows better."

Mamm snorted. "In courting, too."

Amelia didn't let herself be sidetracked. "He didn't seem like that kind of man. He seemed honest."

"With worldly folk you never know." Briskly, Mamm dished up her own helping and sat down. "That's why it's better to sell to an Amish man, if you're going to."

"I'm not going to sell to anyone, Mamm. And I don't want you talking about it like I am. The man asked a simple question, and I didn't have an answer, so I came to get Daed's opinion, that's all."

"A business like that is worth eighty or ninety thousand, I would think," Daed said. He scraped the last of the pudding out of the bottom of his bowl and licked the spoon with satisfaction. "You could do worse."

"Yes, but what would I do with what I got for it?"

"The bank would be happy if you gave them some of it."

"I'm sure they would, but even if I paid off our place, what then? I can't put food on the table with nothing."

"That's easy," Ruth chimed in. "Get married again."

Amelia fought the urge to push back from the table, collect the boys, and walk away into the dark. It took her a moment to master herself and answer quietly.

"I'm not ready to marry again, Mamm. I might have a month left in black, but in my heart I'm still grieving as though it happened last week."

"In time you may feel different," Ruth said mildly.

"By then we'll have all starved to death."

"No one will be starving." Daed's gaze reproached her for being lippy to her mother. "You still have us. You and the boys will always find a welcome here no matter what happens."

She knew it. Daed and Mamm and the farm she'd grown up on were the bedrock of her life — the things she could count on, like the sun coming up and the apple trees blossoming in April. Just last week at church, she'd seen her two brothers and her sister gathered around their parents as though they were warming themselves at the stove. No matter how far apart they spread or how many children of their own they had, they still came back, sometimes for an evening like this one, sometimes for a work frolic at harvest time, and always, always on the Saturday when it was the Lehmans' week for church. Then twenty years would drop away and it was like being kids again, bossed from one end of the yard to the other by both parents as they organized the work party to get the place trim and sparkling for Sunday.

"I know, Daed, and it comforts me. But it isn't really practical, you know. I like having my own home."

"You like having things all your own way," Mamm corrected her around a mouthful of crumble.

"That, too," Amelia conceded. Daed smiled — he knew her well. She answered with one of her own and went on, "But when Mark takes over next year, you'll find things a little too tight in the house if the boys and I are here yet."

Her eldest brother, Mark, had gone off to western Pennsylvania to buy a farm fifteen years ago and much to the delight of Adah, her sister-in-law, had been so homesick for Whinburg Township and his family that he'd sold up and decided to buy into the home place with Daed. By this time next year, there would be half a dozen children playing in Daadi's hayloft and being unwilling guinea pigs for Mammi's latest herbal recipe.

Ah, well. Those recipes hadn't hurt her any, except for that one time when Ruth had made Amelia drink a glass of apple cider vinegar mixed with honey for a cold and she'd *gakutz*ed the lot into the sink five minutes later.

Which reminded her . . .

"Mamm, do you have anything in your medicine chest for circulation problems?"

Ruth perked up like a retriever spotting a shotgun. "What kind?"

Amelia rubbed her hands. "I've been getting pins and needles in my hands for no reason, it seems. The latest one was this morning, when I was getting ready to go to the shop. Even now these two fingers feel like they're going to sleep." She massaged the third and fourth fingers of her left hand.

"Let me see." Ruth took her hand in both of her work-worn ones and rubbed them briskly. "Does this help?"

"I tried that. It does for a little while, and then it happens again. My hand goes numb and I drop things."

"Sounds like a pinched nerve. Maybe in your shoulder."

"But my shoulder doesn't hurt."

"It doesn't have to. It just shuts off the circulation. Dr. Shadle explained it all to me."

Mamm had the kind of faith in her chiropractor that people should reserve only for God. His word was law in her mind, every pronouncement written there in indelible ink. Amelia would think her mother a tiny bit soft in the head if Daed didn't share her opinion. She couldn't remember a single occasion when either of her parents had been to a regular doctor for themselves.

There'd been trips to the emergency room for her brothers, of course, and one for Amelia that time she got food poisoning (she had not eaten any of Mary Lapp's pickled herring since, not once). But her parents either took care of themselves or went to Dr. Shadle.

"You should make an appointment for this week," Ruth told her. "Meantime I'll give you a mustard poultice for your hands, to make the blood flow better."

"Mamm, I don't think —"

"Don't think. Just wait." Ruth hurried the dessert dishes into the kitchen sink and shut herself in her workroom, which had once been the enclosed back porch. Amelia went out to the boiler to get a pan of hot water. Ugh. Mamm's poultices were not just goopy, they usually smelled awful, too.

A few minutes later, Ruth sat her down at the table and wrapped her hands in cheese-cloth soaked in mustard and who knew what else. *Ach,* Amelia choked, twisting her head away and trying to breathe over her shoulder.

"Never mind your noise," Ruth chided. "It's only ten minutes. Any longer and the essence of mustard might burn you, and then you'd be worse off than you are."

She could at least try to sound sympathetic. But Ruth was a little like Daniel Lapp — words went straight from mind to mouth with no stops in between. Especially when it came to her remedies. And yet people didn't seem to take offense. More often than not, when Amelia was walking down the lane after work, someone would be coming up it with a plastic bag full of herbs or looking for some mixture to treat this ache or that pain. She might drive Amelia to distraction, but Ruth had a real reputation as a *Dokterfraa.*

Of course, if a person believed that a mustard plaster would bring her hands back to life, then maybe it would.

After the ten minutes of trying to breathe, Amelia stood at the sink washing her hands and arms all the way up to the elbows. Her hands tingled and burned a little, but under the hot water they still didn't move properly. She'd stop in at the phone shanty and call Dr. Shadle's office. Anything was better than this perpetual needley feeling in her fingers — not to mention the sudden numbness and lack of control. What if she went to cuddle someone's baby on Sunday and dropped it?

No. She'd get this taken care of, and that would be the end of it. She had too much to do to be bothered with such things.

The only pins and needles she wanted were the kind that went into a quilt.

CHAPTER 3

The sermon and testimony at Council Meeting served one purpose — to prepare the congregation's hearts for forgiveness. As a child, Amelia had taken this very seriously, once even going to her brother Mark to ask forgiveness for taking his skates without permission. Since she'd managed to break a blade off one of them by accident and then hidden the evidence, he had a hard time accepting her apology until Mamm had intervened. Then, when Amelia was married, she found that the giving and receiving of forgiveness was a little like exercise. You didn't enjoy having to do it, but once you did, it got easier — and you learned to need it.

Maybe that was what the Bible meant by being "exercised in the spirit."

The second part of the service put the first one into action. When Bishop Daniel spoke aloud his willingness to take part in Communion in two weeks and asked forgiveness of the *Gmee* for any of his offenses in word or deed, Amelia glanced at Carrie. When the minister approached her for her affirmation of readiness, what would she say? Melvin had come home Friday, but Amelia hadn't seen Carrie to find out if the quarrel between her and Aleta had been repaired.

Since Amelia was older and sat closer to the front, she did her part and then listened with all her might to the quiet words passed back and forth in the rows behind her.

"In . . . in all my weakness, I wish to participate." She finally heard Carrie's familiar voice, pitched so low she would have missed it if anyone had coughed or sneezed. "If I've offended anyone, I hope they will admonish me in love, so I can make things right with God's help."

Amelia sat back with a sigh that was one part relief and one part empathy. It could not have been easy to take the humble place with Aleta and apologize first. But Carrie had obviously done it, or she could not say those words. Amelia would have to give her a special hug sometime today.

After the service, no thanks to Ruth's poultice, it turned out that Amelia did not drop anyone's baby — but then, with Carrie around, a person hardly had a chance to get her hands on one anyway.

"If ever a woman was born to be a mother, it's Carrie," Emma said softly when they were helping the Grohl girls set the tables for first sitting. The Grohl house was large enough for the service, but seating was tight for the meal afterward when they put up the tables. So they had two sittings, one for the men and one for the women.

Amelia put down plates the length of the table with the regularity of a clock, Emma matching her on the other side. "I know that people are sorry for her. She must feel it."

"Is that so bad? You don't want her proud, do you, and finding a reason to be offended? Not after what she's just gone through with Aleta Miller?"

"No, of course not. God has heard both our prayers on that score. Maybe I'm just putting my own feelings into Carrie's heart. She's such a transparent person — whatever she feels shows right on her face."

"I hope we find out the whole story on Tuesday."

"Me, too." *Wait a minute.* "Emma, Mandy's wedding is Tuesday. Aren't you going?"

Emma straightened a pair of salt and pepper shakers so that they sat exactly in the center of the table. "Do you know there are no fewer than five weddings set for that day?"

Amelia did a quick count. "Six if you're in my family — my niece up in Smicksburg is getting married then, too. I think Chris and Esther are going, but I can't spend a whole day on trains and vans with the boys just to have to turn around and come back the next day for the shop."

"They'll come for a wedding visit anyway, won't they?"

Amelia nodded. Newlyweds spent the first year of their marriage visiting family and friends, and Mark's girl Emily and her new husband would almost certainly spend the better part of a month in Whinburg when they came. "Most of the family is here, and next year Mark will have moved back."

"She should have waited a year, then."

Amelia had to smile. "That girl has never waited for anything. She even came a month early when she was born."

Emma sighed and moved away to the next table. Amelia could practically hear the unspoken words hanging in the air. *And some of us wait and wait and no one ever comes.*

Or if someone does come, he doesn't stay. Amelia wished her niece everything that was good and right, but there was no getting around the fact that wedding season was going to be hard this year.

And not just for Emma.

Monday was washday, when Sunday clothes were made clean again and ready for Communion Sunday in two weeks. Sheets and towels and workaday aprons, too, the boys' pants and shirts — everything. And since Amelia also had to open the shop at nine as usual, that meant she got up at four on Mondays in order to have everything on the clotheslines — indoors and out — by the time the boys got up at seven.

They had their chores, like chopping kindling, filling the wood box, making their beds, and sweeping the floors. Technically those last were Amelia's, but she saw no harm in having the boys know a few household skills. People who brought dirt into the house ought to know how to get it out again. Enoch had always swept out the mudroom and the porch. When her brothers were boys, they had gotten hold of a library book about knights and jousting, and their mother had an awful time keeping the broom and mop in the closet where they belonged. Many a mock battle had been fought on the lawn until Ruth had declared her kitchen closet off-limits unless they used the contents for their real purposes.

At the shop both Aaron and David were already waiting, as were orders from two Lancaster companies who shipped kitchen appliances. With the sound of the nailer and David's hammer lending a syncopated punctuation to the scratch of Amelia's pen, the morning went quickly.

When she saw someone tying up a horse at the rail in front, she hurried to finish the last column of numbers. Without warning, her fingers lost their strength and the pen did a backflip onto the page.

That did it. Tomorrow morning she was making that appointment. And now she'd lost her train of thought, made an ugly mark across the ledger, and would have to total the column again.

She looked up as the November wind blew a man into the office. He shut the door behind him and settled his black winter hat more firmly on his head. "*Guder Mariye.* Is something wrong?"

"I'm sorry?" She stood to greet him, rubbing her pesky hand.

"You look as though you're angry at something. I hope it isn't me." He smiled, and her frustration faded as she realized that the customer was behaving more hospitably than the shopkeeper.

"No. No, it wasn't you at all. I'm sorry. Can I help you?"

"I don't doubt that you can, but perhaps I ought to speak to the proprietor."

Amelia had this conversation at least once a week. The practiced words rolled off her tongue much more easily with someone in familiar clothes than they had with poor Bernard Burke, Operations Manager. "I am the proprietor, since my husband passed away." She held out a hand, and he shook it. He had a nice handshake — firm, but not too much, like some who were careful to make their point about a woman's weakness in a man's world. "I'm Amelia Beiler."

"Eli Fischer. I'm sorry. I didn't expect to meet a sister in a pallet shop."

"Not many people do. The boys —" She gestured toward the back. "— do most of the heavy work, though I help when it gets busy. Now, what can I do for you? Have you come from far?"

"From Lebanon County, now you mention it. I'm here for the Lapp wedding."

"Mandy or William?"

"Mandy. Her mother, Mary, is my cousin. Our grandmothers were sisters."

Amelia tried to sketch the Lapp family tree in her head but couldn't quite see how closely Aleta Miller and this man might be related. "Are you staying with the Lapps?"

He laughed. "I love them all, but only a small fraction will fit in the house, as big as it is. No, I'm staying with a longtime friend — my cousin Martin King. I believe his boy Aaron works for you."

In a manner of speaking. "Yes, he does. Were you and your family at the Grohls' for church yesterday?" How had she missed them?

"I was. No family with me."

Her first impression of someone older had been mistaken. As he spoke, Amelia realized he probably hadn't seen his thirtieth birthday.

Oh, my. Emma needed to go to Mandy's wedding. Amelia would walk over there as soon as the boys were in bed and convince her.

He went on, "I'm thinking of moving over this way. You wouldn't happen to know of a nice place coming up for sale, would you?"

"Are you a farmer?"

"That's what I'm doing now, but it's a big job for one man. My two brothers want to take over, so I was thinking of selling out to them and taking a ramble to a different part of the country. As a matter of fact, I heard that maybe this shop might be coming available sometime. Is that so?"

Amelia gripped the edge of the desk. She knew she should have talked to Daed out in the barn. It had been a big mistake to say anything about the shop in front of her mother.

"Where did you hear that?"

"A few people mentioned it after church. I don't know how interesting it is to you ladies, but something like that gets chewed over pretty well among the men out in the barn, even on Sunday."

Hmph. "It was lucky you happened to be there."

"That depends on whether it's true."

Amelia teetered, forced into a decision she wasn't ready to make. She had to shut the rumor down now, while it was just a trickle, or it would become a stream, and then the torrent of the community's will would sweep her along until she submitted herself and did what it wanted.

"I don't know," she admitted at last. "I haven't decided. I'm like the colt tied where two ways meet."

"And where are the two ways going to and coming from?" Eli pulled up a straight wooden chair and made himself comfortable, as if he were settling in for some time. "Maybe it would help to talk it over."

Look what talking had done so far. But he

wasn't going anywhere until she gave him something to take with him. She followed his example and resumed her seat behind the desk. "Well, down the one way, I can pay off our place." He nodded, his grave gaze resting on her with attention. "But it's a dead-end road, because then I'll have no way to support my boys and no money left over to start another business."

"Depends on the business. You could sell fruit and vegetables from your garden, like some of the other ladies."

"Anything more than my half-acre kitchen garden is too much for one person, even if the rest of it's only five acres. You've found that out yourself."

"And what's down the other road?"

"I could sell our house, sell the shop, and move back to the home place with my parents. But that would only last for a year, because my eldest brother is moving home next year with his wife and family."

"That wouldn't be so good," he agreed. "Three women in one household."

"Exactly. But there's a third way. A path that isn't really real. It comes and goes when I look at it too hard." Oh, goodness, where had that come from? Why was she being such a *Plappermaul* with this man? Was she really going to tell him the thing she and

67

Enoch had talked over in the privacy of their bedroom?

He raised his eyebrows. What nice eyes he had — dark brown, with crinkly corners, as though he found a lot of humor in the world. Would he find humor in a dream that would never come to pass?

He was still waiting for her to speak, and she couldn't get out of it now. "I could do what my husband and I dreamed of, which is to move the shop onto our place. Build a nice work barn. It would still be a lot to run the business, but I wouldn't have four miles to walk every day. In the winter it gets hard, because I have to drive, which means I have to put the horse somewhere, usually next door with the Steiners' animals." She took a long breath. "I don't want to be a lunch-pail mother. I want to be home for my boys, where I belong."

He didn't laugh. He considered it seriously, frowning as though he were turning it over in his mind. "It sounds like a good plan. It would take a bit of money, though."

She nodded. "I know. That's why it's just a dream right now." She had a little money in the bank, but not enough to build a proper working barn. And with a mortgage already on the place, the loan officer probably wouldn't look too kindly on her asking

68

for another one.

"You could go in with a partner."

She hadn't thought of that. She hadn't really thought of any of this before this week — and she didn't like having to think of it now. "I suppose."

He was silent a moment. "So my coming to see you this morning is probably an imposition. I'm sorry for that. I shouldn't have listened to rumors. Too soon old, too late smart, I guess." This time his rueful smile was directed at himself.

"You're not the first person to ask. I think that's how the rumor got out — last week an *Englisch* man asked me the same question. I didn't know how to answer *him* either. But he left me his card."

"I don't have a card."

Now it was she who smiled. "You're different. I don't need a card to remember you." Then she realized how that must sound, and her still in black. Heat flooded her cheeks. "I mean, you're a Lapp connection and we'll see you at the wedding tomorrow."

"But your situation won't change by tomorrow, I bet."

"At least I know your family. If things change later, they can get word to you." She wondered if Bernard Burke had a family.

He had referred to himself as "a man," not as "us" or "we."

But Bernard Burke was not her business. Not yet, and maybe not ever.

Eli Fischer got to his feet and held out a hand again. "I'll be on my way, then. Just wanted to let you know I was interested, if you do decide to sell."

She shook his hand. "I have to pray on it, Eli. If the Lord has a plan for me, it's best I wait on Him and find out what it is."

"Better to wait on Him than on Whinburg. If it's like my district, folks will be only too happy to give a person direction, whether God has prompted them to or not."

A laugh sprang out of her like a pheasant flushed from a thicket, surprising them both. "Are folks as interested in your business there as they are in mine here?"

"At least as interested. Which is interesting, since I'm a pretty dull fellow."

She doubted that very much. "We'll see you at the wedding tomorrow, then." *I have a friend I want you to meet, and that twinkle in your eye will certainly interest her.*

"*Ja*, you will." He went out the door, and the wind, tricky as ever, blew the rest back to her. "You certainly will."

"I certainly won't."

70

Emma pushed away from the kitchen table and took her pie plate to the sink. She ran warm water and squirted some soap in after it. Unlike Carrie's kitchen, which had water plumbed in but no propane hot-water heater, the Stolzfus *Daadi Haus* had that and other conveniences, too. Like a gas-powered generator in the basement for her mother's oxygen machine, and the phone shanty located just at the end of the lane in case of emergency. Sure, everyone on Edgeware Road used it when they needed to, but Emma had the shortest distance to run.

"His name is Eli Fischer, and he was very nice. And single. He's looking for somewhere to settle, and if he meets a nice girl, he'll be more likely to stay here."

"Then *you* chase him."

Amelia nearly choked on her coffee. "Who said anything about chasing him?"

"Didn't you always say you chased Enoch until he caught you?"

"I did not."

"No? Hmm. Must have been someone else. Maybe your *Mamm* is right. There's nothing stopping you from marrying again."

Taken aback by her tone, Amelia firmed her resolve. "Don't make this about me. I have no desire to marry again, and you know it. I've had my chance, and I don't

71

need another. I have the boys to think of now."

"Ruth will be the first to say that young boys need a father."

"Yes, well, Mamm doesn't get to make that decision. They're doing just fine." Now was not the time to share the tornado-size tantrum that Elam had pitched over going to bed tonight and how she'd nearly cried with missing Enoch, who had been so good with him. She'd been lucky to get over here at all. "But we were talking about you. Please come to the wedding with me. There's room on the seat beside me. I'll even let you drive."

Emma did not appreciate her attempt at humor. "I drive everywhere. I'm not going. If I do, and for some reason he speaks to me, everyone will say I'm chasing him. If he doesn't, they'll say it's because I'm so *mupsich*. I'll do us all a favor and leave him to the *Youngie*. He's too young for me anyway, if what you say is true."

"You look the same age."

"It doesn't matter. I'm going to Sarah Zook's wedding."

"By yourself?"

"If Mamm is feeling well enough, she'll go with me. The oxygen tank will fit right between us."

"And if she's not?" Amelia pulled out the verbal equivalent of the air nailer. "Are you sure you want to walk into the meal alone when the bride has been busy pairing off the courting couples all around you? Do you really want to sit with the oldsters and talk about the latest methods of Dr. Shadle?"

Carefully, Emma put her pie plate on the drainboard. Maybe it was because she wanted to throw it at her best friend.

Amelia softened her tone. "Please come with me. I could use some help with the boys."

"Ruth always helps you." Emma's voice sounded broken somehow, and Amelia got up and put her arms around her.

"I'm sorry, *Liewi.* Don't come for him, then, if you don't want to. Come for me, because I need you."

Emma sighed, then straightened, and finally, reluctantly, hugged her back. "All right. But only because that Elam has me wrapped around his little finger."

With a quick rush of happiness, Amelia squeezed her and went back to the table. "I'm so glad. We'll be there for each other. Because you know Mamm is going to have her eagle eye on me and poor Eli Fischer, too. She might even wangle an introduction. If she does, you have to save me."

"If anyone can save herself, it's you," Emma said, arching one eyebrow in her direction. "Just hope no one tells her he was at the shop. You'll never hear the end of it."

Wasn't that the truth. "I knew I should have duct-taped Aaron King's mouth before he left tonight." She tried to snap her fingers in mock dismay, and they went numb. The snap turned into a feeble wave.

Oh, for goodness' sake. To the phone shanty she would go on Wednesday, and no mistake. She'd take the first opening Dr. Shadle had, even if she had to close the shop. But first she had a wedding to get through.

CHAPTER 4

Mandy Lapp made a beautiful bride in her white organdy apron and cape over a new blue dress. And Mary Lapp made a happy mother-in-law as the groom and the last of her daughters said their vows to Bishop Daniel. Amelia wondered whether Mary would hire a teenage girl as a *Maad* to help with the gardening and housekeeping now that Mandy would have a home of her own. But then Mary was one of the most efficient women Amelia had ever met. She could probably keep up with both on her own — and take Saturdays off to relax on the porch and survey her kingdom.

It would be nice to hire one of the girls as a *Maad*. But what would Mamm say? She had firm opinions about a woman's place, which would set her off on the subject of marrying again, and Amelia could not bear it. The very thought made her feel disloyal to Enoch, and it would hurt his parents dreadfully if they thought her eye was wandering before she'd even taken off her black.

The last verse of the hymn that brought the five-hour service to a close was the signal for the helpers to get up and make their way to the house to put the final touches on the food and begin bringing it out to the shed. Amelia remembered a time when, as a young wife, she would have been among them and, before that, as a teen girl, lingering around the *Eck* and admiring the pretty decorations, hoping a boy would notice her. But now her place was making sure Matthew didn't stick a finger in the cakes to taste the frosting or Elam didn't fall out of the haymow trying to keep up with the bigger boys' games.

While the young men rearranged the benches and made a huge commotion setting up the tables, Mandy and her new husband went outside onto the lawn, where she was soon engulfed in a crowd of *Youngie,* all vying for her attention as she paired them off for dinner. The smart ones had written her in advance. The bashful ones had to get her attention now or find themselves sitting with their buddy bunch while the boy or girl each of them liked was taken by someone else. Of course, a boy's special friend made good and sure she sat with him and no one else.

"Here I am," Emma said quietly in her ear. "If Sarah Zook gets offended that I didn't come to her wedding, I'll send her to you."

"It's the bishop's daughter," Amelia murmured. "How could she be offended? Did both your folks come? Your mother? We could all sit together."

"Pap has a hard time with this many. Church is one thing, but there have to be six hundred people here. Good thing the Lapps have a big shed."

"With five daughters, Daniel Lapp probably started building it while they were still in school."

To her relief, Emma smiled. "Nothing like planning ahead."

"But your folks are well? Who's looking after them?"

"Katherine and her family finally came for a visit. She was worse than you about pushing me out the door. Said it would look bad if our family wasn't represented. Though how anyone would notice in this crowd is beyond me."

"I'd notice." Amelia squeezed her arm and took a firm grip on Elam's little hand. On the other side of the shed, she saw Matthew wrap his arms around his Daadi's waist and go with him. He'd be well looked after until the *Zucker* in the desserts took over, and then he'd go find his school friends, after which she didn't hold out much hope for his good suit. "Come on. Let's find a seat."

The *Ordnung* in their district was lenient about seating arrangements at weddings. Instead of men on one side and women on the other, as it was during a normal meal after church, people mixed it up and families and friends sat together, relatives visiting and catching up on the news since the last wedding or funeral.

Perhaps this was why Amelia, Emma, and Elam found themselves sitting close to the enormous King connection. Maybe it was God's hand, gently guiding them where they should go. Or maybe it was simply her instincts as a matchmaker. Whatever it was, Amelia looked up to see Eli Fischer taking the place next to Aaron King's parents, directly across the table from her and Emma.

If she were a giggling woman, she might have done so from sheer delight. But since she was not, she merely smiled and made the introductions instead.

She wanted to glance to her right to see if Emma showed the slightest sign of interest,

78

but Daniel Lapp raised his hand and the crowd bowed their heads in a silent grace. And by the time the clatter of cutlery on plates and the passing of food began, it was too late. The moment that would have told her the truth before Emma's diffidence covered it up had passed.

Ach, well. It was her duty to help her friend along if she possibly could. If it was God's will that these two were marked out for one another, nothing she could do would stop it. If not, then at least she would have protected poor Eli from the girls looking at twenty-five with such horror that they'd accept a ride home after the wedding from anything in pants.

"So, Amelia Beiler," Martin King began, passing her a bowl heaped with creamy white potatoes, "the rumors of your selling the pallet shop, are they true?"

Goodness. Since Eli was staying with the Martin Kings, she would have thought he'd have gone home and told them what was what. But on the other hand, it was good to know he could keep a conversation to himself.

Awkward for her at this moment, but good.

"I'm not sure yet," she told Martin. She helped Elam to some potatoes and then took two. She loved them steamed like this, with good pork-roast gravy. "Until I find some other way to support myself and the boys, the answer will probably be no."

"I could think of a way." Martin laughed and gave Eli an elbow in the ribs.

Amelia could feel the blood seep into her cheeks. *I will not blush. I will not let him see I have any idea what his silly joke is about.*

"Are you in town for long, Eli?" Emma asked smoothly, passing him a huge bowl of mashed turnips, as golden as the butter melting on top of the mound.

"Not long. I'm here visiting Martin and his family, and I'm invited to not one but two weddings in Whinburg on Thursday. Quite a crop of those this year, isn't there?"

"Lots of *Youngie* hereabouts." Amelia's admiration for Emma's imperturbable calm rose to new heights. How could she keep from coloring up when everyone knew what a sore subject this was? Emma went on, "Whose weddings on Thursday? My sister and her husband went to Sarah Zook's today, and we were going to go with them, but I told Amelia I'd help her with the children."

"We?"

"My parents and I. They're getting old,

and Pap doesn't do so well in crowds anymore."

"Ah. Well, there's Young Joe Yoder's second-youngest boy and Old Joe Yoder's last granddaughter before the great-grandkids started coming. My great-aunt married Old Joe's brother, so you see I had to be invited."

Again Amelia surprised herself by laughing. His eyes crinkled with good nature more than the prospect of the Yoder guest list, which could very well be double the size of the Lapps'. Old Joe had had eleven siblings, after all, and his wife had ten. No one, not even Old Joe, could keep track of the number of nieces, nephews, and grandchildren he had. But it explained, as Mamm often said, why you tripped over a Yoder every time you stepped out the door.

"How are you going to get to both?" Martin wanted to know.

"Easy. I go to the service for one and the supper for the other. That way each group thinks I was there the whole time and they just missed me in the crowd."

"Until they get together and compare notes," Martin's wife, Anna, pointed out. "You might be in trouble then."

"Who is going to waste their time comparing notes about me?"

Anna just looked at him as if he were daft. Only every single woman on both sides of the connection, that was who. Amelia caught her eye, and they exchanged a smile. He might be clueless on that subject, but it showed his modesty, too.

Martin reached for a stick of celery from the jar in the center of the table. "Amelia, while you're figuring out what to do, just remember one thing."

Clearly he was not one of those folks who were sensitive to what a person wanted to talk about and what she'd rather avoid. Amelia resigned herself to listening until he was ready to change the subject — or Emma stepped in again and made him. "What's that?"

"Well, among the rumors I hear was that you were entertaining an offer from an *Englischer.*"

"One of our customers asked about it."

"You won't go selling to someone outside our faith, will you?"

"Have you been talking to my mother?"

He looked a little surprised. "No, not lately. Why, did she tell you the same thing?"

"In almost the same words."

"Then she's a wise woman. No sense bringing in the *Englisch* here when an Amish man could do the job better."

"He just inquired, Martin. There's no harm in that."

"The harm is in putting ideas in your head to look outside the fold for a buyer. You know what happens when we do that."

We get more money for our shop, that's what. The Amish were a frugal people, herself included. If she were a buyer, she'd want the best value she could get. But the view from the seller's side of the fence was different. "I'm not looking anywhere. I haven't given any thought — or hardly any — to selling at all."

"Just be sure you don't sell to an outsider." Martin nodded his head at his plate. "You'd be disobeying God's will. Remember, the children of Israel ceased to prosper when they looked outside the tabernacle to the gods of the land."

Bernard Burke would probably be embarrassed to death that Martin King considered him a god of the land. "I'm not looking outside the tabernacle, Martin." Amelia glanced at Emma in a silent plea: *Help me change the subject.*

"Here, Martin, try some of these pickled beets." Emma handed him a plate piled high. "I put them up a couple of weeks ago — a new recipe with a bit of spice to it. If you like them, I can give it to Anna."

"Denki." Martin took the beets and shoveled some onto his plate. "Eli?"

Eli Fischer took some and handed the plate across to Amelia. He had no sooner let it go than her arm went numb all the way to the elbow, her fingers lost their strength, and she dropped the plate with a crash. It flipped over and landed in the mashed potatoes, staining them fuchsia, and beets and juice arced over half a dozen people, ruining shirts and prayer coverings alike.

Amelia wanted to crawl under the table and burst into tears. "I am so sorry. Oh, Emma, your *Kapp.* Please forgive me."

"Mamm, look at the potatoes. They're purple!" Elam dragged the bowl over and dug another one out.

Amelia, practically weeping with mortification, grabbed as many napkins as she could find and tried to dab the stains off Emma's *Kapp* and Eli's shirt, while Anna reached for more at another table and went to work on her husband's vest. "Lucky thing he wore his purple shirt today," she said. "People will just think he's sweating."

"That's right." Martin's humor seemed to be unaffected by his sudden baptism with pickle juice. "Eating's hot work."

Eli's shirt felt warm from his body heat,

and Amelia realized at just about the same time he did that she was pressing a handful of napkins to the chest of a near stranger. He took the napkins from her, and she sat, a fresh wave of crimson flooding her cheeks. He must think she was the most forward, reckless woman in the whole settlement.

"I'm so sorry, everyone. If you bring your things over to our place, I'll launder them for you tomorrow and bring them back."

"No harm done." Emma grinned at her, wearing her fuchsia-and-white *Kapp* like a crown of diamonds and rubies. "I have others, and if I didn't, I'd make one. Don't go boiling and bleaching on my account."

"If I boil water for one, I may as well do two," Anna said comfortably. "Don't you worry about it. Accidents happen, and rubber fingers happen to everyone."

"It's my fault anyway," Eli told her. "The plate was heavy. I should have made sure you had hold of it before I let go."

Their kindness cooled her humiliation a little, but it didn't help that all the way through dessert, and afterward while everyone was visiting, every time she turned around, she saw Eli, behaving as though nothing were odd about wearing a fuchsia-and-white shirt.

What a kind man. Amelia searched the

crowd for Emma. It was time to get those two together and talking.

Daed had had a horse once that never came when he called it. He finally had to stable it the day before he needed to go anywhere in the buggy, because invariably the horse would make sure it was eating in the farthest reaches of the field whenever he needed to go to town.

Emma was being like that today.

As busy as any of the Lapp women, she pitched in and helped with the cleanup. Of course Amelia couldn't very well stop her when both arms were loaded down with plates and serving bowls. And when the last of the dishes were done, she and Carrie and several of the other young wives wiped down the benches and tables, making sure everything was clean before they went into the wagon for the families hosting weddings on Thursday. In fact, Carrie and Emma chattered as they worked, making Amelia wish she had let Carrie know her match-making plan well in advance. She'd been so taken up with the pallet shop that it hadn't even occurred to her.

With a sigh she left them to it and went in search of Matthew and Elam. Daed and Mamm would be getting ready to go soon. The boys weren't anywhere in the barn, so

86

as she crossed the yard, she kept an ear out for the sounds of play. It hadn't snowed yet, but the ditches were running now, and boys and water attracted each other like magnets.

She kept up a rhythmic rubbing of her left arm as she walked. Surely sometime this afternoon the feeling would come back into it. She couldn't even wiggle her fingers, so numb it was. Maybe it was a good thing she'd closed the shop today. Trying to manage everything one-handed would have been impossible. Perhaps a good night's sleep would relax the arm and get the blood flowing past the pinched nerve. On the way home, she'd ask Mamm for a packet of *Kamille* for tea to help her sleep. At least she knew that worked. That mustard poultice had done nothing more than make her hands stink.

The boys were not in the house. Nor were they in the chicken house, and they wouldn't have gone into someone else's equipment shed or into the granaries. Amelia walked a little faster. All the buggies had been drawn up in neat rows by the older boys in one of Daniel Lapp's fields. Matthew was reaching the age where he wanted to drive, and buggies and horses were a source of fascination. Were he and Elam out here, clambering in and out of the young men's courting buggies to see who had installed a fancy sound system or stuck some new combination of red and yellow reflectors on the back?

Sure enough, she could see short legs and small black hats bobbing as the little boys ran hither and yon. There was Matthew at the head of the pack, with Elam doing his best to keep up. Her steps slowed, then stopped altogether as Eli Fischer stepped out from between two buggies.

"Hello again."

He had not yet changed his shirt. Oh, dear. Maybe he had only the one with him on this visit. "Have you had to explain to a hundred people what happened to your clothes?"

"At least. Maybe two hundred. And I told them all that Amelia Beiler flung a plate of beet pickles at me."

For one frozen second — and because it was exactly what she'd feared — she thought he was serious. And then those eyes crinkled and she realized he was pulling her leg. "Did you say what you did to deserve it?"

His smile broadened. "It depends. To the men I say I offered you too low a price for the shop. To the women I say I was getting fresh and you put me in my place."

She laughed. "Eli Fischer, how can you tell such lies?" But she couldn't help it. The picture of her flinging a plate of pickles at a man for undercutting her sale price was just too funny. Especially when she didn't even have a sale price to cut in any direction. As for the fresh part, that was so out of the question she didn't even stoop to acknowledge it.

"Actually, if anyone was so concerned as to ask, I just told them I was wearing the price of my own clumsiness."

"I'm sorry you have to do any such thing."

"Is that arm all right?" He dropped his gaze, and she realized she was still rubbing the arm up and down, up and down, while they spoke. "Does it pain you?"

"It's a pinched nerve, I think. I'm seeing the chiro this week" — *I hope* — "and it will be set right. Nothing to worry about."

"Are you able to hitch up? Do you want some help?"

Again so kind. "*Denki,* but no. The boys and I came with my parents, Isaac and Ruth Lehman. I think they're getting ready to go, so I came out here to find my two rascals."

"There was a pack of them hounding young Aaron King." Eli turned to point toward a gray buggy at the end of a row, where six or seven of Matthew's little gang were crowding in to look. "Apparently he has had his buggy upholstered in burgundy

89

velvet and has an on-board battery to power the speakers for his sound system."

"My word." No wonder the little boys were agog. "And I'll bet he's not playing hymns on it either."

"Likely not. I'm a bit surprised at Martin King for allowing it. He never did anything like that when we were *rumspring*ing together."

"Anna's had a fancier upbringing. Isn't she from up around Mount Joy?"

"I think so. But she doesn't hold with fancy ways now. Maybe they're hoping Aaron will get it all out of his system and settle down in a year or two."

"It's a shame he doesn't use the wages I pay him to save up for a down payment on a place of his own, like you, instead of wasting it on worldly things."

His smile turned rueful. "Not every young man has an eye to the future, I guess."

She remembered what he'd said in the shop. "You bought your own place."

"My dad left the farm to me, and I bought a section from the man next door with my own money. But it never seemed fair to me. Here I am all alone on that big place, and my brothers making their own way with families to feed. That's why I'm looking about me. They can partner up on the home place, and I'll get something more manage-able elsewhere. At least until —"

He got married? How had such a nice person managed to stay single so long? Or had he been married and lost his wife? Amelia was dying to ask on Emma's behalf but didn't have the courage. Anyway, if the good *Gott* were paying attention, this would be the point at which Emma would walk up leading her horse and ask Eli to give her a hand with the hitching-up. Then the conver-sation could go where it would.

But no Emma appeared. And Amelia needed to be getting on with it.

"Well, I hope you find something," she said. "If I hear of anything, I'll send you word by Aaron King."

"If I can hear the message over the sound of his music." From across the field, the thumping of bass notes had begun as Aaron demonstrated his speakers for his admiring audience.

"I should collect my boys before they go deaf." Amelia stepped away, half her con-centration already on the little crowd.

"*Ja,* you better would," he agreed. "Good-bye."

She smiled and lifted a hand as she hur-ried up the field. But her fingers wouldn't waggle with an answering good-bye.

91

■ ■ ■ ■

The first appointment Amelia could get wasn't until Friday afternoon, and by then her left arm had stopped working altogether. She stayed away from both the Thursday weddings and did bookwork at the shop instead. Both her helpers put in long hours on Wednesday so that they could go, which meant that at least the orders were up to date. And since she was right-handed, she could do the invoicing without calling someone to help. Not that there was anyone to call, though Carrie wrote a nice hand and could be counted on in a pinch.

So Friday found her stretched out on Dr. Shadle's table while he kneaded and bent and worked her arms this way and that.

"A pinched nerve, your mother thinks?" He leaned on her shoulder blade and pushed. All the breath went out of her in a whoosh.

"Yes," she said when she could. "But I'd rather know what you think."

"Based on what you tell me, I wouldn't say her diagnosis was correct. Turn over, please." Test after test, pushing and pulling. "Nope, no pinched nerve here. Yet you say your left arm is numb?"

"Right to the elbow. And now this morning my right hand started getting pins and needles. I have to find out what's going on before I don't have any hands left to use."

"Push against my hand, please. . . . Resist. . . . Relax. . . . Other arm. . . . Wait. . . . What muscles are you using to perform that test?"

She thought for a second. "These." She indicated her upper arm.

"Bend your arm at the elbow and then push against my hand." He waited. "Amelia?"

"I'm pushing, but nothing's happening."

"You have no muscle control at all?"

"That's what I've been telling you."

Test, test, pinch, pull, test. "Amelia, have you been to a doctor about this?"

"Yes. Right now."

"I mean a medical doctor. Because there's nothing wrong with you mechanically."

He made her sound like an engine, made of metal parts. "No. It took me most of a week to get here."

"Well, the good news is, you don't have a pinched nerve. The bad news is, I don't know what's causing the trouble."

Amelia was silent for a moment. "You'd better not let my parents hear you say that." Such a thing had never happened in all the

93

years her family had been trusting him to look after their aches and pains. "I don't know any doctors."

"You might ask around, then. There are a couple in town, but for something like this you might do better in Strasburg or even Lancaster."

"I can't drive that far with only one hand. The only reason I could come here is that I can walk from the shop."

"You could call a taxi."

"Taxis cost money."

"Amelia, you need to get this looked after. Take my advice and find a way."

Good grief. She really didn't have time for this. So much for her hope that she'd leave his office with all her limbs in good working order again, blood flowing where it should and all feeling restored. She should have known that, with the way her week had been going, it wouldn't be so easy. Amelia thanked him, paid for the visit, and walked back to the shop.

Carrie waited for her in the buggy out front. "Thanks for picking me up." Amelia climbed in and settled herself while Carrie made the turn out onto the street. "Did you get all your errands done?"

"*Ja*. I went to Eicher's — they had a big shipment of gums come in, so I got some for Melvin. He's had wet feet in his old ones since last winter. And they had end lots of blue poly-cotton dress fabric. If you don't want it, I'll give it to Emma."

"I'd love it. Light or dark?"

"Light. It's from last summer, and it's a nice weight. You can go to purple after Christmas and be in it by June."

"One thing about black — it doesn't take long to decide what to wear."

Carrie glanced at her, then returned her attention to the street. "So what did Dr. Shadle say? I see you're not using that left arm still."

Amelia sighed. "He says there's nothing wrong with me. Mechanically I'm as sound as a washing machine."

"You haven't seen *my* washing machine, or you wouldn't say that."

"I guess that's my point. He says he doesn't know what's causing this and I should go see a medical doctor. I can just imagine what Mamm will say to that."

Carrie chuckled. "She will be so disappointed to know that her doctor has feet of clay. Maybe you shouldn't tell her."

"I can't keep anything related to medicine and physicks from Mamm. You know how she is."

With a nod of understanding, Carrie said,

"I do. But she did cure those boils of Melvin's two years ago."

"She got him to stop eating that awful cheese he likes. He was allergic."

"It's still a cure."

Carrie was far too generous. When Ruth experimented with something and got it right, word went far and wide, and while it encouraged her, the result was that her family wound up as guinea pigs for progressively odder experiments.

"Do you know any doctors who would deal with this kind of thing?"

Carrie shook her head. "But I bet Emma does. She has a different doctor for each of her parents."

Of course. Carrie was so smart. "I don't know why I didn't think of that. I'll ask her."

"Why not go now? It's on the way." And before Amelia could say *ja* or *nei,* she had snapped the reins over her horse's back and they were off to the Stolzfus farm instead of returning home where she belonged.

CHAPTER 5

Emma lifted her eyebrows and looked from Amelia to Carrie in disbelief. "Dr. Shadle said you should see an *Englisch* doctor?" She set a cup of coffee in front of each of them, then stirred sugar into her mother's cup, handing it to her with a smile.

"He's *Englisch*," Carrie reminded her. He was a friend to so many Amish that it was easy to forget sometimes. "But that's the gist of it."

"I don't know where to start," Amelia said. "When you had to take your parents to different doctors, what did you do?"

"Karen?" Emma's father looked up from his Bible in the front room. "Are you having company? Who is it?"

Emma sighed. "He's not having such a good day," she said in an undertone. Then, louder, "It's just Amelia and Carrie, Pap. They came to have coffee. Do you want some?"

"I never have coffee after lunch. Can't sleep."

"A doughnut or a whoopie pie? They're the lemon ones you like."

"*Nei.* I need to talk to your John about leaving the east field fallow. When's he coming in?"

"Soon, Pap." With a sigh she folded her tall body into a chair at the table. "Sorry. What were we talking about?"

"Don't apologize. He can't help it." How did Emma bear it? Giving her life to her parents' care while all the time her father thought she was someone else? "Doctors."

"Right." Emma paused for a second, gathering her thoughts. "I went to a Dr. Hunter in Strasburg at first, because Mary Lapp had gone to him for her neuralgia."

Amelia wasn't even sure what neuralgia was. Did that have something to do with nerves? "Did you like him? Was he any good?"

Emma shrugged and took a sip of coffee. "It was hard to tell. He listened to me, had a look at Pap, and recommended a specialist in Lancaster, and that's who we've been seeing since. Not that there's anything he can do except write prescriptions."

"But you think this Dr. Hunter might be a good place to start," Carrie put in. "And

98

maybe he'll know what's wrong. Amelia can't even use her left hand anymore."

"It's going to be difficult getting the lid off a jar of peaches in the morning, all right." Amelia smiled at them both to cover up the butterflies that had lifted off in her stomach at the thought. "Good thing Matthew considers himself the man of the house now. He'll be good for that kind of thing until I get this straightened out." She couldn't stand the expression on both their faces — a mixture of confusion and pity. This was just an inconvenience, not . . . something serious. "So we'll see each other Tuesday, *ja?* Have you got all your colors chosen?"

Like a willow tree in the wind, Carrie bent gracefully with the change in topic. "I have green, purple, mauve, and if you let me, I can steal a couple of strips off that new sky blue. If we want to give the idea of a sunrise, it would be perfect."

"You bought it, you can have as much of it as you like. I have lots of black for the background. The sky blue would look good in the skinny border, too, don't you think?"

Emma nodded. "Mamm, can we look in your scrap basket?"

Lena Stolzfus took a deep breath as though she wanted to shout, but only a whisper came out. "You're welcome to any of my scraps. Though they might be too dark for you *Youngie*." She sat back, as if even such a simple generosity were too much for her, and breathed through the tube that ran into her nose from the oxygen tank on its little cart beside her chair.

Lord, I bend to Your will for my life, whatever that might be, but please don't let me end up like either of Emma's parents.

One was giving up his mind and the other her body. There were lots of ways to come to the end of life's road, but Amelia hoped these two ways wouldn't be in God's plan for her.

That plan, for the moment, seemed to indicate that she should seek out an *Englisch* doctor. So to Dr. Hunter she would go. And then, she hoped, he could give her some medicine and all this nonsense would be behind her.

Later, when they were in the kitchen preparing a bite to eat, Emma took advantage of the fact that they were out of Lena's earshot and leaned close to Carrie. "I was glad to hear your voice on Sunday."

Carrie hesitated a brief second, then reached for another handful of oatmeal chocolate-chip cookies and arranged them on the plate. "If I hadn't spoken, there would be too many questions."

Amelia gave her a sharp glance. "You mean you haven't made it right with Aleta?" Carrie wouldn't say she was prepared to participate in Communion in front of the whole congregation when she wasn't, surely?

"I mean that I apologized and she is taking her time realizing that she has an apology to make, too. My conscience is clear."

Amelia would bet it was clearer than the atmosphere in the house. "But, Carrie, to take Communion you have to be at peace with each other. And last time I looked, peace came from both sides."

"Which is why I'm praying that she'll be able to humble herself enough to say those two words by then." Carrie smiled at them both and took the plate of cookies in to Lena.

Emma glanced at Amelia. "She's still offended, apology or not. This isn't good."

"And yet it's so hard to blame her," Amelia said with a sigh. "I'm lucky in my in-laws. Enoch had a much worse trade."

Emma chuckled, and then her smile faded. "We need to pray for her."

"I already do — every night. For you and her both. But I'll add this as well."

"What things do you pray for me?"

"That God will show you His will. That

you'll find happiness in it."

"Not that I'll find a husband?"

Amelia couldn't tell if Emma was being deliberately flip or if the humor had an edge to it. "I don't get specific with the Lord, I'm afraid. Whenever I do that, I find He either turns the tables on me or gives me so much more than I ever expected I have to do a whole new round of praying to be able to handle it."

Except this thing with her hands. There she'd been getting very specific. She could only hope that the good *Gott* didn't mind.

On the Sunday before Communion, Amelia and the boys usually joined Ruth and Isaac, as well as her brother Christopher and his wife Esther, and their family, at the Lehman farm for a morning of devotions, reading the *Christenpflicht,* and a story or two from the *Martyrs Mirror.* They would ask forgiveness of one another for any little hurts and spend the day quietly, visiting and doing their best to prepare themselves for the following Sunday.

The early fathers had known what they were doing, Amelia thought, to give families a chance to make things right in private. Even though something big might be confessed and forgiven at the Council Meeting, the little daily annoyances and disagreements had to be dealt with, too. And where better than at home, with those who knew all your faults the best?

During the eight-hour Communion Sunday service, Amelia was busy trying to listen to the sermon while keeping the boys from wiggling too much, whispering to each other, or playing too enthusiastically with the single wooden toy each was allowed to bring. But when it came time for the foot washing, her antennae went up. Carrie had dropped a hint at quilting the other day that had made Amelia wonder — something about going the extra mile to show someone the right direction to walk in. Amelia hadn't asked then, but she wondered now if Carrie meant to act on her thoughts.

Sure enough, there she was, whispering in Aleta Miller's ear. And to Amelia's astonishment, Aleta sat and waited while Carrie brought the basin and towel over to her.

Her throat closed up, and she concentrated on teaching Matthew that washing his brother's feet didn't really mean that he had to get between the toes and scrub the way he did at home. "It's a symbol," she whispered, her voice cracking with emotion. "Christ washed His disciples' feet, so we take the humble place and do the same for each other."

"Mamm, why are you crying?" little Elam asked.

"Because I'm happy, *Schatzi*. Now you trade places and do the same for your brother."

How could anyone hold an offense close to her heart when the so-called offender was willing to humble herself so? Amelia risked another glance at the side of the room and this time saw Carrie take her place on the bench while Aleta slowly, ponderously, got down on the floor with the basin.

Oh, my.

There could be no thorns of resentment or pride left to torment those two women, not if one was willing to humble herself and the other was willing to forgive.

Thank You, dear Lord, for working in the heart of my friend whom I love and for giving her the strength to do the right thing in front of all these people. You know she was supposed to wash the feet of Erica Yoder, who's next to her in age and length of marriage, but You moved in her heart to do this for the one person who most needed it, even though the cost was great.

Oh, Lord, I hope I'll be as willing for what You'd have me do, no matter what it costs me.

It was a prayer that came back to her now and again during the following week. Because it took several days to get in to see Dr. Hunter, days when she wondered more than once what the best course of action was. By midweek her left arm had regained its feeling — and just when she'd begun to breathe normally and hope that maybe this strange episode was over, the pins and needles came back. And by the weekend her hand felt as if she were holding it too close to the stove.

"What do you mean?" Carrie asked when she came to drive her into Strasburg on Monday for her appointment. "Did you burn yourself?"

Tears of frustration surged just below the surface, and Amelia restrained herself from snapping — barely. Her best friend didn't deserve that. "No. I mean my hand feels like it's burning. Hot, sore. I can't explain it."

She couldn't do much better with Dr. Hunter. He pushed the sleeve of her dress up to her shoulder and poked and prodded while she tried to describe how it felt. He took blood pressure. He measured her responses to stimuli — which netted him nothing. Her arm lay cradled in her lap as unresponsive as if it had come off, the surface of her skin feeling as though it were on fire.

He glanced up at her from beneath bushy white brows that looked like coconut macaroons on a head that was perfectly bald. "You say it's been like this for two weeks?"

"On and off. Earlier the feeling came back, and I almost called to cancel. And then it went away again, except for the pins and needles and this burning feeling."

"I'm glad you didn't cancel." He took a sharp instrument and poked each of her fingertips. "Feel that?"

"I know you're doing it because I can see you, but it doesn't hurt."

"Hmm."

"It's not a pinched nerve?"

"Hmm? No, no." Prick, tickle, prick. "Nothing so simple." That didn't sound good. "I'm going to send you for some blood tests and then an MRI."

"What is that?"

He took a breath to say something, then seemed to change his mind. "I forget who I'm dealing with here. It's like a big camera. You lie on a big tray, and it takes pictures of your insides."

Amelia's imagination failed her. What on earth?

"It's up to you, of course, but without it I

don't have a way to see exactly what's going on. There's nothing to worry about, Mrs. Beiler. It's fairly standard procedure."

For him, maybe. She'd never heard of such a thing. "Is it expensive?"

"A couple thousand dollars, I think. Unless you have health insurance."

"No." She didn't have a couple thousand dollars for such things either. How could a camera that took pictures of your insides be so expensive? She couldn't hand over the little bit of money in her savings for something so outlandish — especially when it might not be able to tell them anything. "Could there be another way?"

He gazed at her while she tried not to look at his eyebrows. "I suppose you could wait until your symptoms get so bad that the conclusions become obvious. And then we put you on medication for pain and to try to slow the symptoms down. It would be better to know now, though. So we can do the right thing, right away."

It sounded like he already knew what was going on. But she didn't want to be forward and ask impertinent questions when she knew nothing and he was the authority. "Do you . . . have an idea . . . ?"

"I have lots of ideas, Mrs. Beiler. Can you speak up?"

Oh, dear. He was getting angry with her. "Of what it could be."

He shifted, straightening his back as though he were getting ready to argue with her. "Your symptoms are consistent with a number of maladies. But an MRI would pinpoint exactly which one." He paused. "I understand the church has a fund for medical emergencies. I've had Amish patients before, and there's never been any problem getting procedures paid for."

"Even an . . . MRI?" What did that stand for? Never mind. She didn't have the courage to waste his time by asking.

"Even one of those. I recommend you speak to your bishop and see if they can free up some money for you."

Daniel Lapp had the final say, but, as deacon, Moses Yoder had authority to make decisions on medical procedures, since he handled most of the financial transactions for the *Gmee*. She could just see herself explaining to him that she needed two thousand dollars for a giant camera to take pictures of her insides. Her insides weren't the problem. Her hands were.

"Mrs. Beiler?"

"*Ja*. I mean, yes. I'll try. But what if our deacon says no?"

"Then we'll go on our best assumptions.

There are medications that can slow the symptoms and even put you into remission."

"Remission?" Why did he keep sounding like he already knew the answer? Why insist on the MRI, then, and put her through the trial of asking the church for money?

"Let's get some facts to work with first. I don't want to alarm you unnecessarily."

"I'm alarmed now." Her voice, though carefully quiet, carried an edge that she'd never heard in it before, even on her worst days. She plucked up her courage, even though it went against a lifetime of practice in submission. If she could get out of going inside his camera with a few little questions, then she would. Even if it meant taking up a few minutes of his time. "Could you tell me your idea?"

But he shook his head. "We need the blood tests and the MRI, Mrs. Beiler. Otherwise it's just educated guesswork." He rose and helped her down from the padded counter shaped like a bed. "Go talk to your bishop . . . er, deacon, and then call my office to schedule the test, all right?"

He was already walking her to the door, so she didn't have much choice but to submit. There were a dozen patients in the waiting room who probably had serious things wrong with them, like cancer or epilepsy or broken bones. Not pins and needles and numbness and burning sensations that came and went like fireflies in the grass.

Carrie stood when Amelia came out into the waiting area, clasping her hands over and over. She waited until they were outside before she said, "Well?"

Amelia shrugged and patted the horse's glossy neck before she climbed into the buggy. "Not much to tell. He wants me to take a test called an MRI. Do you know what that is?"

Carrie backed the horse away from the hitching rail, and Amelia handed her the reins when she climbed in. "It's when you lie in this big tube and it makes a bunch of noise taking pictures of you. One of my sisters had to go for one once, when she tripped over something on the stairs and fell down half the flight. She wrote and told me in great detail all about what the inside of her head looked like."

What did the inside of someone's head look like? "Did she see the pictures?"

"She must have. So it was a good thing. Are you going to have one?"

"I don't know." Amelia sighed. "Why does it have to be so complicated? Why can't I just go and get some medicine and have that be that?"

"Some things are meant to be simple," Carrie said, "but our bodies are complicated." She made the turn from the main road through Strasburg to the long stretch across the valley to Whinburg. In the silence punctuated by the horse's rapid clip-clop, Amelia heard the rest. *And some women have families of twelve without trying, while some cannot conceive a child no matter how joyful its welcome would be. Bodies are complicated, and only God knows them.*

And only God knew what she should do. Because Amelia certainly did not.

That evening, as she did the supper dishes, the answer came to her. *Ask Daed if he will go to the deacon on your behalf.*

Relieved at a solution that had clearly come from God, Amelia scrubbed one-handed at the roasting pan with renewed energy. But if she thought she could get the boys into bed and slip away early, she had another think coming.

Elam struggled to pull his hand away as she led him up the stairs to brush his teeth. "*Nei!* I don't want to go to bed."

"Maybe not, but go to bed you will. Brush your teeth first, like your brother."

Around the toothbrush Matthew said, "He's just a baby. Hey, Elam, maybe *es Ungeheier* will come and get you tonight 'cause you're such a baby."

"Matthew! There's no need to be cruel. What's this about a monster?"

The face of her eldest had sobered at the sharpness in her tone. "Nothing."

She knelt and took Elam into her arms. Tears swam in his eyes as he tried not to let them fall in front of his brother. "What is it, my little man? What has you so afraid? There's no such thing as monsters — God did not create them. It says so in the Bible."

"Miss Hannah says there's a leviathan in the Bible, and that's a monster," Matthew informed her from the sink with all the confidence of the scholar.

"There are no leviathans in Whinburg," she informed him right back. "To bed with you, young man, without another word."

Elam clutched at her. "Don't go down, Mamm. Sing the golden song?"

It was a delaying tactic, but she didn't have the heart to refuse it. "Teeth, then prayers, then the golden song."

Maybe it was the comfort of the old and familiar. Maybe it was the fact that she sat with them, singing one of the modern songs she used to with the *Youngie* on Sunday nights. Whatever it was, she sent up a prayer of thanks when Elam's eyes finally slid shut and his breathing lengthened.

Monsters in the dark. Goodness. In daylight she would have a little talk with him and find out what was really behind his fears. If it was Matthew, making scary noises in the night, there would be *Druwwel.*

She tiptoed downstairs, put on her coat, and set off down the lane in the cold twilight.

When she stepped into her parents' front hall — oh, blessing — she found Daed alone by the kitchen stove, reading.

"What do you have there?" She closed the door behind her firmly with her hip, so no chilly breezes could get into the warm house. Sometimes the door stuck when it got cold.

He held up the book. *Modern Farming and Husbandry.*

"I guess I shouldn't be surprised."

"It's not for me," he said. "I got it for Mark. Thought he might be interested in some of these newfangled ideas. I'm planning to mail it off to him tomorrow."

Surely this was God's will. "So you'll be in town, then. Any plans to go by Moses Yoder's place on the way back?"

"I could. What's on your mind, Amelia?"

She peered into the living room, but it was dark. "Where's Mamm?"

With his chin he indicated the porch behind him. "In her room concocting something for Lizzie Stolzfus. Seems she has those warts you had when you were a girl, so she wrote to ask for a cure."

"So Mamm is preparing those drops and giving her a scrubbing brush?"

Isaac nodded, and Amelia resisted the urge to say what she wanted to say, which was that the scrubbing brush would do just as much good with or without the drops. She considered telling Emma to tell Lizzie, her sister-in-law, but then decided against it. The drops would do no harm.

"Do you want to see her?" He put his book on the arm of his chair and made to get up.

"No, no. It's you I want to see."

Settling back, he raised his eyebrows at her. That was one of the things she loved about her father. No fuss, no muss. Just settling down and preparing to listen.

"I take it this has something to do with our deacon?"

"Yes." She paused a moment to pull a chair over. "I wonder if you would ask him on my behalf for some money."

Her father blinked. This was obviously not

what he had expected her to say. "Why would you not come to your mother and me if you need money? We don't have much, but —"

She shook her head. "It's a lot of money. A couple of thousand dollars." And that was just to start. Who knew how much more it would be after that?

"Are you adding on to the shop?"

She saw now she had started at the wrong end of the conversation. Jumped in with both feet off the rope swing instead of wading in a step at a time. "No. I — It's for medical purposes. Something called an MRI." When he looked blank, she explained what that was as well as she could. "It's because of my hands, Daed. It's not a pinched nerve. I went to Dr. Shadle, and he said he couldn't help me. So I went to a Dr. Hunter in Strasburg, because that's where Emma took her dad. And he seems to think I need this MRI. But I don't have the money to pay for it."

He nodded, slowly, taking it all in. "The church keeps a fund for medical purposes. I see now. He should be able to tell you, but he'll likely ask all the elders for counsel. So this is what you'll need? Two thousand dollars?"

"More or less."

"Less is no problem. More? I'm not so sure."

"I don't know yet. Dr. Hunter says he'll be able to proceed once he sees the pictures. I have no idea what that will mean for money."

"We'll take it one step at a time. Would you like to come with me to see my friend Moses? I'll do the talking, but he may have questions."

"I'd rather not, Daed. I have the shop to run." And tomorrow was Tuesday. With all these unsettling medical visits, she needed the strength of her quilting frolic in the afternoon. If Moses Yoder sent her a direct request in his role as deacon, then of course she would go. But until he did, she needed to be with Carrie and Emma.

"All right, then. I'll come by tomorrow evening and tell you what he says."

She got up and hugged him. "*Denki,* Daed. I can always count on you."

But he didn't release her, even after he stood. "You're all right, though, aren't you?" Concern lurked in his deep-set eyes.

"Of course." She couldn't move her fingers in his hand. Did he notice? Gently, she pulled out of his grip. "It's probably nothing more than a circulation problem. I'm hoping he finds out what it is, gives me

116

some pills, and I'm back to normal by Communion Sunday — or at the latest by the time Christmas baking starts."

"I hope so, too. I wouldn't want to miss your pumpkin pie." He smiled, but the worried look didn't leave.

Sometimes she loved her dad so much she couldn't breathe. But he would be deeply embarrassed if she told him so. "You'll have your pie."

"You won't stay and have a cup of *Kaffi* with us? Your mother won't be much longer."

"I don't think so. I can't leave the boys for long. Don't say anything to her. I don't want to worry her for nothing."

She slipped out before the door to the closed porch on the other side of the kitchen could open. If her mother found out she had to go for fancy, expensive tests, she would never hear the end of it. In her mind, if Dr. Shadle couldn't fix something, it was obviously God's will and a person should bow to it. How did Mamm not realize that people got cancer and pneumonia and all kinds of awful things? They didn't just bow down to those — they went to doctors and got help.

She wasn't alone. Others had asked the church for help before this. There was no reason for them to refuse. And in the absence of a husband, she'd done right to ask Daed to appeal on her behalf.

Her feet crunching on the gravel on the side of the road, Amelia looked up into the night sky, crisp and glittering with stars.

She just needed to trust that God would see her through.

Isaac did even better than he had promised. He went to see Moses first thing in the morning and then came by the shop on his way to the post office. By the time Amelia got home, packed up what she needed for the afternoon, and met Emma at Carrie's, she was practically bursting with the need to share the good news.

"Goodness, Amelia. Tell us quick." Carrie hustled her over to the table, where Emma was unpacking her tote bag of fabric. "Look at this girl, Emma. She has good news, I know it."

Emma put down a pile of fabric squares. "Did you see the doctor? What did he say?"

Amelia filled her in as she unwound her shawl and tossed it over a chair. Then she said, "And Daed went to see Moses Yoder first thing this morning. Wouldn't you know, Bishop Daniel was there, because the two of them were getting ready to go look at a horse, so Daed didn't have to go chasing all over the district to find them. And they said yes!"

"To what?" Emma wanted to know. "I'm missing something."

"To giving me the money for the MRI. Mind you, I have to pay some of it. But the church will take the greatest burden. Isn't it wonderful *gut?*"

Emma drew a long breath, a smile dawning like the sun. "I would say so. But how could you doubt it? They would hardly say no when a sister is in need. The church is paying for Mamm's oxygen and Pap's medication, because goodness knows after the harvest we had, there isn't much left over."

Amelia felt giddy with relief. "I know. I was foolish to doubt it. But I've been so worried and frightened —"

"Frightened?" Carrie's smooth brow wrinkled in a frown of concern. "About the money?"

Amelia shook her head. "About my hands . . . the shop . . . how I was going to manage if I didn't get better."

"Don't borrow tomorrow's trouble." Emma dug her good shears out of her bag. "Today's is enough. So when do you go in for this test?"

119

"I'll go see Dr. Hunter tomorrow and find out. I have to go to Lancaster for it, so Daed said he would come with me on the bus."

"Oh, I'm glad." Carrie looked apologetic. "I'm glad we can't drive in the city. It scares me to death. What would you do if your horse bolted into traffic? Much better to go by bus."

"We'll leave the horse at my brother Saul's place in Intercourse and take the bus from there. It will mean an early start, sure."

"But at least it will be done. You'll find out what's wrong and be able to do something about it." Emma's tone was bracing. She held up several pieces of blue and purple fabric. "This is where you are right now, in the dark before the dawn. But dawn will come. What do you think of these for our bottom row?"

It was a relief to think about something other than herself. Amelia and Carrie bent over the colors, moving pieces around to find the best blend. "You know what? I think these would look better on green rather than the black," Amelia said. "It just seems more hopeful. Like you said, the sun rising over the green and fertile earth, *ja?*"

Carrie studied the pieces scattered over the length of black fabric Amelia had brought. "It's a shame not to use this, though."

"There's enough to make a cape and an apron or two, but I already have enough. I suppose I could use it to make pants for the boys. Matthew is growing so fast I can hardly keep him dressed."

For a wedding quilt, the black would be awfully dark. She couldn't say that in front of Emma, though. "What do you think, Emma?"

Pursing her lips, Emma arranged the squares and triangles on the dark green. "I think you're right. The green seems to make the other colors brighter. And the quilting stitches will show up better."

"I don't know if we want mine showing up." Amelia rubbed her hand. It was becoming a habit, as though she hoped she could rub the life back into it. "I've never been able to load ten stitches on a needle on the best of days, and now with these hands I might be down to only four or five."

Emma nudged her with one hip. "This is just for us. By the time we get to the last stitches, you'll be back up to eight or nine, because the medicine will be working. We'll see your journey back to health in this quilt — it's nothing to be ashamed of."

"We have a few weeks of piecing ahead of us anyway," Carrie put in. "Who knows? By the time that's done and we get ready for the quilting, you could be cured."

Please, dear Gott, *let that be so.*

"The green it is, then. We'll save the black for another day."

CHAPTER 6

Instead of going to the examination room to give her the results of the MRI, Dr. Hunter led her down the hall to his office. He indicated the padded chair in front of his desk. "Have a seat, Mrs. Beiler."

This was going to take a long time, then. Fortunately, Daed was immersed in *Newsweek* out in the waiting room, so he wouldn't miss her even if it took half an hour.

She seated herself, tucking her skirts around her and smoothing down her apron. She wasn't sure what to do with her shabby leather purse, which no one would guess held two thousand dollars in cash, so she laid it in her lap and folded her hands on top of it.

Dr. Hunter gazed at her across the glass top of his desk. A large manila folder rested on it, and reading upside down, she saw her name typed on the label. "I'd like to go over the results with you."

She nodded. A picture of her insides. This disappointingly flat envelope was the result of that dreadful glassed-in room, where they'd put her in a big tube like a roast in the oven and commanded her not to move. She'd lain there, hardly daring to breathe, while the machine went crazy all around her, banging and clacking like a bunch of boys beating on the corrugated-tin walls of a culvert to scare a possum out. When they'd finally slid the table from the tube and let her get up, her muscles had been stiff — both from obedience to the technician's directive and from sheer anxiety.

She'd had every sympathy with the possum.

"While the image itself isn't a hundred percent conclusive, when I put it together with your symptoms, your situation becomes clear." Her gaze didn't move from his face. "Mrs. Beiler, it seems evident that you have multiple sclerosis."

As though someone had flapped reins over her head, her mind took off at a gallop. Multiple sclerosis. Lila Esch had come down with it in her forties. Within five years she'd been confined to a wheelchair. By the time she was fifty, she'd been unable to sit up without a strap around her chest and her speech had become a series of unintelligible noises. Soon after that, she was dead, and six months later her husband married the Mennonite girl who had nursed her.

Multiple sclerosis. Dear *Gott,* no.

She was going to end up like Lila Esch. And who would look after the boys? The next ten years would see them grow up and become teenagers, and who would make sure they became good men? Certainly not a helpless, speechless body strapped into a wheelchair.

Oh, no. No. This couldn't be happening to her. The diagnosis must be wrong.

"Mrs. Beiler, I realize this must be a shock, but it's not the end of the world."

Only the end of hers.

Dear Gott, mein Gott, *why have you forsaken me?*

"There are a number of medications that have been proven to slow the symptoms, and some patients have even responded so well that they've gone into complete remission."

Still she could not speak, though questions tumbled through her mind in a waterfall of fear.

"Would you like to see the MRI image so I can show you what we're basing our conclusions on?"

She nodded, though she really didn't see what good it would do to look at a picture. The Lord had been right to command His children not to make graven images. They only brought trouble.

The doctor slid a large plastic sheet out of the envelope and pushed it toward her. She looked down because he expected her to — looked and did not comprehend. A mass of color and swirly lines and black circles. What on earth? Her insides resembled nothing so much as the floor that time Matthew had eaten green crab apples and hadn't made it to the compost bucket fast enough.

"I don't know what I'm seeing," she finally said — the first words she'd spoken since she sat down.

Dr. Hunter reached over, pointing. "This is your skull, and this is your neck area. The camera takes slices — cross sections. Like when you slice potatoes. Think of this as pulling one of those slices out, laying it down, and looking at it from the top."

She tried to wrap her imagination around someone slicing her like a potato and gazed at the image again. He pointed to some circles and wiggly lines. "This is the area we're concerned with. See these lines? They could be lesions, here, below your brain, consistent with the ones generated by MS.

The loss of feeling in your extremities is caused by these. The body is attacking itself. Basically, what it's doing is eating away at the nerve casing, so your hands are reporting those sensations, not what they're actually feeling. Do you understand?"

"My body is attacking itself. And my hands are feeling the attack, not whatever is actually touching them." Her voice sounded high, strained, foreign.

Her body wasn't hers anymore. Not even her voice belonged to her. Her life was being taken away, nibbled bit by bit, the way a rat gnawed at a tomato in the garden until nothing was left but a dead stem.

And the tomato sat helplessly, knowing what the rat was doing but unable to do a thing to stop it.

"Mrs. Beiler, you look very pale. I know that this is a shock, but as I said, there are a number of things we can do. Would you like a glass of water?"

When she nodded, he went out into the hall and murmured something to someone he found there. A moment later a nurse leaned in with water in a paper cup.

"*Denk*— I mean, thank you." She took a sip, then drank the whole of it down.

Dr. Hunter reached for a prescription pad. "I'm going to give you a course of medication to start with. Take two of each a day, and if they make you sick, back it off to one a day."

Make her sick? Weren't pills supposed to do the opposite? "What are they?" He told her something that sounded like a foreign language, which did not help at all. "What I meant to say is, what will they do inside me?"

"These will inhibit your pain receptors, which will stop the burning sensations, to start with."

"That will be good, but what about curing the MS?"

He gave her a long look. "Mrs. Beiler, MS isn't curable. You have to live with it. Our goal is to make you as comfortable as possible and slow it down as much as we can. I'm going to have you come in for more blood tests so we can pinpoint the drugs your body will respond to best."

Drugs. Prescriptions. "How much will this cost?"

He tore the sheet off the prescription pad. "I won't lie to you. It will be expensive. A thousand dollars a month — maybe less, if we can get you into a discount program. Is your income below twenty thousand a year?"

He'd lost her at "a thousand dollars a

month." The pallet shop brought in enough to tithe, to pay the rent on her space and make the mortgage payment and household expenses, with a little left over to put into savings. That little bit certainly didn't amount to a thousand a month for pills. How could something so small be so expensive?

"Mrs. Beiler?"

She gazed at him. "I don't have a thousand a month for pills."

"That's what I'm saying. Maybe we can get you on the discount program, and the church will pick up the remainder."

"For how long?"

His eyes were kind under those strange eyebrows. "For the foreseeable future, I'm afraid. We'll reevaluate periodically, but other patients have been and will be on some form of medication for the rest of their lives."

Which would be the next ten years, if poor Lila was anything to go by. A thousand a month for twelve months times ten years . . . oh, dear. Daed had been able to get two thousand from the bishop. Would he be so amenable if the sum were a hundred and twenty thousand? You could almost buy a house and five acres for that.

"Is there —" Her throat closed, and she

cleared it. "Is there any other way? Any treatment other than these drugs?"

For a moment he didn't answer, just gazed at her. "I'm not sure what you mean."

"Well . . . some of our folks up in Bird-in-Hand went to Mexico for a special kind of cancer treatment."

"You don't have cancer, Mrs. Beiler."

She was not communicating very well. And did he have to sound quite so sorry for her? "What I mean is, could I find a way to help this without it being so expensive? I just don't know if I could ask the church for a thousand dollars a month for the next . . . for the rest of my life."

"Such are the benefits of a health plan," he pointed out.

She straightened. "We don't believe in those." Why did he even bother to mention it? She needed to deal with what was, not what he thought it should be.

"So I understand. What I believe you're asking is if there are alternative treatments. The answer is yes, of course there are. But most of them are bunk, in my opinion. Behind every offer of a miracle cure, you'll find a charlatan more interested in taking your money than giving you actual solutions."

He was not going to help her. If she went

with his plan, she might impoverish the church. Even though the whole district tithed, was there enough money in the coffers to keep her in pills and help others, too? Could she justify the entire community sacrificing for her when she could give nothing back?

And in the end, even in the best of cases, he'd said himself these drugs wouldn't cure her. They'd just slow things down, drawing out the payment of money even longer.

Amelia's shoulders drooped with the weight of all that obligation. And what about the boys, who would be left to care for her instead of finding the wives God had prepared for them and starting their own lives? Even if she made them go, what would she do? Return home and be a burden to Mamm and Daed?

Dr. Hunter pushed the slip across the desk, and she took it automatically. "I'll call this down to the pharmacy, and it will be ready for you by the time you get downstairs. Take your time, Mrs. Beiler. Do you have someone with you?"

She nodded. Stood. Walked to the door like a scarecrow held up by nothing more than crossed broomsticks, then down the hall, her sense of direction taking her back to the waiting room.

Daed looked up from his magazine when she stood silently next to him. "I'm convinced that the world is crazier than ev—Amelia? What is it, daughter?" The magazine fell from his hands and landed upside down on the floor, like a bird that had been shot out of the sky. "What did the MRI tell you? What did that doctor say?"

She told him.

Told him again. And when he finally understood, when his dear, lined face had gone so white that she thought he might crumple up in a faint, that was when she finally began to cry.

It wasn't until they'd taken the long bus journey back, retrieved the horse and buggy, and were rolling down the road at a smart pace a mile out of Whinburg that she remembered she hadn't given the doctor his two thousand dollars.

"It can't be true. Why, Lila Esch —" Carrie stopped abruptly and picked up the iron before it burned a hole in her neat Crosses and Losses block.

"She's the first person I thought of, too," Amelia admitted. "I can still see her, strapped in her wheelchair, trying to say *Guder Mariye* to the bishop and not being able to get a single syllable out." Her lips wobbled, and a shot of fear arced through her stomach the way a shooting star fell across the sky. "Surely it isn't God's will for me to . . ." She couldn't finish.

"It was His will for poor Lila." Carrie left the rest unspoken. *If it's His plan for you, you have to be willing. There is a purpose for everything, even being strapped in a wheelchair.*

"Let's not talk about God's will until we know for sure that the diagnosis is right." Emma dropped three completed blocks on the table, alive with several shades of green — sage, slate, and even a lime that could only have come from someone's underslip. Certainly a color that vivid would never be worn where anyone could see it, lest it attract attention.

"You mean I should get another opinion?" Amelia asked her. "But you said Dr. Hunter was a good doctor."

"He is. But he isn't the only one in Lancaster County. After all, didn't he say the MRI wasn't a hundred percent conclusive? And he used words like 'I believe' and 'appears to be.' Not 'I know' and 'is.' "

"Doctors never say anything for sure, just in case they turn out to be wrong," Carrie said.

"But I'd take that 'not a hundred percent'

and put my hope there." Emma sounded so firm. Amelia wished she felt half as confident. But then, putting one's faith in how a person used his words didn't mean much when you had the reality of little boys and running a business to deal with.

"What should I do?" she finally said. At least her feet still worked. She got the treadle sewing machine going and used her left hand to weight the triangles of blues and purples as she fed them under the needle while she kept them lined up with her right. Thread and fabric. A person could count on these. She might be floundering in an internal sea of fear and indecision and lack of knowledge, but on the outside she could control color and cloth.

"I would go and see Milner Esch," Emma said, "and ask him who Lila went to."

"Whoever that was didn't help her much," Carrie pointed out. "We want someone who can tell us something different. After all, didn't Dr. Hunter say Amelia's symptoms could be a couple of things?"

"True," Emma admitted. "Well then, what would you suggest?"

But Carrie couldn't think of anything. "The only time I go to the doctor is to get a filling in my teeth. And that's not the right kind of doctor."

"What about the Clinic for Special Children?" Amelia said suddenly.

"Are you a special child?" Emma grinned, and Amelia stuck out her tongue at her.

"They take care of kids with strange diseases. Maybe they could recommend a doctor closer than Lancaster who might know something. Maybe even one of the doctors there."

"That's a good idea." Carrie looked at her the way her teacher in the one-room schoolhouse used to do when she got an arithmetic problem right on the blackboard.

"We can stop by the phone shanty on the way home and call," Emma said. "They'd be in the phone book."

Whoa. Slow down. That was just like Emma — from thought to action in two seconds. "Maybe I should talk it over with Mamm and Daed."

"Why?" Carrie wanted to know. "You're just asking. And if there's no one there who knows about MS, ask if they can refer you. Someone around here has to know about it. After all, Lila didn't get her diagnosis out of a box of laundry soap."

The picture made Amelia smile.

"That's better," Carrie said. "I've missed that smile."

"You have to admit, I don't have much to

135

smile about."

"But you have us," Emma said. "You're not going through this alone. Carrie and I will be by your side the whole way, whether that means looking after the boys or giving you rides to the doctor." She looked at Carrie. "Isn't that right?"

Carrie nodded, the sun glinting off her blond hair where her *Kapp* rested on it. "Whatever you need. I probably have more time than Emma, now that Melvin has decided to go up to Shipshey again."

Amelia's foot ceased its rocking on the treadle. "He's leaving? Already? For how long?"

"For the six weeks between Thanksgiving and Old Christmas." Carrie swallowed. "And again in February. Apparently they need relief men in the RV factories to cover for people who are taking holidays."

"And they don't have enough men in Indiana for this?" Amelia couldn't believe it. Indiana was a long train ride away. And what if Carrie needed her husband during those six weeks? What if something happened? And how would she stand it, all alone for such a long time?

"His cousin is getting him in, and because he worked there before and they liked him, it was easier. And we . . . we do need the money," Carrie said softly. "What is he going to do with himself all winter if he doesn't go?"

What the other men did. Take care of his horses. Repair the harvesting machinery. Work on the barn. Fix things around the house.

But Melvin didn't have the gift for fixing things that other men had — or the lifetime of training. He was the son of a harness maker who for some unfathomable reason had decided to take up farming far away from his family.

"Has Melvin ever considered moving home and going in with his father in the harness shop?" Amelia asked.

Carrie began sorting burgundy, pink, and red triangles, laying them out this way and that, looking for an order that pleased her. "His dad and the shop are sore subjects. Besides, his brothers bought in when he left, so there isn't really room for a fourth."

"Why a sore subject?" What a relief to talk about someone else's problems. "Don't Melvin and his dad get along?" First his mother and his wife, now his father . . . What had gone wrong in that family that there was so much tension?

"He never says much about it, but from what he lets slip every now and again, his dad has a bit of a temper. Melvin always tried to please him but never seemed to be able to. And it just got worse as he got older."

"Like me and Karen," Emma muttered.

Carrie looked up from her focus on the fabrics. "It must be awful to be the one taking care of them and all the time your dad thinks it's Karen."

Emma's face had set in pale lines. The sullen skies outside the window didn't help — even the light seemed to conspire to wash her in shades of gray. "It is awful. Sometimes I'd just like to scream at him that it isn't Karen cleaning him up after he has an accident or feeding him when he has a bad day and can't manage the fork and spoon."

"But you wouldn't do that," Carrie said, looking a little shocked.

"Of course not. He's my father, and if I did scream at him, he'd probably still clout me." She took a deep breath, as though she were searching for her usual calm. "Mamm's my example. With all she has to live with, she still does little things for him. Still tries to help me. She can hardly get from her bedroom to the kitchen, and there she is at seven in the morning putting the water on for porridge for all of us, with her oxygen tank following her around like a pet dog."

138

Amelia dropped her gaze to her seams and pumped the treadle. In comparison to Lena Stolzfus, right now she didn't have much to complain about. She could get into town and work. She could still cook, though they weren't eating so many vegetables that had to be cut up fine, like cabbage, and she was teaching the boys to help with meals. They liked helping with that part, egging each other on to see who could cut his carrot the fastest. If their root vegetables looked lopsided, she didn't care — they all went down the same way.

"Amelia," Carrie said slowly, "getting back to Melvin leaving . . . Would you ever consider — I know this is an imposition, but do you think . . . What if you found a place for him in the shop over the winter?"

The needle stopped halfway through a stitch. "Melvin?" In her shop? Could the man even handle a hammer, much less an air nailer?

"It would be such a gift to me if he didn't have to go so far away at Christmas." Carrie's words picked up speed, as if she were hurrying to convince Amelia before she could say no. "And I know he could do the work — he repaired the porch here, and that's pretty straightforward, like pallets."

This probably wasn't a good time to point

out that the porch boards curled up on the ends because he'd nailed the green wood camber up instead of down. She had to watch her step every time she came over or she'd stub a toe.

She couldn't hire Melvin. But neither did she have the heart to quench the hope that shone in Carrie's eyes. "I already have the two boys on the payroll," she said as gently as she could. "I'm not sure I could afford to take on another man."

"But haven't you told us fifty times that Aaron King doesn't pull his weight? If you let him go and hired Melvin, he could do the work of two men. And you'd have someone trustworthy there on the days I took you to the doctor."

Behind the sewing machine, Amelia winced. When had Carrie developed the ability to use guilt like that? Because how could she ask Carrie to help her when she stood by and did nothing to keep Carrie's husband at home?

She didn't know what to say, and Emma was sorting fabric with such attention it was obvious she wanted to stay out of the conversation. "I don't know," she said at last, sounding lame even to herself. "I'll have to pray about it, *ja?*"

"I'm doing enough praying for the two of

us," Carrie said quietly.

Oh, dear. If she refused, would it damage their friendship? Do so much harm that she would lose the woman she looked on as a sister — as much or more than her own sisters? Because you couldn't choose your family, but she, Emma, and Carrie had chosen one another as friends way back in the schoolroom.

"Let me talk to Aaron, all right?" It would only delay the inevitable, but at least it would give her some time to find the right words. Words that wouldn't hurt. Or divide.

Carrie let out a breath, as if she'd been holding it. "Of course. Maybe Aaron wants a reason to quit anyway. One of my brothers used to do that — be so slow or so sloppy that my dad would finally elbow him out of the way and do it himself."

"Maybe." Amelia didn't think that was the case. Aaron's parents might have bought him his new buggy, but all those fancy additions still had to be paid for, and Aaron took money very seriously.

If Melvin came to work for her, how would that be? Teenage boys were one thing — they hadn't quite gotten out of the habit of obeying their parents and saw her as a mother whose bidding they still had to do. But a full-grown man? How would he like

141

taking instructions and orders from a woman — particularly one he was used to seeing chattering and laughing in the kitchen with his wife? How would he react when she showed him how to work the air compressor? Would he want to change how Enoch had done things?

Oh, dear, oh, dear. This was why God made the worlds of men and women separate. Each had their own work, and each grew up learning what to do. How these *Englisch* women in big companies maintained their authority over the men who worked for them was an utter mystery.

Emma glanced at the sky and began to pack up her fabric. "We'd better start for home, Amelia, or we're going to get wet. And just between the three of us, I'd rather not be here when Aleta gets back from the Lapps'. I hardly know what to say to her."

For the first time that Amelia could remember, she was glad to get out of Carrie's house. As soon as they left the lane and were in the quiet of Moses Yoder's field, Amelia spoke.

"Do you think I should do it, Emma?"

"What, hire Melvin?" She glanced at Amelia. "I saw how uncomfortable you were. Do you think you could stand to have him around?"

"I'd have to watch him every second, and I don't have time for that."

"David would be with him, though. He can show him the ropes."

"Sure he can — at first. But Melvin's a grown man. Will he take kindly to being managed by a boy? Or a woman?"

"If he has the spirit of a lamb, he will."

"A lamb who's all thumbs."

Emma laughed. "Look at it this way — he can't be worse than Aaron, can he? At least you'd know he was dependable and not running off to band hops on Fridays without telling you."

That was true. "So you think I should do it?"

"I think Carrie needs one good thing to happen." She glanced over toward the road, as if making sure Aleta's buggy was nowhere in sight. "If it's in your power to give her that, you might think about it."

Hadn't she just been thinking of all the things she had *no* power over? Now here was one thing that God had dropped into her lap, and she was pushing it away with both hands.

"I'll talk it over with Daed. And Aaron. To be fair, I have to speak with him first."

"Of course. And if he —"

"Emma!" On the other side of the field,

143

they saw Karen, her skirts hiked up in both hands, running toward them.

"Oh, no," Emma breathed. She broke into a run.

"Emma, it's Pap!" Karen called when she was close enough. Her chest heaved, and her *Kapp* had slipped sideways. And were those *leaves* caught in her hair? "He's wandered off again and none of us can find him!"

CHAPTER 7

"Where was the last place you saw him?"

They were gathered at the *Daadi Haus* where Emma lived with her parents, separated by the lane with its double row of poplars from the big farm now run by Karen and her husband, John.

"Right here on the back porch," Lena Stolzfus said from the rocking chair, bundled up against the weather, her voice trembling with age and fear. "He was right here, looking out over the yard, and then he wasn't." Four of her grandchildren, all under twelve, clung to her chair anxiously.

"Looking out where?" Emma asked. "Which direction?"

Lena gazed past her, as if to recall her husband's figure silhouetted against the gray skies, and met her daughter's gaze once more. "I don't know. Just out. And he was in his shirtsleeves. He didn't even have a coat."

"All right." Karen's John shrugged on a heavy coat and took charge. "I'll take the buggy and young Phil and go a mile in either direction on the road. Emma, you and Karen take the younger kids and walk our fields. And, Amelia, if you wouldn't mind, could you walk Moses Yoder's fields between our place and yours?"

That would cover all four directions. Amelia nodded and squeezed Emma's hand. The latter looked as though she were about to cry. No matter how bitter she got, underneath it all she loved her dad and couldn't bear to think of him coming to himself out there all alone, not knowing where home lay.

"We'll find him. How will we let each other know?"

"Bring him back here to Mamm, then run over to the farmhouse and hit the dinner gong hard," Karen said.

"Everybody take an umbrella," Lena said. "It's raining already."

They scattered, umbrellas bobbing away over the lane and into the fields. Amelia wished she could have gone with Emma, but time was in short supply if they were to find Victor Stolzfus before he slipped in the mud and hurt himself or got a chill from being out in the wet with no coat.

Once she left the well-worn path over the fields between her place and Emma's, the going was difficult. Amelia's shoes sank into the soft ground, which had been roiled into ridges by the harvester's wheels a month earlier. She struggled up the slope to the highest point and, breathing hard, tipped her umbrella back to see through the driving rain and the bluish mist that seemed to rise off the ground as the day cooled into late afternoon.

Nothing moved except a flock of crows in a stand of hawthorn bushes. She turned in the other direction and, away at the bottom of the field where it butted against the highway, caught a flash not of movement but of light. Blue, then red, over and over, dancing behind the trees that lined the road.

A police car.

Amelia's heart kicked into a gallop. A police car plus a missing man added up to nothing good. They were half a mile away, but she didn't hesitate. She dashed into Moses Yoder's barn and found him hitching up his buggy.

"Why, Amelia Beiler!" he exclaimed. *"Was tut Sie hier?"*

"Victor Stolzfus is missing," she gasped out. "And there's a police car out on the highway with its lights flashing. Can you take me down there?"

"Amelia . . . don't jump to conclusions."

"Please, Moses. Just to make sure it's not — And with the rain —"

He nodded, his movements crisp and efficient as he finished with the straps. "Get in."

Five minutes later — far less time than it would have taken her to run across half a mile of mud — Moses wrapped the reins around his hands and pulled up the horse behind the police car. By this time another had joined it, and there was a third car, too — sitting catawampus across the shoulder with a broken windshield. A man with slumped shoulders was talking in jerky sentences to one of the policemen, off to the side. Something lay still on the ground, with an orange tarpaulin over it. The only sounds were the squawk of the radio in the police car, the voices of the men, and the patter-patter-patter of rain on the tarp.

"Moses —" Amelia grasped his left arm with damp fingers and her throat closed. "Can you ask them . . . ask if . . ."

Even as she spoke, an ambulance flew over the top of the hill and skidded to a stop between the police cars. The flashing lights were giving her a headache, and she squinted, turning the deep brim of her black "away" bonnet to block out the jittery lights. Two men in paramedics' uniforms jumped out, and one ran to the tarp while the other stopped to talk to two more policemen. One of them finally turned toward the buggy, rain dripping off the visor of his cap.

"Folks, turn around and take the next road east, please. This is an accident scene. We're not letting any traffic through."

"What happened here?" Moses asked, leaning out of the buggy.

"It's under investigation, sir. Please turn around."

"One of our people is missing." Moses sounded as calm as a pond on a summer day. "We have a concern that he might have come to some harm."

"What do you mean, 'missing'?" The cop's eyes narrowed.

"He is old and has the . . . the . . ." Moses looked at Amelia.

"Alzheimer's," she whispered.

"He has the old timer's disease. He forgets where he is, and he wanders off."

"Can you describe the man?"

"Sure. He is Victor Stolzfus. He had his seventy-sixth birthday in August, and he lives on his son-in-law John's place about half a mile up that way." Moses pointed.

The cop looked to his partner as if seeking advice, and in the silence Amelia heard the *Englisch* man on the side of the road say, "I'm telling you, he just walked out in front of me, didn't look or anything. This is a county road, I was doing fifty at least, and in the rain . . . I tried to swerve, and next thing I knew, he was flying over the hood and there's glass everywhere."

"May I look at this man?" Moses Yoder asked quietly. "If it is our friend, someone will have to tell his family."

The policeman hesitated. "It's for the family to identify him, down at the morgue. I don't think —"

His partner lifted a hand and nodded toward the buggy. "It's the Amish," he said in a low voice. "You gotta be flexible with them." Moses took that as permission and got out. Biting her lips together to keep them from trembling, Amelia looked down at her hands, studying them instead of what lay under the tarp. Less than a minute later, the buggy tilted under Moses's wiry weight.

He sighed. Picked up the reins. Turned the horse around. Only then did he answer the question in her gaze. "Victor and I have been friends for sixty years. Better Lena should hear it from me than the *Englisch* policeman."

Amelia nodded, her heart weighing like a

stone in her chest. It was so like Moses to put Lena before himself — he probably wouldn't even allow himself to grieve until the day was over and he'd gone out to be alone in his barn. Emma would be just the same, seeing to everyone and everything before herself. But where would she go to grieve?

Oh, Emma.

Amelia gazed straight ahead over the horse's back, seeing nothing through the rain that ran untrammeled down the glass storm front of the buggy.

The Stolzfus clan scheduled the funeral for Saturday, and Thanksgiving became a quiet celebration of Victor's life. Lena even shooed her daughter Katherine and her husband off to the wedding they'd been invited to. "Death, marriage, and birth are part of life," Lena told them. "They go on with or without us, all part of God's will."

Amelia marveled at Lena's spirit of acceptance — deep in her own heart, where no one except God could see it, she still hadn't accepted Enoch's death, and it would be a year on Sunday. But Lena just shook her head. "I've had a good many years to prepare myself. And he's in a better place — with his right mind and with his

Savior. I couldn't ask for better gifts for the man I love."

Such a full, sweet spirit in a body that was so frail you could practically see through it.

Amelia wished that Emma could share some of her mother's spirit, because she looked positively haggard in her funeral black. As the long line of buggies rolled slowly down the highway out to the cemetery, the horses' hooves a slow clop and the wheels shushing them on the wet pavement, Emma let Matthew take the reins. She had offered to drive Emma and Lena, but the enormous Stolzfus connection had swept all the arrangements before it and had hardly left mere friends a corner to serve in.

Which, she supposed, was the way it should be. Family came first — though in her most private thoughts she reckoned that Emma would have been more grateful for the family's help in the ordinary day-to-day care of her father than she was now, where every moment was dictated by tradition and everyone knew what to do.

When you were on your own and the mental disintegration of the parent you loved produced a different kind of crisis every week, even one of those casseroles lined up on the tables and stacked on the kitchen counter in the big house would have been a gift from God.

But it was done now, and all that was left was the grieving — and, after that, the missing.

The turn into the cemetery was coming up, and the buggies had all slowed to a creep. "I'll take the lines now," she said to Matthew.

"I can do it, Mamm." He sat straight on the bench, every muscle in his little body behind the reins, sensitive to every movement of the horse. "I see the turn up there. Daed taught me. I'll show you."

Her instincts, long trained to hold back, to keep close, to prevent, urged her to take the reins from his hands. But in her memory she heard Enoch laughing as he walked beside Daadi's pony cart. "That's the way, Matthew. Hold him back. Show him who's boss. You don't want him running away with you — and I don't want to go chasing you down the lane and *plotz* in a puddle."

She nodded and sat back. "*Gut,* then. You show me."

She needn't have worried. The procession was moving so slowly that the turn between the stone walls of the cemetery might as well have been a straightaway on an open road, so easy to manage it was. She didn't have to take over until they approached the hitching rail, and even then he jumped out to loop the reins over it.

"Well done, *Schatzi*," she said, resisting the urge to give him a big hug. He was turning into a young man so quickly — and besides, a group of his friends had gathered to watch him drive, their eyes huge under their black hats. It would never do for her to treat him like little Elam in front of an audience.

She kept both boys next to her at the gravesite. There would be no running around as there would at a wedding. And anyway, between the rain and the solemnity in the crowd, the boys seemed to be content to stay close, sheltering under the big umbrella. How could it not bring back memories of Enoch's funeral? They had stood one row over, under that big pine, and listened to the bishop pray, just as he was doing now. They had held hands then, though, Amelia clinging to her boys as though they were life rafts and she a drowning swimmer. Elam was content to hold on to her skirt and press close now, but Matthew stood beside her, not touching, his back straight and his face solemn.

Ach, they grew up so fast. Before she could turn around, they would be going on *Rumspringe* and badgering her for buggies of their own.

When the last hymn had been sung, the crowd moved and scattered. Since she was standing near the back, it was no trouble to walk the few steps to Enoch's grave. Simple and unadorned, it carried only his name and the dates of birth and death.

"Thirty-two years, a month, and seventeen days," Matthew said. "That's what you get if you subtract the first date from the second."

There were trees not ten feet away that had lived longer than her husband. "So short a span to be born, grow up, get married, and have you two, isn't it?"

"Daed and Victor Stolzfus are in heaven, aren't they, Mamm?" Elam tugged on her sleeve.

"They are. God took them to be with Him for eternity."

"Will we see Daed when we die?"

"Well, we won't have the bodies we have now; we'll be made of spirit," she said slowly. "But it says there will be no sorrow there, only joy, so I'm thinking that means we'll be together with Daed again."

"So he's not really down there in the dark?"

The dark. The pieces fit together in her head as Elam looked up at her, his face white with apprehension. "No," she said softly. "His body is going back to the ground that God made Adam from, but there is no dark where he is now. No dark, no monsters, nothing to fear . . . Only light and singing for joy at being with God."

She fell silent, wondering if she'd said too much. But Elam wasn't finished. He pressed even closer. "And Emma will have her papa, too?"

"Yes."

"She should be glad, then, shouldn't she?"

"I think she will be, in time. At the moment she's missing her father, like we miss Daed still."

"You should tell her she'll be with him in heaven, Mamm. That would cheer her up."

She touched Elam's cheek, whose color was returning, and still with its baby roundness yet. "You can tell her, at the house. I think she'll be glad if you remind her."

And so he did. Matthew had responded to the more cheerful atmosphere of the house and gone with his friends out into the orchard to find windfalls. But Elam had waited until Emma was by herself near the window, and when she leaned down, he whispered in her ear. Amelia watched her hug the little boy, bent over him as though he were the only thing holding her up. Then

156

she straightened, made sure he had another helping of gingerbread cake next to his Auntie Esther, and walked out of the house.

Amelia grabbed Carrie. "Come on. Emma needs us."

Emma walked rapidly across the lane and along the well-worn path to the *Daadi Haus*. Amelia practically had to run to catch up, the heavy lining of her apron beating against her thighs as if to tell her to slow down, to act more becoming. Right behind her, Carrie said, "She wants to be alone. Shouldn't we give her that?"

"That's the last thing she wants." Amelia remembered how it was. "She needs friends with her."

"The big house is full of friends and relatives. She needs her family."

"We're her family, too." Amelia pushed open the kitchen door and stepped into the warm quiet, holding the door until Carrie slipped through.

"I don't think I've ever been here and found no one in the kitchen," Carrie whispered. "Where is she?"

"I'm out here." Emma's voice was muted.

When Amelia rounded the corner into the living room, she found Emma standing by the window, gazing out at the same fields she'd been looking at her whole life. "Are

157

you all right? We saw you leave, and we got worried."

Emma turned and took their hands, gripping them so hard they shook. Then her face wavered and collapsed as she released their hands and flung her arms around their shoulders. They stood together, the two of them wrapping her in patient love while she cried.

Carrie slipped out to the downstairs bedroom and came back with a white cotton handkerchief. *"Denki."* Emma blew her nose and mopped her eyes, then tucked it into her sleeve as she sank onto the narrow, uncomfortable sofa. "I don't know what came over me. I've been trying so hard to stay strong for Mamm, and all of a sudden . . ."

"It will get easier with time," Amelia said softly.

Emma huffed out a breath that on any other occasion might have been a laugh. "I wasn't even crying over Pap. I guess . . . I was just so grateful that it's you two and I can be myself. I didn't mean to let it all go."

"You can't be yourself over there?" Carrie asked. "But it's all your friends and your family."

"Do you know what it's like to have a

houseful of Stolzfuses?" Emma's gaze was wry — almost like herself. "Every woman convinced she's the only one who knows how to arrange things and everyone trying to do for Mamm, when all she wants is to sit by the window and remember the old days with her buddies. You know, when she was first married and they were all making mistakes together. When Pap was strong and handsome." She sighed. "There aren't so many of those ladies now. It seems like God calls one home every few months."

"We should go back, Emma." Carrie glanced out the kitchen window, though there was nothing to be seen but the poplars, the last of their gold-coin leaves sifting to the ground in the rain. "They'll be missing you."

"No one will miss me. Not for ten minutes. I just need to sit here and be quiet with you. I feel all *verhuddelt*."

"Life is *verhuddelt* right now," Amelia told her softly. "Put yourself in God's hands, and He'll make it come out right."

Emma fidgeted. "My word, this couch is awful. The first thing I'm going to do is get a new one."

Amelia had meant to offer her comfort, not provoke an abrupt change of subject. "The first thing after what?"

"After everyone goes home."

"A couch?"

Emma wriggled and finally stood up, resuming her place by the window. She gripped her elbows as if she were cold. "Pap would never let us change a thing. He brought that couch home in the market wagon in nineteen fifty-something, and here it stayed all this time. Mamm never sits on it. Says it makes her back hurt."

"Maybe you should —"

"Karen will have a fit." Emma talked right over Carrie as if she hadn't spoken. "She's just like Pap — doesn't want things to change, even when they're for the better. Well, she can have the couch. Mamm and I are going to get something we like."

Carrie glanced at Amelia with concern in her eyes. "Emma, please sit. Not on the couch, in your reading chair. It's not good to make too many changes after . . . after something like this. Give it a few months and then see how you feel."

"I'll have a sore back, is how I'll feel."

This wasn't right. Emma wouldn't sit. Instead she paced back and forth, as if coming to join them and then changing her mind and walking away, her hands fisted against her apron. Something more than a couch was at stake here.

"Emma, what's really going on? You never get het up about silly things like furniture. I don't think I've heard you talk about a couch, ever."

Emma turned on the ball of her foot and stalked the seven steps over to the bookcase. And back. When she looked up and met their concerned gazes, she exhaled on a long breath that carried something of relief, something of despair. "Is it wrong to be glad he's gone?"

CHAPTER 8

Glad?

That was the last thing Amelia had expected her to say. For a moment she couldn't think how to reply.

How can you be glad your father is dead? But no, that was Mamm's voice she heard in her head. The voice of guilt, of expectation, of caring what everybody thought.

Was it really so bad, looking after him? She couldn't say that either. Cleaning up the head of the household after he had messed himself really *was* that bad, no matter how much love lay between you. And deep down she couldn't bear to know. At some point someone — Matthew? Mamm? — would have to do that for her. Maybe sooner than she thought. Who had done it for poor Lila Esch when the Mennonite nurse was not there?

Carrie said softly, "No one is here but us, Emma. Sit down and tell us everything."

"I know it's wrong to feel this way — I loved Pap." Emma's voice sounded hoarse — as if even her body were trying to prevent her from saying the words. "I know he sacrificed for us kids growing up, so it was my place to sacrifice for him when he needed me. But . . ."

"But?" Carrie prompted when the pause grew into a silence.

"But why is caring for my parents the only thing God has held out to me?" Emma wailed. "Why can't I find a husband like Karen or Katherine? Why do I have to be the senior single and watch the years go by from this window?" She hid her face in her hands. "I'm so ashamed, only thinking of myself. But I can't help it."

"You're grieving him," Amelia said slowly. Her heart hurt for Emma — and it wasn't the first time any of them had thought those very questions and had never dared to say them out loud. "But you're mourning yourself, too. And I don't see anything so wrong with that."

The rain ran down the gutter spout, as if the very world around them joined in.

"It's selfish," Emma whispered. "Remember JOY? Jesus first, others next, yourself last?"

"I know, but, Emma," Carrie said, "we're

only human. We can strive for the best, but sometimes we don't hit the mark. That's where God's grace and forgiveness step in. I don't think He is going to blame you for having these thoughts. I know we aren't."

"Maybe things will be different now, after you've had a little time to grieve and adjust." Amelia didn't have any answers. But that didn't mean they weren't out there. God, after all, knew what He was about, even if to them His plan looked as obvious as a dirt road in heavy fog.

"I don't think you're glad your dad is gone," Carrie said. "I think you're relieved. And that seems to me to be pretty normal."

Emma nodded, her gaze on the plank floor of the living room, polished to a shine by her own hands. "Relieved." She looked up. "That's the very word. I feel as if a weight has been rolled off me, like I'm a balloon bobbing in the air just waiting for a tree to catch me."

Amelia grinned. "Maybe that tree will be wearing pants."

To her huge relief, Emma attempted a smile. "Or maybe it will be holding a —" She stopped, changed her mind about the next word. "A new couch." She stood. "We should get back. You're right — Mamm will be wondering where I am."

She hugged each of them in turn — that was twice in one day from a woman who wasn't usually given to displays of affection. As they walked back to the big house, Amelia rubbed her left hand. It was a habit now, though it never did any good. What had Emma been going to say before she'd stopped herself? What besides a husband did she think was going to catch her and make her life change?

Ah, well. When she was ready to tell them, she would. That was one of the things Amelia loved about their friendship. They had no secrets from each other.

Amelia found her horse, Daisy, in the Stolzfus field, snorting and jostling for the choicest grass with everyone else's animals, and walked her over to the buggy. Amelia wanted to stay with Emma for the evening and help Victor's daughters clear up, but at the same time she was nervous about driving at night with hands she couldn't depend on and the boys along. After Enoch's death it had taken everything she had to drive at all. Even now she walked everywhere she could — except today, when everybody had gone out to the cemetery in the rain. Some days you just had to pull up your socks, wipe away the pictures in your mind, and do what had to be done.

She was backing the horse between the rails when a voice spoke behind her.

"May I give you a hand?" Eli Fischer's experienced hands tightened straps and fastened buckles, and before she could protest, he had the job done.

"*Denki,*" she said at last. "It's very kind of you. But I thought you had a wedding to go to?"

"I got a ride back in a van, which shaved a day off the trip." The shoulders of his waterproof jacket were slick with rain, and a steady drip came down off his hat over his left eye, but in spite of it his eyes twinkled and he looked as if he were perfectly content to be harnessing her horse in a downpour. "You would not believe the number of people in that house. It was another Lapp wedding — one of my cousins on my mother's side, which means Mary and Daniel Lapp were there, though they left early so they could come back for the funeral. I gave the bride my good wishes and a set of yard tools, and I made sure Mary saw it so she could write and tell my grandmother, and after that I was a free man."

He was the most provoking person, making her laugh when the occasion was so serious. Good thing they were out in the field, with no one closer than forty feet but one of Emma's brothers and his teenage boys.

"Well, I appreciate the help. It's hard to harness a horse with one hand." She waggled her left, since the fingers wouldn't respond properly. "At least it's good to hold the umbrella yet."

"What does the doctor say, if you don't mind me asking?"

She should mind. She hardly knew him, despite his disconcerting habit of appearing when least expected. But somehow the look in his eyes was sympathetic rather than nosy, as though he were honestly concerned. "He says it's multiple sclerosis." Those brown eyes widened, and she went on hastily, "I'm getting a second opinion. When I'm at the shop tomorrow, I'll start making calls."

"It's good that you have a phone there, if you need to use it for such things."

She nodded. "I never expected to use it for more than answering customers' questions and taking orders, though."

"Will this affect your decision not to sell?"

Amelia felt as though someone had pulled the collar of her coat open in the back and let the cold rain pour in. Was that what he was interested in, then? Was he just trying to butter her up by helping?

167

She took the reins from his hands with a little more authority than he was probably used to. "No." The single syllable was as final as the stiffness in her face. "Thank you for your help."

She got into the buggy and would have flapped the wet reins over Daisy's back without even saying good-bye, except that he slid open the door and leaned in.

"Amelia. What did I say? Did I offend you?"

She tried to find words that would offend less than the ones she'd just heard. "I suppose it's a sensible conclusion to come to — that I'd be more likely to sell if I were sick." He made a sound that could have been distress, but she didn't allow him to speak. "I'm not convinced it is MS, though, and until I am, the shop is not for sale."

"Amelia, I didn't mean it that way."

"Didn't you?" The black brim of her bonnet framed him tightly in her field of vision, blocking out the fields on either side. His brows wrinkled in the middle, and his gaze never left her face. That annoying trickle of water off the brim of his hat made her want to reach over and turn it so it leaked onto the back of his jacket. But that was a gesture that would be misinterpreted by him and anyone watching, and besides, she *was* offended, sin or not. "It sounded so."

"About the shop — I respected the answer you gave me when I asked, and if you change your mind, you'll tell me. I simply meant that — I wondered if — That is, I was afraid it would make things harder for you, this trouble. That's all."

Amelia felt the hot blood of shame seep into her cheeks, her forehead, her neck. She'd been too quick to judge — done the very thing she disliked most in her own mother and had vowed never to do with the boys. Only proud people got offended. And here, at the first opportunity and right after he'd helped her when no one else had thought of it, not even her own brothers, who were over there in the barn with the Stolzfus men . . .

She reeled in her galloping thoughts and forced herself to relax her grip on the lines. Poor Daisy was backing and stepping, with no idea what Amelia wanted her to do. "Easy, girl," she crooned. "It's all right." She forced herself to turn and look Eli Fischer in the face.

"I'm sorry," she said. "I took offense when I shouldn't have. I should have known your intentions were not — that you — I mean —" Now it was her turn to stumble and stammer. "I — I need to find the boys and take them home before it gets any darker."

"Of course." He closed the buggy door and stepped clear. "I'm glad to see you looking so well anyway. And I hope the second opinion is better."

She flashed him a half smile and shook the reins, wheeling Daisy around and heading her over to the yard, where Ruth had the boys corralled on the porch.

He thought she looked well.

Goodness. It had been a long time since a man had said such a thing to her.

Just you never mind thinking thoughts about Eli Fischer. You're in no position to be looking into his eyes and imagining nonsense. You can't lead a man on and then disappoint him. Because if this second opinion you're after agrees with the first one, there will be no one after Enoch. No one.

She paled at the thought, thankful as they drove home that Matthew and Elam were more interested in the horse than in the unruly thoughts of their mother.

On Monday, Amelia arrived at the shop determined to start fresh and new and have it out with Aaron King. She found the place empty but for David out in the storage yard, organizing the lumber into neat stacks as tall as he was. Aaron wasn't lounging on the step waiting for her, and he certainly wasn't with David or doing some other useful thing while he waited for her to unlock the doors.

At ten minutes past nine, he finally ambled into the office, where she was laying out the jobs for the day.

She looked rather pointedly at the clock on the diner across the street and two over, which displayed the time in a circle of pink neon, night or day. Oblivious, Aaron kept going, heading into the back. Amelia stood and intercepted him.

"Aaron, I'd like to have a talk."

He smiled and parked a hip on her desk. "Sure, Amelia. What up?"

Had he forgotten how to speak good *Deitch?* Instead of switching to English, she went on in their own tongue. "Is there a reason you're late this morning?"

Surprised, he leaned to look out the window at the diner's clock. "Am I late? It's only ten after."

"We open at nine, as you know very well."

"But it's only ten minutes." He sat there, long drink of water that he was, mystified.

"It may only be ten minutes, but in those minutes you could have had a job laid out. If a customer came, what would he think of a shop that's empty and silent, with no work being done?"

"Um . . . well, *you* were here. And I hear David out there. Besides, there's no customers here yet. It's too early."

She resisted the urge to roll her eyes, and resisted another urge to give him the spanking that his parents clearly should have given him years ago. All her good intentions of asking him his plans, of not rocking the boat in Melvin Miller's favor, flew out the window on the wings of exasperation.

"Aaron, I'm not happy with this. You're late to work three days out of five, and when you are here, you don't pull your weight. I've spoken to you about it before, and I don't see any improvement."

Under his shaggy thatch of hair cut in the *Englisch* fashion, he at least had the grace to look abashed. "I got a lot of things going on, Amelia."

Sure he did. Parties and running around in his flashy buggy, that's what. "Is that all you have to say for yourself? What kinds of things?"

"My dad, mostly. He needs help on the farm, even though he has my two older brothers to help him. I was up at four this morning milking."

"And I get up at four on Mondays to do the wash. We all have our work at home as well as here. You're not the only one."

"Yeah, but you don't have my dad down your back. He's got me working all the time I'm at home. I have to leave if I ever want to —" He stopped, and two scarlet patches flared in his cheeks.

So he had the ability to blush. Never mind, it was none of her business. "Well, I'm thinking that obeying your dad is your first responsibility, but I need someone I can depend on. I'm going to have to let you go, Aaron."

He gazed at her, stricken, as if she'd slapped him the way she'd wanted to a moment ago. "You're firing me?"

She was a little surprised to see that he cared this much. But at least he had alternatives. Carrie had none. If she didn't give Melvin a job, he'd have to go to Indiana, and Amelia wouldn't be able to bear her best friend's distress if that happened. "*Ja.* This is two weeks' notice. But if you decide to go today, I'll write out your check."

He slid his bottom off the desk and stood on his own two feet. "How are you going to manage without me?"

Look at him, standing there with one hip cocked, as if her business would crash without his hard work and determination. Hmph.

"I'll manage. And if I can't, I'll hire

173

someone else." He didn't need to know that she was going to ask that someone else immediately — probably this evening, so he could start on Monday.

"You know, Amelia, I don't feel comfortable working the two weeks if you don't respect what I do for you. I'll just take my check now, if that's okay with you."

Now? As in right now? "Aren't you going to finish out the day?"

He shook his head. "I don't want to be where I'm not wanted."

"Oh, for goodness' sake, Aaron, stop playing hard done by. Of course you're wanted. But I need someone who wants to be here, too, day after day. And I don't think you do."

She thought she heard him mumble, "You got that right."

"And that's fine. Building pallets isn't for everyone."

"You make it sound like some kind of career."

"We both know it isn't. But it's good, solid work, and it's needed, so I do it. You know perfectly well I'd rather be at home, but God didn't set me on that path."

"I know." At least the attitude had leaked away. "But I can still have my check?"

"Yes. Just let me write it out."

When she gave it to him, he had the grace to extend a hand and shake hers. "*Denki, Amelia.* Good luck."

Businesses didn't run themselves on luck, but she wasn't going to explain that to him. "I hope you find the work God means you to have, Aaron."

He just smiled the kind of smile that Emma used to when she had a secret to keep, and loped out the door, shoving the check into the tight front pocket of his worldly jeans. With a sigh Amelia resigned herself to running the air nailer with David, and turned to gather up the job slips. But when the phone rang, her hands jerked and all the slips flew up like doves frightened out of a tree.

She grabbed the phone. "Whinburg Pallet and Crate, Amelia Beiler speaking."

"Aunt Amelia, it's me, Marie — your niece?"

She had twelve nieces, and Marie was her sister Donna's second girl. "Hi, *Schatzi. Wie geht's?*"

"I'm well, thanks. Mamm says I'm to say hi from her, and she's looking forward to seeing you at Christmas."

Donna lived away up in Lebanon, and they got to see each other only a couple of times a year, usually at Christmas and in the spring when her brother-in-law brought the family down for the mud sales. "I'm looking forward to seeing her, too. But . . . why are you calling? Does she think I'm taking too long to answer her letter?"

"No, it's not about that. Mammi called us last night. She says you're looking for a second opinion on an MS diagnosis?"

Mammi needed to mind her own business. "Yes, I am. But what —"

"I'm calling because I have a job now, Auntie. At Dr. Stewart's office in Strasburg."

"Strasburg?" That was miles from Lebanon.

"*Ja*. I'm on my own now, sharing a house with two other girls. Anyway, Dr. Stewart is a really good doctor, and since I make her appointments, I can put you down for tomorrow morning if you can make it. Can you?"

Amelia's jaw hung in the wind, swinging open and shut like a gate without a latch. How could she have been so dense? Worrying about finding a second doctor in the phone book when all she had to do was put the word out among her own family that she needed help?

Pride again. She'd become so hardened, so used to thinking she was so capable, that she just never thought of giving someone else the chance to serve.

"That would be wonderful. But . . . but what is Dr. Stewart's specialty? She's a lady doctor? Does she know about MS?"

"She knows about all kinds of things, Auntie, including that. She's a holistic doctor. You wouldn't believe the number of people who walk out of here well, sometimes for the first time in years. And half her patients are Amish. You'll be in good hands, I promise." Holistic. Did that mean whole? Never mind, Marie was speaking again, making the appointment for the next day. "I just need one thing. Can you ask your doctor to send your MRIs over here? Dr. Stewart will want to look at them, too. And it will save you the cost of getting another set."

After Amelia agreed to make the call, she sent her love to Donna and the family and hung up.

Maybe it was her mother, getting overinvolved the way she did every time the subject of health came up. Or maybe it was God's hand, directing her to the very person she needed to see.

Amelia just hoped that in the end this new doctor would have the right answer.

CHAPTER 9

Carrie loved it when the boys came over, so as soon as the dishes were done, Amelia got them into their coats and gum boots and hitched up the buggy for the trip to her house. Carrie squealed with delight and pulled them all into the kitchen, which was warm and smelled of fried sausages and cinnamon.

"I'm so glad to see you. I'm trying to make these pumpkin cookies, and I could really use your help." She set Elam in front of a bowl of cooked pumpkin chunks and handed him a potato masher. "Why don't you mash this while I talk to your mama. And, Matthew, can you measure out two level cups of flour?"

"Actually, I was hoping to talk to Melvin." Amelia shot Carrie a meaningful look and was gratified to see her brighten as though someone had turned up a wick behind her eyes.

"Sure. He's in the sitting room reading the newspaper." With a smile, she returned to her worktable. "That's it, Elam. Really mash it good."

Melvin looked up as Amelia crossed the room and sat in Carrie's rocker. "Hello, Amelia. What brings you our way on this windy evening?"

Even as he spoke, she could hear branches tapping on the side of the house. They ought to be trimmed back, but nothing would make her say so.

"Carrie loves to see the boys, and with school they don't get over here as much as they used to. And I wanted to speak to you." He folded the paper, which was open to the Help Wanted section, and gave her his full attention. "I wondered if you might be interested in a job at the shop."

He paused, as if he were unsure she actually meant him. "Your shop?"

"Yes. I let Aaron King go this morning, but if I don't find another builder by Monday, I'll be running that air nailer myself. I just don't have the time or the strength to do it."

"You're asking me. But Amelia . . ." He took a breath. "I don't know a thing about building pallets."

"You helped build RVs, didn't you?"

179

"Sure, but that's different."

"Probably a lot more complicated. Believe me, if I can build a pallet, you can. And David Yoder will help you. He knows as much as I do about it — more, in fact."

She'd expected him to jump at the offer. Why was he sitting there looking so uncomfortable? "Are you set on going to Shipshey instead?" Part of her hoped so. Then she'd have done the right thing without having to pay the price of his ineptitude.

"No, it's not that. It's just —" He toyed with the edge of the paper. "We're both from the same kind of families, Carrie and I. Plainer maybe than you. I don't know how I'd feel working with your power tools. They'd be a temptation for me, you see."

That was the last thing she'd expected him to say. "They're not powered by electricity. They run on gas."

"But you just said you used an air nailer. That seems like a fancy tool to have when a good hammer serves us well and always has."

"You can't use a hammer and ordinary nails to build a pallet."

He smiled. "Can't — or won't?"

Men who need work shouldn't question the faith of those who offer it. "Can't. If you did, the minute the customer's forklift slid its

180

prongs into the loaded pallet, the nails would rip right out and the whole thing would end up all over the ground. Which wouldn't be so good if the customer were shipping eggs."

He stared at her, clearly not understanding.

"We use special coated nails with a twist in them. Almost like a screw. The air nailer inserts them properly so they don't pull out under the stress of the forklift."

Understanding dawned. "I have a lot to learn, don't I?"

"Maybe a lot. But it's not so hard. So you'll take the job and not go to Shipshewana?"

With a glance out at the kitchen, where Carrie was laughing at something Matthew had said, Melvin nodded. "I see that my wife has been talking to you. And Emma, too, probably?"

"Yes."

"You didn't fire poor Aaron just to give me work, I hope."

"No. I was thinking of letting him go anyway. He doesn't pull his weight, and I need someone who does."

"I'll do my best. I may not be the smartest farmer in the world, but I think I can manage your air nailer with its twisty nails."

Again Amelia felt ashamed of her opinion of Melvin. She loved and respected Carrie. Would Carrie have married a stupid man? He had just admitted he knew his own limits. There must be depths to Melvin Miller that the casual observer couldn't see. Maybe he would be a gifted pallet maker.

She held out a hand. "Welcome to Whinburg Pallet and Crate. I'll see you at nine o'clock —" She hesitated. Tomorrow was the doctor, then quilting that afternoon, and David was off on Wednesdays. But she couldn't very well make Melvin wait until Thursday. She didn't want him thinking she didn't trust him to do his work if she wasn't there. David would just have to handle it. "Tomorrow."

"And don't be late?" He grinned at her as he shook her hand.

"I can be a hard boss," she warned. "Don't get ideas."

The smile faded. "Thank you," he said. "I know you're doing this for love, not because I have any talent at building things."

"And you're working for me for love," she said. "You want to see Carrie happy as much as I do."

"More. There's nothing I wouldn't do for her. Even rent my land to my neighbors so I can work in town."

And if you do that, and you're content with your work, maybe a baby will come faster. But Amelia only smiled and went back out to the kitchen to see how the boys were doing.

Carrie looked up from the table, where Matthew was scooping out tablespoons of batter and Elam was carefully pressing them on the cookie sheet with a fork, peanut-butter-cookie style. Both of them had more batter on their faces than there was in the spoon.

Carrie's face held so much hope that Amelia could have leaned over the worktable and hugged her. But she didn't — merely nodded — and that was enough. Carrie squeezed her eyes shut, clasped her hands under her chin, and jumped up and down in silent joy.

Elam turned to look at her. "Auntie Carrie, did you burn yourself?"

"No, sweetheart," Carrie said on a shaky breath. "I just had a very happy thought, that's all."

"Did God give it to you?"

Amelia smothered a smile. During prayer time Sunday night, they had talked about where thoughts come from and whether you let them roost in your mind or chased them away like starlings out of the vegetable garden.

"Yes, He certainly did." Beaming, her eyes damp, Carrie ruffled his hair.

"So you will let it stay?"

"I sure will. Lots of good things will be staying. Like these cookies, if we don't hurry up and get them in the oven. Would you like to take some home with you?"

Dr. Stewart looked so young that Amelia wondered if she had gotten out of medical school only the week before. She was smaller than Amelia herself, and her red hair was pulled back in a French braid that lay against her white lab coat in a fat rope.

"I've looked at the MRI slices, and from what you've told me and the motor-control tests I had you do, I don't think I can add or subtract anything from the diagnosis you got from Dr. Hunter."

Amelia's stomach bottomed out, the way it did when she'd swung too high on the rope swing as a child. She sat on a couch across a low table from the doctor, smoothing her apron flat across her knees. "So you agree with him?" She needed to hear it, definitely, one way or the other.

"Yes, I agree with him. What medications did he put you on?"

Amelia dug in her purse and pulled out the prescription paper. "I haven't had time to do anything with this yet."

The doctor scanned the paper in less than a second. "Just as well. Your niece may have told you that my methods are a little different from the mainstream's?"

"She said you were a holistic doctor."

"Right. I treat the whole person, not just sore legs or headaches or — in your case — the immune system. So I think you have a choice to make, Mrs. Beiler. We have some options to look at, or you can do as Dr. Hunter suggests and go on medication."

"How long will the medicines take?"

The doctor's eyes were the color of moss. "You mean, will there ever be a point when you're off them?" Amelia nodded. "No. You're looking at the rest of your life, probably."

Amelia sagged against the back of the couch. She knew that. But somehow it was worse when it came in a woman's positive tone.

Dr. Stewart went on, "But the church is good about looking after its people. I know of patients in Ronks and Intercourse with this condition, and their medications are paid for, no problem. If that was worrying you."

"It was. Is. I don't want to be a burden to my neighbors, even if the fund is for that very thing. I pay my hundred and twenty-five dollars into it every month, just like everyone else, but I'd be taking out much more than that."

"If you decide to go that route. There are others."

"What others? Dr. Hunter didn't mention any."

The doctor smiled, the freckles on her cheeks seeming more prominent than ever. "I know Dr. Hunter. A fine practitioner. But with eyebrows like that, you'd think he'd have more imagination, wouldn't you?"

Amelia chuckled. "I couldn't take my eyes off them. They look like coconut macaroons."

"A perfect description if ever I heard one. I'll have to tell him that."

"No!" Amelia sat up in alarm. "Please don't tell him I said something so foolish."

"Of course not." Dr. Stewart made patting motions in the air, and Amelia settled down. "I'll steal it and pass it off as my own. No, what I meant was that he doesn't pay attention to what's going on outside his little pharmaceutical world. There are experiments and research out there that make me very optimistic that we can get you some

186

help. Maybe even remission, eventually."

There was that word again. It seemed to represent hope as fragile as smoke. "Like what?"

"Like anger therapy, for one. MS has been called the disease of anger, and the reason it's so prevalent in women is that we turn our anger in on ourselves instead of going out and kicking something."

Amelia stared at her. "I'm not angry at anyone." That wouldn't be Christian. Didn't the Bible say the people of God were to put away bitterness, wrath, and anger? A person had to forgive, as Christ had forgiven. As Carrie and her mother-in-law had forgiven. You couldn't lug that burden around with you anyway — it would eat you up from the inside.

With a tingle of shock, Amelia realized that this was exactly what the doctor had just said.

"No? Well, I'll leave you to think about that one. Then, in Mexico City, a group of researchers have had a lot of success reintroducing myelin to the body. That's the stuff that's getting stripped off your nerve casings."

"Yes, Dr. Hunter explained it to me. How can they do that?"

"They use myelin from cows."

Amelia stared at her. First anger, now cows? What kind of quack was this woman?

As if she'd read her mind, Dr. Stewart smiled. "I can see what you're thinking. But cow myelin is very similar to ours, just as pig valves work perfectly well in human hearts. With regular injections of this substance, patients down there have gone into remission or their symptoms have backed off to the point where they have relief. From what Marie has told me, you're a young mother with two little boys and other than this you're in excellent health. I think you'd be a very good candidate."

"What would I have to do?"

"Travel to Mexico City. Stay there for two to four months while you undergo the treatment. And begin a course of exercise and vitamins afterward to bring your immune system up to snuff."

"I can't be away from my boys for four months!"

She lifted her shoulders, as if to say, *Your choice.* "Maybe the boys could stay with family members. Maybe a family member could come with you to look after them. There are ways to accomplish it. Think about it."

Amelia had already thought about it. It was out of the question, something so outlandish. But then she heard herself say, "What would it cost?"

"Other than getting down there and a place to stay, it would run you about fifty grand."

Well, that was that. "I don't have fifty thousand dollars."

"There is the church fund."

Amelia opened her mouth to say they would never let her have that much money when she remembered Old Joe Yoder's cancer treatment in Costa Rica, years ago when she'd been a girl. The elders had taken nearly a week talking it over, but in the end they had agreed to fund it, and it had come to over a hundred thousand. And here he was, decades later, hale and hearty, with grandchildren and great-grandchildren like bunches of cherries on the branches of his family tree.

Maybe there was a chance.

No, no. If *she* thought that extracting myelin from cows was quackery — and possibly against God's will, having an animal's parts inside you — what would Bishop Daniel think?

Dr. Stewart waited quietly across from her, which Amelia appreciated. Dr. Hunter had made her feel rushed and foolish. At least this woman made her feel calm, even if all these odd suggestions tempted her to smile.

"Think it over," the doctor said quietly. "Talk about it with your family. And then let me know if you want to go ahead with something like that or stick with the mainstream and take medication for the rest of your life."

Amelia left the office with a big packet of papers and brochures, feeling even more confused than when she'd gone in. A second opinion was one thing. But choosing between a well-trodden path that others had been down versus a path that led to the wilds of Mexico . . . That was something else again.

She needed to talk to her family. And her friends. Carrie hadn't been able to come with her this time, but thank goodness she could see her and Emma in just a couple of hours. While they laid out their quilt blocks in neat, pleasing rows, they would help her decide what to do with this disruption in the order of her life.

And speaking of disruptions . . . how was her new employee getting on back at the shop?

Daisy had waited patiently outside the doctor's office, but she was ready to lengthen her stride when she realized they were heading back to Whinburg. Slowly, awkwardly, Amelia unhitched her in the shed the Steiners kept for their horses behind their cabinet shop and hurried around the side of the building to her own shop. A quick glance around the office as she struggled one-handed with her coat told her that no disasters had happened there. But a cold feeling sank into the pit of her stomach as she hung up her away bonnet and opened the door to the back of the shop.

David straightened as he saw her. "Hallo."

"Hi, David. Where's Melvin?"

A board slapped the concrete floor behind the stack of waiting lumber, and she jumped. "Right here." Melvin came around the stack holding a board and handed it to David. "Try this one. Amelia, what's wrong? You look very pale. Did it go badly at the doctor?"

Her gaze jumped from one to the other. "Yes. I mean, no. It would be hard to say. Is everything all right?"

Melvin smiled, a smile so humble and filled with pain that she dropped her gaze. "Did you expect me to burn the building down on my first day?"

He may as well have struck her, she felt so sick. What did she think? That he would live down to her expectations? That was her sin.

Judging people before giving them a chance.

"No, of course not, Melvin. I'm sorry. It's just that with the power tools — and when I didn't see you just now — I thought . . ."

David rescued her. "It's okay, Amelia. He's doing fine. I was showing him how to fit the pieces together, and we split a plank, that's all."

Breathe. Bad enough you think so little of him. Much worse that you showed it. He is your best friend's husband, and when you think critically of him, you do the same to her.

"Sorry," she said again. "Of course. Do you need me to help?"

Both men shook their heads, and she got the message. *Leave us to our work and go organize your papers.*

Back in the office, she collapsed into her chair behind the desk. She must really be rattled if she was showing her emotions so clearly. Orders and invoices would settle her. She pulled a stack toward her and began to sort them by due date, but the numbers faded in and out, competing with the pictures in her head.

"Amelia, concentrate," she whispered.

But she could not.

Finally she pulled the phone book out of the bottom drawer and flipped through the yellow pages in the back.

There.

"Strasburg Travel, may I help you?"

"*Ja,* I wonder if you could tell me how much it would cost to take the train to Mexico City from Lancaster?"

There was a pause. "Ma'am, did you say *Mexico City?* As in *Mexico?* A train?"

"Yes."

"Why would you want to do that when you could fly?"

This had been a very bad idea. What had possessed her? "Because I am Amish, and we do not fly in planes."

"I see. I should have known that as soon as you said the word *train.*" Another pause, filled with the clacking of keys. "Ma'am, you might want to choose another destination, then, because Mexico suspended all its passenger train service about ten years ago. The only way to get to Mexico City is by bus, and, frankly, our government doesn't recommend that people do that. It's not safe, especially for a woman on her own."

"I would not be on my own. I would have my two boys and a friend with me."

"A male friend?"

Amelia felt herself blush. "No. Female."

"If you're set on going, then, it would be much safer to fly. For all practical purposes, it's the only way to get there from Pennsylvania."

Amelia gave up. All she wanted was a number, not a lecture. "Fine, then. How much would it cost to fly?"

The young woman sounded much happier when she replied briskly, "Departing when?"

"Um. Does it make a difference?"

"It sure does. It's much more expensive if you go in the winter versus the spring or summer."

"Oh. Well, I don't think I can wait until spring. Next month?"

"Christmas is a very popular time to travel. Do you have a special reason to fly then?"

I need to go before I lose my right hand, too. No, she couldn't say that. "How about early January? Would that cost less?"

"Quite a bit less. How long would you be going for? A week?"

"Oh, no. Four months. Maybe five."

"Lucky you. Well, to give you a ballpark price, let's say you leave January sixth and come back on May sixth." Keys tapped in the background, and someone in the travel office let out a great boom of sound. Maybe he'd just been handed his bill. "We could get you there for as little as five hundred dollars a person, round-trip."

Two thousand dollars. The price of the MRI, which Daed had wound up taking to Dr. Hunter in its brown envelope.

"And you'd need somewhere to stay. I don't recommend a hotel for that length of time. There are plenty of condos available. You could probably get a nice one for six or seven hundred a month, give or take."

Amelia added up the column in her head. Thirty-five hundred dollars. She could almost buy a new buggy for that, or a good band saw and a new air compressor both.

This was foolish. Crazy.

"Ma'am? Are you still there? Do you want to book the trip?"

"No. Not right now. I have to think about it. Thank you for your help."

"Anytime. Give us a call back when you decide."

She had already made up her mind. Leaving the flying out of it, how could she stay in a strange country for five months, bewildered by strange customs, strange language, and no fellowship? And what would they eat? It wasn't likely she could find beef and potatoes and root vegetables there, was it? Didn't they have palm trees? Wasn't it hot? And she'd be injected with cow myelin, and who knew what that would do to her?

Amelia shuddered and pushed the phone book back into its drawer.

It might cost more, but she'd best stick with the pills. At least then she could stay at home where God wanted her.

CHAPTER 10

"Mexico?" The sewing machine stopped while Carrie stared at her and, out in the kitchen, Emma turned from the coffeepot to hear what she would say.

Lena Stolzfus had asked if the quilting frolic could be at the *Daadi Haus* that day so that she could help, so Amelia had set her to pairing triangles. Lena didn't fuss about the fact that Amelia couldn't get the edges to match up. She didn't have the control in her hands now even to put two small pieces of fabric right sides together, but she would not let Lena suspect that she envied the skill in those thin, frail fingers that did what she could not. It was for the best to meet here today, despite the fact that Lena's presence kept them quiet on certain subjects. They could piece twice as many blocks, and they would be able to keep Lena company.

Up until now the girls' feet had kept a

steady rhythm on the treadles.

"*Ja,* Mexico." After a second or two, Carrie bent to her task, pairing the triangles and sewing them down their long sides in a continuous chain, which she snipped apart afterward. Amelia went on, "This Dr. Stewart says that the treatment would be four or five months, and I might go into remission."

"As opposed to taking pills for who knows how long," Emma finished. She filled the coffeepot and put it on the stove.

"I know how long. The rest of my life." Amelia told them everything the doctor had said, and she ended with a laugh. "I'll never say it to my niece, but I probably won't go and see her wonderful lady doctor again. Mexico and cows! Who would believe it?"

"And besides the strangeness, think of the expense," Carrie said. "The *Gmee* might be able to handle a hundred and twenty thousand over all those years. But fifty thousand all at once?"

"It would be more, Amelia," Emma put in, joining them. "These things always cost more in the end. Trust me."

Amelia nodded. "Mamm told me that if it's God's will for me to endure this disease, then I should set my mind to enduring it. There must be a purpose for it. At least if I take the pills, I'll be right here at home. I may never know until I see Him in heaven what the purpose was, but if I have to endure, it would be easier here."

"What did the doctor tell you about the other patients who went to Mexico?" Lena's voice was so quiet that Amelia almost couldn't hear it above the flywheel.

"She said that in many of them the disease was arrested. But not all."

"So you would rather live with it and go steadily downhill than do something to try to stop it?"

Amelia halted the sewing machine's movement and turned the flywheel so the needle went down into the fabric to hold it. Those few seconds let her say what had to be said with respect. "I would rather be treated here at home by doctors our folks trust than go on a wild-goose chase."

"Those geese aren't wild. It seems they're curing people down there. Or close to it. I think you should go."

"Mamm!" Emma sounded shocked.

"You do?" Carrie looked from one to the next. "But the money."

Lena calmly paired triangles as if she had not just tossed a rock into the pond of Amelia's hard-won calm. "You can try to do this thing and see results within the year. Or you can go for years and years paying

199

for pills and losing your muscles and wonder the whole time if you should have done something different." She looked at Amelia over the metal rims of her glasses. "It may be God's will for you to endure this disease. But it seems to me He has also provided a way of escape. He has worked through your mother before."

Amelia thought that Dr. Stewart might have more claim to that than her mother did, who had made a phone call because she couldn't resist meddling in people's medical affairs.

"I . . . I never really thought seriously of going," she said at last. "What if the elders say no? And how will I get there if I can't fly?"

"How do you suppose Old Joe got to Costa Rica? Do you think he swam?" Lena's eyes twinkled. "They will seek God's will in this matter, just as they did for Old Joe, and when they find it, you would of course accept what they say. But you should at least try. You owe it to your boys to do what you can."

The boys had been first in her mind from the very beginning. But this was a new way to look at it. A way of escape. She wasn't sure what this experience would teach her, but if the elders said yes, then that was a clear indication that she should take the way of escape, no matter how strange it seemed to her. Because there were other people in her situation, and they had gotten well. Some of them at least.

Oh, if only Enoch were here to talk this over with! The ache in her heart, which had dulled over the months to the pain of a bruise, now flared up again as if someone were pressing fingers against it. She could ask people's opinions until the cows came home, but his was the advice she'd always sought first. He had such a reasoned way of looking at things, and he was smart when it came to worldly matters like travel and getting things done.

If only . . .

But there was no sense in longing for "if only." That was like chasing a hat down a river — always just out of reach.

"I'll talk it over with Mamm and Daed," she said when she realized that Lena was not going to let her get back to work without an answer. "And I'll tell them what you've said."

Lena nodded and turned her attention back to her triangles. Amelia glanced at Emma, who was looking at her mother as if she'd never seen her before, and it was only because she was sitting in the same room that she kept her mouth firmly shut.

But her eyes told a different story. And in them Amelia saw the same fear and doubt that lay in her own.

There was no point in wasting time. She practically invited herself to supper at her parents' house, and when the boys had gone outside to see if they could follow the barn cat to the litter of kittens they were sure it had hidden somewhere, Ruth spoke up.

"What's on your mind, Amelia? You sat through my pork and kraut like that chair was covered in tacks. Here, that bread pudding needs more caramel sauce."

Amelia let her pour some more over her untouched dessert. Then she picked up her spoon and toyed with it while she told them the whole story — Mexico, cows, money, everything. "I talked it over with Carrie and Emma, and they agreed with me that I shouldn't go, that I should just accept God's will and start on the medication."

"Ah." Ruth sat back. "So that's what you've decided."

"Well, I thought so. But then Lena spoke up and said that if God had provided a way of escape in the form of this Mexico plan, then I should take it. Otherwise I'd spend the rest of my life" — *however long that turns out to be* — "wondering if I'd done the right thing." She dug into the pudding, still warm from the oven. "So now I'm back at the beginning, not knowing what I should do. I have to make arrangements to pay for medication either way. But do I ask for the money for this treatment? Or for the medication, which might end up costing more over the long run?"

"Amelia," Daed said.

"*Ja?*"

"Put the pudding in your mouth and eat it."

Amelia looked down at her spoon. "Oh. Right." The pudding tasted delicious — but then Ruth's favorite part of any meal was dessert, so she always put extra care into what she made.

"We should go to the bishop and ask what is best," her father went on. "I saw Daniel Lapp in his yard yesterday and stopped in to say hello. He asked after you, and we talked a little. I think you'll find Moses and the others prepared when we go to speak with them."

Amelia felt the burden slip a bit from her shoulders. "Do you think so?"

"I would be very surprised if they have not already been praying about it. How soon would you like to go?"

"This week would be wonderful *gut.* But I

know that Daniel is probably busy with wedding season, and doesn't one of the ministers have a girl getting married soon?"

"I think they can spare an hour for you, if you don't mind giving a little to come when they're available."

She'd give quite a lot if it meant finding out which path to take and getting some peace. "I'll come, no matter when."

So when her father called her at the shop on Thursday to say that the elders would gather on her behalf on Saturday at eleven at her parents' farm, she didn't hesitate. "I'll be there. *Denki,* Daed. I know it took some wangling on your part."

"And what better reason to wangle than my own daughter? Bring the boys, too. Your mother wants to take them to Shoe Barn and get new gums for them."

"She doesn't have to do that."

"*Ja,* but she wants to. Until Mark and his wild bunch get here, she misses having little ones around the place to cuddle and spoil."

"But —"

"Amelia," her father said quietly. "Let her do something for you. You're so independent sometimes, I worry."

Luckily, there was no one in the office to see the hot blush of shame that scalded her cheeks. "I know. I'm trying to conquer it, but it's hard. Even calling on the church for money sticks in my craw."

"Each part of the body is designed to depend on the other parts. There's no shame in that. We all work together."

"I know. See you Saturday, Daed."

"It will work together for good, you'll see."

So Saturday morning found her on Edgeware Road, holding the boys' mittened hands in her own as they crunched the frosted grass on the waysides, soil hardened to concrete by the cold.

Either Ruth had been baking all of yesterday instead of sewing or she'd already had an array of coffee cakes, pie, and soft pumpkin cookies on hand just in case a crowd dropped in. She and her two grandsons left for town in the buggy just before the elders arrived. Amelia's father, Bishop Daniel, Moses Yoder the deacon, and the two ministers all settled at the kitchen table while Amelia moved from one to the next, filling coffee cups and making sure everyone had at least one of everything her mother had left for them. If she came home and found that a big dent hadn't been made in all this baking, she would think Amelia hadn't been a good hostess. When they all had what they needed, Amelia settled into her old place at the table, a disjointed prayer gabbling at the back of her mind.

Bishop Daniel cleared his throat and put down his half-eaten cookie. "So, Amelia. You're here to make a request of this congregation?"

"I am."

"And what would that be, child?"

Amelia told them, though in more succinct terms and with much less humor than she'd told Emma and Carrie. She added in what she'd found out from the travel agency, ignoring her father's soft intake of breath when she got to the part about taking the boys with her. When she finished, she twisted her fingers in her lap and waited for one of them to speak.

"This treatment with the cows, could you tell us a little more about that?"

She pulled Dr. Stewart's packet of papers out of her bag and pushed them across the table to him. He put his spectacles on his nose and read them through, then gave them to Moses Yoder, who read them with equal attention and gravity while Daniel spoke again.

"I don't understand this cow myelin business."

"I don't very much either, but apparently when they inject it into you, it starts to grow on the nerve casings."

"And this takes four to five months?"

"The injections do. I don't know how long it takes for . . . for things to start growing."

"And it's in Mexico."

Something about the tone of his voice made Amelia's heart sink. And since when did she care so much? When had something so laughable become a possibility, then hardened from that to a decision? Until she heard the doubt in him, she hadn't known the certainty in herself.

"Isaac Lehman, may we have the room to ourselves in which to pray and talk this over?"

"Of course. Amelia, come with me out to your mother's porch."

It was the longest half hour of her life. Her father tried to make conversation, but under his words she found herself listening for a sound through the door, a phrase, any indication at all of which way the talk might be going.

Finally one of the ministers opened the door and leaned in. "Will you come now?"

They settled themselves in their chairs.

"It's been our practice to support every member of the church in their medical needs," Daniel said slowly. "The *Englisch* doctors, they know what they're doing, and our people have received the help they need.

207

Even Lila Esch, when she came to us, got the money for her medications during her lifetime."

During her lifetime. Which was now over, as God saw fit.

"We support treatments that are accepted medical practice, Amelia. Treatments where we know that the hard-earned money of our people will be put to good use, and we've seen the results among us."

Moses Yoder spoke up. "But it would be difficult to explain to the church members that we've taken their money and used it to put substances from a cow's body into yours. To be honest, I'm not even sure that would be scriptural." He glanced from Daniel to Isaac. "For this reason we don't believe in organ transplants, and we certainly don't believe in putting animal parts in a human body. That is blasphemy. Other congregations may find reasons to do so, but we here in Whinburg cannot."

"But the rate of remission —"

"Have you spoken to these people?" Daniel indicated the paperwork, which now lay neatly next to her dessert plate. "Do you know this to be true? We cannot spend so much money based on words on paper, or on the word of a doctor we do not know."

"But many Amish go to her and have been

treated for their problems. My niece Marie says they have been made completely well."

"For a skin rash or the flu, possibly they have. But have they had to go all the way to Mexico for it?" Had they forgotten Old Joe Yoder? He'd gone to Costa Rica, hadn't he? But if she brought that up, they'd think she was being disobedient and argumentative and showing a bad spirit.

Moses's eyes were kind, and she knew he honestly believed they were doing the right thing for her. Daniel's next words confirmed it. "The church will be willing to fund your treatment using accepted medications, such as those Lila Esch used. But we cannot in good faith send you so far on such a crazy scheme. We have prayed about it, and we believe the Lord wills that you stay home with your boys."

Amelia struggled for even a few words — for a breath. But she had nothing.

Her father spoke up. "What if she were to find a way to go to Mexico and have the treatment on her own? Like Old Joe Yoder, or Marianna Grohl that time years ago?"

"We would not stop her," Daniel said slowly. "Old Joe paid his own way, and it was the Lord's will to make his trip a success. But the cases are not the same. Having the substance of a cow injected into the

209

body of one of God's children? We would have to lay that at His feet." His gaze rested on Amelia. "It is possible that you would be breaking His will as we know it in the *Ordnung*. And the punishment for disobedience is separation from His people."

If she'd had trouble breathing before, she was suffocating now. Shunned? For getting a treatment that might possibly work and leave her able to care for her family and be active in the church? How was that possible?

"We will put things in motion for getting you started on your medications," Moses said. "When the money is in place, we will let you know, and you can tell your doctor."

The bishop rose, and the men stood up with him. "Peace be with you, Amelia," Daniel said kindly. "I know this has been very difficult."

She could not present another argument, even if she could think of one. To stand up and speak again once the elders had made their decision with the help of God was not only proud but selfish, too. Her place now was to submit, and to show it, she should get up and go with Daed to see them to the door. She should thank them for their time and care, as he was doing.

But it took everything Amelia had just to

draw her next breath — and not allow the cry of despair in her throat to escape.

Amelia pulled her knitted shawl more closely around the shoulders of her coat as she walked. When Ruth got home with the boys, she would feed them a snack, and then Isaac would bring them home. She and her father had talked a while longer, trying to puzzle out why a medication made from cow myelin was so offensive, but in the end they could come to no conclusion. It was no use anyway.

"Even if you went and had this treatment, Amelia," Daed told her sadly, "we would lose you as surely as if you had died. Your mother and I and your brothers and sisters would have to obey *die Meinding,* and what about the boys?"

She could hardly bring herself to think of it. They were too young to be baptized in the church, but even so, if she were under the *Bann,* they would join her in her shame. They could go to her parents' house with her, but she would have to eat at a separate table, and they couldn't so much as take a bowl of potatoes from her if she passed it to them. She could drive them to church but could not go in. Would she gradually drift away from the church and deprive the boys

211

of their family and traditions, because the pain of living among the *Englisch* was less than living among her own people, separate and unequal?

This can't be Your will for me, Lord. Please show me what I'm to do. I want to go to Mexico and have a chance at remission. I don't want to go on medication and die a slow death like Lila Esch. Show me a way to convince Daniel Lapp that having the injections is just as harmless as . . . as eating beef stew.

The clip-clop of hooves drew closer behind her, and out of habit she moved off the shoulder into the crisp grass. The sound slowed, and the horse snorted and stamped as its driver brought it to a halt on the side of the road instead of in a safe yard or a barn.

"Amelia?"

She turned to see Eli Fischer in the buggy, his hands firm on the reins.

"Can I offer you a ride?"

As if waking from a dream, she looked around her. Acres of harvested corn. Fence in perfect repair. A long hill with a stand of maples at the bottom, the last of their red leaves still clinging stubbornly to the bottom branches.

Old Joe Yoder's farm. She had passed her

own drive long ago, which meant she'd walked three miles or more in this daze. Was the disease beginning to affect her mind, too?

"*Denki,*" she said at last, climbing into the buggy. "I was thinking so hard I walked right past my place."

"Are you headed home or somewhere else?" He flapped the reins over the horse's back and clicked his tongue.

"Home. I just forgot to turn in, I guess."

He looked up and down the road carefully before guiding the horse in a U-turn, and a moment later they were moving briskly in the opposite direction. "That must have been some pretty hard thinking."

"*Ja.*"

His silence invited her to share what it was, but she couldn't do it. How could she tell this kind man that he was giving a ride to someone he might have to shun later? So instead she said, "Were you on your way to visit Old Joe?"

"No, I was coming back from town. I'm staying with him for a few days now, you know, to give Anna and Martin a break from company. His daughters-in-law gave me a huge list of ingredients they needed for the baking Wednesday, when I said I was going to get parts for the baler, so I'm pretty full back there." He nodded over his shoulder to the back of the buggy, which was crowded with cardboard boxes and grocery bags. "They needed me out of the house anyway. Church is there next week, and they've been in a frenzy of cleaning and washing for days."

"So you're not going to your home right away, then?"

"No." After a moment of silence filled only with the sound of hooves and wheels, he said, "I might get invited to another wedding, you know, and I'd only have to come back for it." When she smiled, he seemed to take it as encouragement. "Where are the boys today?"

"My mother took them to get boots before the snow flies."

"Her timing is good. It won't be long." He drew in a long breath. "I feel it in the air."

She did, too, now that he mentioned it. The sky seemed to have lowered and become sullen and gray, and in the air was a peculiar chilly silence that meant snow and not more rain.

"I'm glad you came along, then. I might have walked all the way to Strasburg and got myself caught out in it."

"I'm glad, too." His hands tightened on

the reins and then relaxed, as if by an effort of will. "That must have been the reason I got myself invited to stay — it was to make sure you were all right."

His tone was light, but his hands continued to flex and relax, flex and relax, his thumbs in their woolen gloves rubbing at the leather.

"I'm all r—" She stopped herself in the middle of the lie. She wasn't. Maybe she never would be again.

Eli slowed the buggy as he took the right turn at Edgeware Road, and before she thought, Amelia averted her head from the scene of Victor Stolzfus's accident. At the top of the hill, they saw a lone male figure walking on the side of the road, and because he wore no hat, she saw by the unruly brush of blond hair that it was Aaron King.

Amelia smiled as Eli pulled up. "Hello, Aaron." The young man nodded, hitching his coat up on his shoulders.

"I'd give you a ride home," Eli said, "but I'm full up. Amelia, she takes up a lot of room."

Aaron's smile didn't even show a tooth. "It's okay. *Denki.*" With another nod he walked on, and Eli shook the reins.

"That's odd," Amelia said. "I wonder what he was doing out here. The Kings are a mile or more south."

"Maybe he was visiting a girl."

"There aren't any on Edgeware Road." Well, except Emma, and a boy of seventeen wouldn't have much to say to her after *Guder Mariye.*

"He might have been delivering something to John Stolzfus for Martin," Eli said. "Parts or something."

That was possible. He'd had a package under his arm.

Eli pulled a little on the reins, and the horse slowed to take the turn into her drive. "Amelia."

There was only so long you could speculate about the walking habits of young men. "Yes?"

He brought the buggy to a stop in the yard. With no one home, the house looked cold and lonely, though she'd left a fire going in the stove. "Amelia, I —" His throat closed, and he cleared it. The horse bent its head to crop some grass at the edge of the lawn, and he let it — a sure sign in a man that his mind was otherwise occupied.

"Eli, what is it?"

"I wonder if you . . . if it would be all right if I came by from time to time. To see — to help you. There must be things that I could do around the place to make it easier for you."

She was so surprised that she couldn't think what to say.

He flushed, his cheeks going rosy between his coat collar and his black felt hat. "I didn't wangle an invite to Old Joe's so that his girls could get their flour and sugar delivered. I did it so I could be on this side of the settlement. To be more useful to you. If you needed me, that is. If I could help."

Plain folks didn't place much stock in words. A man could say whatever he wanted, and his words would blow away on the wind. But his actions were different. They meant something — had permanence, substance, and the results of them lasted. If a man wanted to show his feelings for a woman, he didn't tell her. He showed her.

The way Eli wanted to show her now. If she would let him.

But she could not.

Oh, she wanted to, and no mistake. What a gift his help would be — cutting wood, bringing it into the house, wrapping the pipes for the winter, cleaning out the eaves while she dug the last of the potatoes out of the garden before the ground froze and didn't thaw once the sun came up — the

217

myriad things that had to be done even though she wasn't running a farm.

The things Enoch had done.

But if she let him, her actions would have meaning, too. If she accepted his help, allowed him to give her these gifts, it would mean she was prepared to accept more. His courtship. Maybe his love, someday.

And that was what stopped her. Even if she left out the fact that she wasn't ready for a new man to put his boots by the back door, how could she let him court her when he would be making a bad bargain? Who wanted a wife in a wheelchair? Or worse, one who might be under the *Bann* by the time he got around to proposing?

Oh, no. As tempting as it was, she would not use a good man like Eli Fischer as a sort of unpaid handyman, drawn in by a promise she wasn't willing to make.

She lifted her gaze to his. He was watching her patiently, waiting for her answer to his stammered question. "*Denki*, Eli. It's very kind of you to offer, and I'm grateful to you for thinking of it. But I — Between Daed and my brothers, I have all the help I need."

She slid open the buggy door with her good hand and fled into the house, keeping

her back to him even when she waved good-
bye.

She could not bear to look into his face.

CHAPTER 11

There was no church the next day, but Amelia and the boys were invited to the Stolzfus house for the midday meal to say farewell to the last of the relatives who had come for the funeral. So of course, when she most wanted to avoid the topic, it seemed everyone was determined to bring Eli Fischer to her attention. Oh, not that she was so self-centered as to think they were doing it on purpose. Surely they weren't. But it was embarrassing just the same.

"I hear Eli Fischer is still in town." Emma bumped her shoulder after dinner, while she was out in the yard watching the boys floating leaf boats down the creek. If the older boys got to horsing around, they might make little Elam lose his balance and fall in, so Amelia felt it was prudent to watch from a distance. "You'd think he'd have things to do at home after all this time away."

"I'm not sure he does," Amelia said finally, when the silence had grown so long that Emma had begun to regard her with more concern than curiosity. "His brothers run the farm with their dad. He's out here looking for work to do."

"Maybe he's looking for more than that." Emma gave her a sidelong glance. "I also hear he gave you a ride home yesterday."

Amelia swung to stare at her, mouth open. "How . . . ? What . . . ?"

"My sister was on her way back from town and happened to see you getting into his buggy. What were you doing all the way out there?"

There was no escaping the Amish grapevine. It was more efficient than the *Englischers'* Internet. "I was walking. Thinking. I'll tell you and Carrie all about it on Tuesday, when we have some privacy."

"We have privacy now. Let me get Carrie. You can't tease me like this and expect me to wait two days for the rest of the story."

And before Amelia could say a word, Emma hurried off into the house. When she came out again, Carrie was with her, buttoning her coat. The snow that had fallen last night was only a promise of greater things to come, but it still forced them all to put gums on over their shoes. They crossed the lawn, covered now with footprints and animal tracks, and joined her at the top of the slope, where they could see the boys hunched on the stones next to the water watching the bright leaves race away on the rumpled current.

"Eli gave you a ride home yesterday?" Carrie asked breathlessly, tugging her knitted scarf tighter around her throat. "And we're only hearing about this now?"

"It wouldn't even be now if Amelia had her way," Emma told her. "She was going to make us wait until quilting day."

"What kind of a friend would do that?" Carrie's sparkling eyes belied the severity of her tone. To look at her, you'd think they were all sixteen and exchanging secrets about who had come with a flashlight and shone it in whose window in the middle of the night. But that was back before they'd joined church and gotten serious about life. Things were different now.

"The kind of friend who doesn't think it's worth sharing," she said. "Yes, he gave me a ride home. And no, it didn't mean anything."

Carrie's eyes narrowed with speculation. "I bet it meant something to him."

Drat the blush that insisted on rising in

her face. "Maybe it did. He offered to give me a hand around the place, too."

Emma gasped. "What did you say?"

"I said I had all the help I needed from Daed and my brothers, and he went away."

"Amelia!" Carrie's gloved fingers went to her mouth. "How could you?"

"What was I supposed to say? You know as well as I do that if he came around to help, Mamm would start planting celery for a wedding and everyone else in Whinburg would talk up a storm."

"It's not the talk you're afraid of," Emma said flatly. "It's Eli."

"No, that's not true at all." She wasn't going to think about whatever Emma was hinting at. "I like him, as much as I like Melvin or any of our men. I want good things for him. That's why I had to turn him down."

"I don't understand you." Emma lifted her hands and let them fall, empty. "I'd give anything if —" She cut herself off and closed her mouth, its usual generous lines narrow and grim.

"I'd give anything, too, not to have this disease." Amelia's voice roughened with emotion. "How can I lead him on, allow him to court me, if all I have to offer him is a future with another Lila Esch? He doesn't

223

want a wife strapped into a wheelchair, Emma. Or one he's going to have to wash in her bed and clean up after. I wouldn't inflict that on any man."

"You don't know that's going to happen." Carrie's lips trembled, and she drew a deep breath. "People can go for years without being as bad as poor Lila. Why, look at Janelle Baum at the post office. You'd never know there was anything wrong."

"And what about this Mexico treatment?" Emma said. "If you do that, maybe it will stop the disease."

Amelia told them what Daniel Lapp and Moses Yoder had said.

"Oh, my." Carrie's shoulders drooped. "Well, if the church won't fund it and you still believe in it, we'll just have to think of another way."

"We could sell the quilt we're working on," Emma suggested. "If we go through the auctions in the spring, we could get maybe a thousand dollars for it."

Any other time a thousand dollars would have seemed a fortune. "I'm afraid we'd have to sell sixty of them to get enough to go to Mexico. I'll be an old lady by then, and it wouldn't be worth it."

"There must be something," Carrie said.

"I'll write a novel and sell sixty thousand

copies," Emma said.

Where did the girl get her outlandish ideas? "Then you'd be put under the *Bann,* too." Amelia's tone was glum.

" 'Too'? What?" Carrie gripped her arm. "What are you talking about, under the *Bann?*"

"If I go to Mexico, Daniel Lapp said I risked *die Meinding.*"

"What on earth for?" Carrie's voice rose, and Emma shushed her when one of the boys looked up over his shoulder. "People go to other countries for these new cancer treatments," she said more quietly. "Old Joe was never shunned when he went, was he?"

"I don't know. That was years ago. All I know is that because these injections come from cow myelin, they're bad. At least Daniel seems to think so. Like putting a pig's heart inside you."

"It's not the same thing at all," Emma said hotly. "If we were all put under the *Bann* for putting cow parts inside us, the whole community would have to shun itself. What do they think their Sunday roast is made of?"

"That's what I thought. Maybe you should write a letter to the elders and explain that to them."

"I certainly will, if you think it would help."

"Emma, I was joking," Amelia said quickly, putting out a hand as if to stop her from marching into the house and finding a pen that very minute. "You know we can't do any such thing. If the elders say I can't go to Mexico and have this treatment, then I will not go."

"They don't know everything," Emma muttered, but Amelia let the words drift off into the air, harmless as smoke. There was nothing more to say. The only solution pleasing to God was obedience, and the only solace was sharing it with them, for the relief of it, the way either of them would grab the other handle of a wash basket or a tub of vegetables and help her carry it in. She could do it on her own, but it went better with someone on the other side.

Usually obedience brought her more peace, though.

At four in the morning, when she got up to do the Monday washing, peace was as elusive as when she'd hugged her friends and called the boys up the slope, wet around the edges and ready to go home.

No peace about the treatment.

No peace about Eli Fischer.

In the cold dim of early morning, lit by the lantern hanging on the laundry-room wall, she watched the shirts and aprons agitate in the machine, tucked her hands into her armpits, and gave herself up to prayer.

It calmed her, even if she was too jangled inside for true peace — the kind that came with acceptance of God's will. But she would settle for calm, particularly when she opened the shop a couple of hours later and found that one of the pipes serving both her part of the building and that of the Steiners next door had broken and there was an inch of dirty water all over the workshop floor.

With a cry of dismay, she hurried back into her boots, and when Melvin came in, he found her frantically sweeping water out into the yard.

"Get a mop out of the cabinet!" she said, forgetting even to say *Guder Mariye.* "We have to get this out before it damages the wood any more!"

David came in right after that and borrowed a space heater from next door to dry the wood once they got the floor clean. The orders scheduled for that morning were half a day late, and the truck idling out in the yard for an hour did nothing to soothe her nerves. If she had been at home, she'd have gone to the fridge for something to eat. As it was, even after she ate the lunch she'd packed, she still felt twitchy. She reached into her desk drawer to see if there was anything to snack on.

Hmm. One hard candy. That was no good. She wanted something crunchy. Hadn't she tossed a bag of nuts in here sometime? Away at the back, she found it — a partial bag of mixed nuts that had probably been in there since Enoch was alive. Whether they were stale or not, she didn't care. She crunched into a nice fat Brazil nut and felt something snap, and pain lanced up into her head.

Owww. Shell. She'd bitten into a shell. These were supposed to be shelled already. She felt around with her tongue and spat the hard object into her hand.

It wasn't a dark brown bit of shell. It was silver. She'd broken a filling, maybe even a bit of tooth.

With a groan Amelia sagged against the back of the chair and berated herself for letting her mouth get the better of her. If only she'd gotten absorbed in her work instead — that would have taken her mind off her troubles and done something profitable at the same time. She tossed the twisted little piece of metal into the trash can.

I don't have time to deal with this.

You have to deal with it. What if it gets infected?

She got up and went into the toilet, where there was a mirror over the sink. "Ahhhh." The molar second from the back on the right side gaped at her, naked and vulnerable.

She trudged back to the phone and dialed the dentist her family always went to. His mother had been a cousin of Daed's, and while he'd never joined church, he had settled near Whinburg and ran a pretty brisk practice.

"You lost a filling?" the receptionist, who doubled as dental assistant, said sympathetically. "It happens. How soon can you come in?"

Not today — it was nearly closing time and the boys would be home. And she wouldn't give up quilting tomorrow, tooth or no tooth. Wednesday was David's day off, and she didn't feel right leaving Melvin on his own yet. Thursday and Friday were booked with orders, and the dentist wasn't open on the weekend. "I'm not sure. Next week?"

"We usually treat these like emergencies, Amelia. Dr. Brucker will probably put a temporary cap on it. I'm looking at your chart, and it was pretty old anyway. You're probably going to need a crown."

Crowns were vanity. Having a gold crown

in your mouth drew attention to you every time you laughed or yawned. The plain people didn't even wear gold wedding rings, never mind carry around that amount of gold in their mouths.

"I . . . I would probably just have it pulled."

"Pulled?" The assistant paused. "Oh. Right. I forgot. Well, that means oral surgery, maybe two or three weeks out. I don't know if you'd want to hang on that long. Bacteria will start working."

She couldn't face it. The pain, the swelling, the sheer aggravation of it. She could not. "Can I think about it a little while?"

"Sure. I just wouldn't think too long. Call us back tomorrow, okay, and make the appointment?"

"Yes," she said, because the woman was waiting for her to say so. "*Denk*— I mean, thank you."

Amelia set the receiver back in its cradle. Looked at the abandoned package of nuts.

And then she put her head down on her arms and cried.

Sometime later — it could have been five minutes or half an hour — she heard a soft sound and realized that the door to the shop had closed. Next to her elbow stood a plastic bottle of water that had clearly come from a gas station or a convenience store, because she kept no such thing on the premises. She stared at it stupidly for a moment, then scrubbed her eyes on her sleeve, held the bottle next to her stomach with her arm, and twisted off the cap with her good hand.

Water. So simple and so comforting. And as cold and refreshing to her rough throat as a dip in the creek in August.

"For whosoever shall give you a cup of cold water" — or the modern equivalent — *"to drink in my name, because ye belong to Christ, verily I say unto you, he shall not lose his reward."*

She pulled her hankie out of her sleeve and blew her nose, then went into the back. Melvin squatted next to the air compressor, turning the nailer over in both hands.

Her stomach rolled in sudden alarm. "Don't point it at your face!" she called. "You could trigger it by accident and —"

"It's all right, Amelia." He waved the nailer as casually as if it didn't weigh nearly ten pounds. "It's empty. At least I think it is. No nails are coming out, so I —"

The thing made a sound like a shot, and a nail thunked into a nearby stack of lumber not three feet from her. "Melvin!" She ducked behind the door and peered through the glass.

"Sorry! Sorry." Cautiously, he laid it on the concrete next to the air compressor. "Are you all right? I thought it was empty."

"Once in a while, a nail will get stuck." Years of practice at self-control prevented her from screaming at him as if he were Matthew teasing the cows at Mamm and Daed's, practically under their hooves. "If it's not feeding properly, just take off the little door and look at what's left in the cartridge."

But when she stooped to show him, he didn't look at the nailer. "Sorry if I scared you."

"It's nothing we all haven't done." Her breathing was still shaky. "Get David to tell you about the time he shot a coffin next door."

Melvin chuckled. "I bet that's a good story. Are you feeling better?"

That was as close as he would come to asking if there was anything wrong. "You left that water for me." When he didn't answer, only turned off the air compressor, she knew she'd guessed correctly. "It was kind of you." And the couple of dollars he'd spent were more than he could afford for such a silly thing. She had a thermos of coffee and one of juice in her desk drawer at this very moment if she was thirsty — but they hadn't refreshed her like that water.

Kindness didn't know everything. It only acted. Maybe Carrie had known what she was doing when she'd chosen Melvin Miller over any of the boys from home.

Neither of them said another word about the scene in the front office or what might have caused it. She showed him how to clear the jam in the nailer and how to load it so it would be less likely to seize up the next time. When David came back from his errand, they both behaved as if nothing had happened.

But something had — and it had nothing to do with flying nails or bottled water.

Melvin glanced up at her through his fringe of hair. "I forgot to tell you. While I was at the horse auction on Saturday, I got to talking with these *Englisch* from Harrisburg."

"What were they doing all the way out here?"

"Looking for cheaper prices, I suspect. They work at a manufacturing plant, and they'll be needing pallets to ship their parts. For boat engines or something. I told them about you."

"We can always use the business." Despite how the morning had gone. "And they were at the horse auction?"

He shrugged. "They weren't bidding or anything. I think they were there with someone who was."

"Well, thanks for letting them know about us anyway."

"I'm better at talking about pallets than making them." He regarded the nailer sadly.

"There's nothing wrong with your work. That stack is as good as anything David has made." She waved a hand at the pallets waiting for pickup.

"That's because it was mostly he who made them. I just handed him lumber."

"That's how you learn. Give yourself a chance, Melvin. You've only been here a week."

Listen to her — the woman who had to be pushed by her best friend into giving him a job. But he was right. The man was better at talking than building. What a shame there weren't jobs just for people who talked.

When she left the shop on Tuesday at noon, she felt marginally more confident about leaving him and David alone. But even if she hadn't been, nothing would keep her from the quilting frolic. If Melvin had shot one more nail into a defenseless board, she would have given him the afternoon off and gone anyway.

The frolic was at her house today, which meant she could use her sewing machine. Hooked up to a battery, it would run all afternoon. And the advantage to its being at home was that when the boys came in from school, there would be a warm kitchen, snacks, and a hug waiting for them.

Carrie was full of sympathy about the lost filling as she unpacked her squares and triangles and organized them on the work-table. "That happened to me last year. I had to chew on one side for a couple of days until I could get in to get it pulled." She opened her mouth wide. "See?"

One of her molars was missing. Amelia grimaced. "I can't bear the thought of having it done, not on top of everything else."

"At least you have no worries about paying for it," Emma said. She had loaded her sewing machine into the buggy and brought it over. Luckily, it was one of the lighter models — if it had been an old one with its own cabinet, the three of them would have had a hard time moving it across a room, never mind into a buggy.

"It just makes me mad," Amelia confessed. "One more thing to deal with when my plate is already running over the sides."

"The Lord has His reasons for these things, even if we can't see them," Carrie said, laying a comforting hand on Amelia's shoulder as she rounded the table. "And His cup of mercy is running over the sides, too."

"But why now? I've been praying for peace, but it doesn't come."

"Peace about the medical things? The Mexico plan?" Emma didn't say "about the multiple sclerosis." Amelia didn't like to say those words either — as if the more she said them, the more real the fact of the disease would become — entrenching itself deeper into her body.

"That. And . . ." She took a deep breath and plunged in. "And Eli Fischer." Carrie and Emma exchanged a glance — one that told her they'd already discussed this interesting subject between them, even though she'd insisted to Emma that nothing was going on. "Both of them have been dangled in front of me like lures in front of a trout, leading me on with the wonderful possibilities, only to be taken away."

"Eli hasn't been taken away," Emma pointed out. "Not if he's giving you rides and offering to help you around the place." She gestured out the window, where a man's world was.

"Maybe not, but you know why it's impossible." Miserably, Amelia dragged the subject back to where it had been. "Why would God show me a way of escape and then slam the window shut on my fingers? No matter how much I pray, I can't figure out if He wants me to try again to go to Mexico, to prove how much I want to get well, or look at it like a test of obedience, meant to bring me low because I'm getting too proud and independent."

"I don't think it's that." Carrie's blue eyes were full of sympathy.

"But how can I know?"

"Have you really decided against the Mexico plan?" Emma asked. "Maybe you've shut that window on your own fingers."

"I don't see that I have a choice. The elders have as much as said they'd put me under the *Bann* if I went."

"They didn't say that exactly, though, did they?" Carrie said. "Didn't Bishop Daniel say they would have to pray about it?"

"Sure they have to pray. I want them to. Yet in the end I think all it will do is let me down slowly."

"But what if it doesn't? What if you went before they had a definite answer?"

Amelia narrowed her eyes at Carrie over the spool of thread on top of the sewing machine. "What are you saying?"

"Well, as of this moment it's not a sin,

because they haven't received a conviction from God. All they have is their own human opinion."

"Bishop Daniel does go by that from time to time," Emma pointed out dryly. "Remember when the power company came to Moses Yoder and wanted to put that windmill in his field? Daniel Lapp didn't take two seconds to decide that it was too much like actually having electricity on the farm, even if it didn't run to the house or the barn, and Moses had to say no."

"They offered him a lot of money, too." Amelia remembered the flap it had caused in the *Gmee,* particularly since Moses was a deacon. She supposed that was why Bishop Daniel had to lay down such a firm line — because Moses and the other elders were examples to the entire flock.

"But they've said they're going to pray about it, not just give an opinion," Carrie persisted. "I think you should go before they get a definite answer. Then, when you get back, you go before the church in the members' meeting if you have to and ask forgiveness," Carrie said. "Can you live with being shunned for six weeks?"

Amelia and Emma both stared at Carrie, then at each other.

"Better *die Meinding* for six weeks than

the disease for the rest of your life," Emma said at last. "Carrie is so smart. You could have your treatment and forgiveness, too."

Amelia began to shake her head before Emma had even finished speaking. "That sounds so . . . calculating. Like I'm deliberately trying to get away with something."

"You're not trying to get away with something," Carrie said. "You're trying to accomplish something."

"Not like this. It feels . . . deceitful."

"How?"

Exasperation welled up in her, the same as all the times she'd tried to explain to Matthew why they did things the way they did when the *Englisch* ways he'd seen seemed so sensible. Like having a telephone in the kitchen, where you could call if someone got sick, instead of having to run a quarter mile down the road.

"It feels like I would be taking advantage. I know the spirit of the law, even though the letter of it hasn't been written yet."

"You *could* see it that way," Emma mused. "Or you could see it as that window being lifted off your fingers so you can do something with them. Like climb out."

CHAPTER 12

Surely they didn't mean she should deliberately disobey the bishop and the deacon and then have the nerve to ask forgiveness afterward? Amelia turned back to her seam and concentrated on matching triangles and squares under the slow march of the needle.

Emma pulled a chair over in front of her treadle but didn't go to work. "Have I offended you, *Liewi?*"

Amelia shook her head. "*Nei.* It's just that Daed has already chastised me for being too independent, and here you are telling me I should be more so. Disobedient, even."

"It wouldn't be disobedience yet," Carrie put in, giving her layout a critical eye. "Do you think I have too much peach here?"

Emma got up and joined her. "I think the pink might be better below it and the peach at the very top."

Carrie rearranged her triangles and considered them. "But look. What if I do this?"

She reversed the loose pieces of the block in the middle of her row. "See? Then the line of light triangles goes up and down, almost like a butterfly in the garden."

"But we're not doing butterflies in the garden." Amelia didn't feel like she could agree with anybody today. "We're doing a sunrise over green fields."

"But we still want some movement," Carrie persisted. "If you do them all facing the same direction, it just looks frozen. But if you reverse the middle block, it looks like the colors are moving, the way the sun is in constant movement."

"First butterflies, now sun. Make up your mind."

Emma raised an eyebrow at her, and Amelia ducked her head with shame. "I'm sorry. I'm in a bit of a state right now. I probably should have stayed at the shop and made sure Melvin didn't shoot anything else."

"What?" Carrie dropped a peach triangle, looking horrified. *"Was sagst du?"*

"Oh . . ." Amelia blew out a breath, like a winded horse. "A nail got stuck in the air nailer, and it shot a wild one by accident into the lumber pile. No harm done." Except to her nerves.

"But aside from that he's doing all right?"

241

Carrie sounded diffident. "Maybe it's none of my business."

"A woman's husband *is* her business, I would think," Emma said.

"But his work isn't. I shouldn't have asked, should I?"

"You're not talking to the man in charge of that RV company," Amelia pointed out with a smile. "It's just me. Of course you should ask. And other than shooting the odd length of board, he's doing fine."

Even from her seat at the sewing machine, Amelia could see Carrie's long breath of relief. "Have you been worried?" Amelia asked gently.

Flushing, Carrie nodded. "It's so difficult for him. Working with his hands, I mean. He's just not cut out for it."

"Some aren't," Emma agreed, still gazing thoughtfully at Carrie's blocks. Was she trying to see the butterflies that Carrie saw? "God gives us all different skills, even if they're not ones we can use right where we are at the moment."

Amelia looked up as she clipped her threads. "God always gives us what we need."

"Sure He does. But maybe Melvin needs to put himself where he can use the skills God has given him."

Amelia nodded. "I was thinking just today what a shame it is that a man can't get a job talking for a living."

"You can if you're *Englisch*. Look at those people on the radio, talking all day long."

"I meant in Whinburg. In the church."

"So what does it say if God puts you among His people but gives you skills that are only useful outside?" Emma had turned, looking at the piecing from a different angle.

"How would you know you had them, if you were in the church and never thought to use them?" Carrie asked.

"Melvin knows he can talk better than he can shoot nails," Amelia pointed out. She lined up her next seam and set the needle going. "That doesn't mean he can do that to make his living."

"Maybe God is going to make him a minister," Emma said.

"Oh, goodness." Carrie's voice sounded muffled. "Don't say that. I mean, I know we must all be willing, but . . . don't say it."

"Not ready to be the minister's wife for the rest of your life?" Emma teased. "It won't kill you. And if anyone could do it, Melvin could."

"That is up to the Lord," Carrie told her. "Don't you go hurrying Him." She picked up the triangle of pale peach and laid it in its place. "I really think we should do it this way."

"However you like," Emma said, relenting. "Have your butterflies if it makes you happy."

Carrie's quick glance over at her reminded Amelia that they were supposed to be making this one for Emma, so her preferences ought to come first. "Are you sure?" Carrie said. "It's your quilt, too. If you think it's better the other way, then that's how we'll do it."

"No, no." Emma waved a hand and went back to her treadle. "You see colors and patterns better than I do. If it were words we were arranging, that would be different."

"Or people's lives," Amelia muttered to her bobbin race.

"I heard that," Emma said.

"I just can't believe you both advised me to disobey." Amelia eased a seam into place. "You're supposed to be helping me."

"Leaving the cow myelin out of it, the elders have no problem with you going to Mexico with your own money?" Emma asked.

"If I had the money, they'd have no problem with it — even the flying part, it seems, since they allowed old Joe to do it when there was no other way to get there.

244

The church just can't finance something that hasn't been proven. Which is reasonable."

"So if you found the money and went for the treatment, then came back with the disease in remission or stopped, you'd be useful to the church again."

Emma's thinking echoed her own. *"Ja."*

"So I think that outweighs the cow myelin problem. And even if you have to ask forgiveness in front of the church, they would see as time went on that it is a proven cure. And maybe the next person wouldn't have it so hard."

"Maybe." And maybe Emma should go in with Melvin and they could both talk for a living. "But I still can't find the money."

"You could if you sold the shop."

The words fell into Amelia's quiet front room like a flurry of hail on the roof. "I've already thought of that. But how would I make my living when I got back?"

"You and Enoch started from nothing before. You could do it again."

"And have two competing pallet shops in Whinburg?"

"A little competition is good. Didn't you say that man from the seed company is interested? If you get a good enough offer from him, maybe you could afford the

Mexico trip and start a new business, too."

She didn't want to be in business in the first place, never mind start up another one. But God had given her this row to hoe, and it was up to her to do the best she could with it. All she needed was equipment. If she got a good price for the shop, there might be enough left over for an air compressor and a nailer, and enough lumber for Daed and her brothers to build her a shed right here on her five acres. It would be small, but if she let some of her smaller customers know, they might come along with her, leaving the industrial customers for Mr. Bernard Burke.

"She's thinking," Carrie said to Emma.

Yes, she was, God help her.

Because to do this, He would have to.

BERNARD BURKE, OPERATIONS MANAGER.

Amelia laid the card gently on the desk next to the phone. It was Wednesday, David's day off, and the regular sound of nails being driven into wood sounded from the shop, meaning that Melvin was too busy to interrupt. He'd started on a hundred-piece order right after he'd come in, and the sound of the air nailer had hardly stopped since then.

If she picked up the phone and dialed the

number on the card, she couldn't go back. She would have set herself on a course that had no exits, only a finish line.

Lord, help me to know Your will. Am I looking through a window You have opened, or is it just my own will I see? How can I risk the Bann *unless I know that this is the course You want me to take?*

She waited, but no answer came. No sign but a car that rolled down the street, a rooster tail of slush coming up off its back tires. Even through her window, she could hear the sloppy sound it made.

Was that *Englisch* car a sign? Call the *Englisch* man?

If a buggy had gone by instead, what would that have meant?

She picked up the card again. Looked at the phone.

Opened the drawer and dropped it on the stack where it had been sitting for weeks.

Sat.

Sighed.

When the phone rang, she jumped like a pheasant flushed out of a hedge. It took two more rings before she could calm her breathing enough to speak.

"Whinburg Pallet and Crate, this is Amelia Beiler speaking."

"Mrs. Beiler?" a male voice asked, though

247

she had just given her name.

"Yes."

He cleared his throat. "Right. Sorry. You said that, didn't you?" When she didn't respond, only waited, he went on, "This is Bernard Burke, from the Lincoln Seed Company. Remem—" At her intake of breath, he stopped. "Mrs. Beiler? Are you okay?"

No, she was not. Amelia wilted into her chair, the fingers in her good hand feeling as rubbery as the ones that didn't respond to her anymore.

"Mrs. Beiler?"

"Yes . . . yes, Mr. Burke, I'm well. I . . . I was just thinking about you."

He chuckled, a sound that should have been comforting but was tinged with nerves. "In a good way, I hope."

"Yes, it was." *Calm down, Amelia. The poor man probably just wants to place an order.* "What can I do for you?"

"Well, I was wondering . . . I'm going to be down your way in the next couple of days, and . . . I wondered if — I mean, would it be convenient — Were you still thinking . . . ?" He stopped. "I'm making a right fool of myself here."

"It must be difficult dealing with a female voice when you're used to talking with

Enoch," she said in an attempt to put him at his ease. He was such a big man, too. You think he'd feel as though he owned the earth.

"No, no. It's *your* voice I was wanting. You, I mean. Uh, not like that. I mean I wanted to talk to you."

His embarrassment was catching. She felt her cheeks heat up, as though it had communicated itself to her over the phone line. "What about, Mr. Burke?"

"I wondered if I . . . if you'd be . . ." Another breath. She could practically hear him counting to ten. "I wonder if I might take you out to lunch one day this week."

Amelia nearly dropped the receiver.

When she finally got it under control, she had to smother the urge to laugh. Once she started laughing, she might never stop until Melvin came out to see what was going on. Did it never rain but pour?

"M-Mr. Burke, I'm afraid I could not do that," she finally said when she had herself under control. "It would not look right, you see."

"Do you have a better offer?"

Again she reined in a shriek of laughter. "I would not say better, though I believe he is a good man. But —"

He made a noise, something like an explo-

249

sion. "Mrs. Beiler! Miz . . . Amelia — Oh, no, I didn't mean that. I wasn't asking you for a date!"

Now that blush came back with a vengeance — so much that she felt she might actually catch fire, right there in her chair. How could she have been so *batzich* — so filled with pride that the first thing she thought of was that a man would want her?

She could not bear it. She should just hang up this phone right now, lock herself in the toilet, and never come out again.

Bernard Burke stepped bravely into the breach. "What I meant was, I'd like to take you to lunch so that I could lay my proposal — er, I mean, my proposition before you. A business proposition. That is, if you were still giving thought to selling the shop."

She had asked for a sign, and here in the plainest terms was an answer.

Too bad she'd made such a complete and utter fool of herself first. What man would want to talk business with such a ninny?

"I *have* given it a little thought," she managed. "I was just looking over your card this morning."

"Then maybe I could pick you up tomorrow — say around eleven-thirty? We could talk more openly if we went to a restaurant, and I'm partial to the Dutch Deli out there on the county highway."

"Oh, no, that would not be good." Carrie's little sister Melinda worked in the kitchen there. Imagine the furor in the church if she happened to walk by the service window and saw Amelia in the company of an *Englisch* man, cozily eating lunch with their heads together, having a very private conversation.

"Well then, do you have a preference? I like just about anything."

"I'm afraid I could not have lunch with you no matter where it was, Mr. Burke. Everyone knows everyone here, and it would look very bad."

"But I only want to talk business."

"I know, and so do I. But the trouble is, people would think — I mean, they would very likely assume that —"

"Folks would talk," he said heavily. "I s'pose that's the case anywhere. If I took my accountant to lunch here, there'd be those who'd gossip and say I was having an affair. Which is impossible — that woman is old enough to be my mother, and she's way too smart to be seen with the likes of me."

In spite of herself, Amelia smiled. "Could we talk business right now? If this is a good time for you."

"Sure, if that's what you want. I'm just

251

sitting in the truck in the parking lot on my lunch break, watching it snow."

From what she remembered of the Lincoln Seed Company's checks, they were based in a town about fifty miles west. "Oh, dear. More snow is coming, then?"

"Forecast is for more tonight, then a big dump of it on the weekend."

And church on Sunday all the way out at Old Joe's. She'd better ask her father if she and the boys could ride with them.

"So then, Mr. Burke," she prompted him.

"Right. Well, I'll just pretend I'm sitting across the table from you and I've just buttered you up with a great big Reuben sandwich. The Dutch Deli makes the best in the county."

"It was delicious." Smiling, she played along. "And so is this coffee."

"I haven't really had a good look at your shop, but I've been there a time or two and been impressed with the operation. You keep your equipment in good repair, the place is as clean as a whistle, and it seems you make a pretty good living."

"We get by."

"Sure you'd say that, but to make a practical offer I'd need to know about how much it brings in in a year. Ballpark."

"Would you like to see our tax return?"

"If we go any further, that accountant I mentioned would probably want to, but for now just a rough estimate."

"Last year we had a net profit of forty thousand."

He whistled. "Not bad for a little place."

"Our customers are local, but we also have some big outfits in Lancaster, so it balances out."

"In that case, Mrs. Beiler, I'd be willing to make you an offer of a hundred thousand for the business."

If this conversation went on any longer, she was going to have to put the receiver down and speak into it with her useless hands in her lap.

"A hundred thousand?"

A trip to Mexico, airfare for four, and accommodation for four months. There. Just laid out before her like a Christmas gift. And some money left over to start again, like a pretty bow on top.

"I'm not a rich man, Mrs. Beiler. I'll tell you straight, I'll have to take a loan out for part of it. But like I told you, I'm ready to retire, and I want a nice little business to keep me active in my golden years."

"Doesn't the seed company give you a pension for driving the truck?"

He paused. "I don't just drive the truck,

ma'am. I own Lincoln Seed with my son Frank."

It was a few seconds before she could say, "Oh."

"He's got big ideas, so he's going to buy me out. I'll move to Whinburg, find me a nice widow who can cook as well as they do at the Dutch Deli, and settle down . . . again."

"The cook at the Dutch Deli *is* a widow," she said automatically, her mind spinning with figures and possibilities.

"Then it's a match made in heaven. So what do you think, Mrs. Beiler?"

Amelia scrambled to find her common sense, which was like trying to catch one starling in a flock wheeling up off the lawn. "I hardly know what to think. I need a few days to . . . to get counsel and think it over. Would that be all right?"

"Sure, sure. Take as much time as you need. I'm not going anywhere. Well, except out of this parking lot and back on the road, eventually."

"I believe I should tell you, Mr. Burke, that one of . . . well, another party has expressed interest, too."

"Has he? No dummy, I expect. Well, if I get beat out, I do, but I wanted to lay my cards on the table. No fuss, no ulterior motives. Just my figure and my feelings about it."

"I respect that. May I let you know later? Perhaps next week?"

Maybe the elders wouldn't come to a decision before then. She had no idea how long it would take a sale to go through, and she was not a woman who rushed things. But at least she could make a decision in a week's time, couldn't she?

"That would be great. I'll give you a call then."

"As long as it's not lunch."

He chuckled, and this time there was no embarrassment. "I'll have them deliver that Reuben to your shop. Lunch is on me — and if what you say about that widow is true, I might just place my order in person."

Laughing, she hung up.

It took a few minutes of hard thinking before she came to herself and realized that the back of the shop had gone silent. How long had it been since she'd heard the percussive sound of the nailer?

Had Melvin been listening?

And just how much had he heard?

CHAPTER 13

"I'm out here." Through the open sliding door, Amelia saw Melvin wave from behind the lumber pile. "Just getting some studs. Did you need me?"

"No. I'll come and give you a hand. Just let me find my gloves." With a cheery return wave, Amelia said nothing, merely went back into the office. Her gloves sat by the door in the basket with the others, but she had something to do first.

She was foolish to mind whether or not Melvin could have heard her end of the conversation. Things like this had a way of getting out — she'd be lucky if her secret survived until Sunday. She had no reason to believe that he would be interested in buying the business. Neither he nor Carrie had ever mentioned it, and how could he do it, anyway, without selling the farm?

No, she wouldn't think about Melvin. But she did need to think about Eli Fischer. It was only fair to tell him about Mr. Burke's offer, and the sooner the better.

She rifled through the desk drawer. Aaron King had a cell phone, which his father did not know about. But she did. Where was the number? Under a package of erasers, she found a slip of paper with his untidy scrawl, and she dialed.

"Yo."

"Aaron, it's Amelia Beiler. Do you have a minute?"

"Yeah." She heard the clang of metal and a whoosh of water. "I'm just cleaning out the milking pen. Wassup?"

"Is Eli Fischer still with you? He hasn't left town yet, has he?"

"No, but he's planning to. Friday, I think."

She had no time to lose, then. "Could you ask him if he would be free to come to my parents' house for dinner tonight? Six o'clock?"

It would not do for him to come to *her* house now that he had let his feelings be known. The last thing she needed was for people to think he was courting her. Of course, once it got out that he had offered on the shop, it would be the first thing they'd think. Lucky Eli, they would say. A wife, a family, and a business all in one stroke. The only thing that would prove the whole district wrong in its assumptions would be her departure for Mexico.

"I don't know if he's here, Amelia. I haven't been in the house in a couple of hours."

"As soon as you see him, then. If it's before four, maybe you could call me back here at the shop and let me know."

"Okay. I gotta get this place cleaned out before my dad comes back. Later."

"*Denki,* Aaron. You won't forget, will you?" But he had already disconnected.

When the phone rang at three-thirty, it was Aaron — for once doing what he said he'd do. Eli would be happy to have dinner at the Lehmans', and Aaron's mother would send along a coleslaw.

That left only her parents. Amelia caught a ride home with one of the Steiner boys from the shop next door and crunched her way up the drive of the home place. Her sons had been watching from the front window and, as soon as they caught sight of her in the twilight, ran out onto the porch to meet her.

She squatted to hug little Elam as the warm lamplight spilled out through the doorway like a blessing. "*Schatzi,* here you are in your sock feet. *Es ist zu kalt fer dich.* Into the *Haus* with you!"

Matthew pressed himself against her side and beamed up at her as they went in. "Mammi is making mincemeat pie, and she's letting me cut out leaves to put on top."

"Mmm, that sounds wonderful. You will be quite the baker, between Mammi and Auntie Carrie."

The kitchen smelled spicy with the jars of mincemeat Mamm had put up. "Will you have room for one more tonight? I hope it's all right that I asked Eli Fischer to come."

Ruth stopped rolling out pastry dough to stare at her, and Amelia could practically count every question as it crossed her face. She held up a hand to stem the flood.

"No, it's not what you think. He is not courting me, and he never will, so put that out of your mind right now. But I need to have a talk with him about the shop, and it would look better to have it here than at my house."

"What's that?" Daed walked in from the living room, folding the newspaper. He laid it on the stack in the cardboard box next to the woodstove, which was piling up now that it was winter and the stove was never allowed to go out. "*Was machst* with the shop now?"

Matthew returned to his careful cutting of

leaf shapes from some leftover pastry, so Amelia sat at the table and pulled Elam into her lap for a cuddle.

"The man from the Lincoln Seed Company called this afternoon and made me an offer," she said simply. "I want to give Eli a chance to do the same before I call this man back with an answer."

"You're going ahead and selling?" Her father's eyebrows lifted.

"How much did he offer?" Ruth draped the pastry over the pie dish and cut away the excess with a knife. That was her mother all over. Get straight to the point, with no messy extra details.

"One hundred thousand."

With a clatter, Ruth dropped the knife, but before it had stopped rocking on the table, she'd corralled it so it wouldn't hurt either Matthew or the clean pastry. "So much!"

"Not so much after you take out the cost of the treatment in Mexico, getting down there, and somewhere to stay while I'm there."

Daed gazed at her. "I did not know you had decided on this course. Do Daniel and Moses know of it?"

"Not yet. But as soon as it gets out that I'm selling, I'm sure they will."

Her father did not allow her to slide out from under the real question. "But I was in the room when they told you they had to lay this matter at the Lord's feet. Have they received an answer so soon?"

"Not that they've told me." She raised her head and looked at him directly. "I'm going ahead with it, Daed. I can't do anything else, for the boys' sake."

"But if it goes against the *Ordnung,* will you wish you'd done something else?"

She ran a hand over Elam's head. His hair was getting long. Time for a haircut, before all the family got together at Christmas.

"Amelia?" Her father was not taking silence for an answer.

"Maybe," she said at last. "But I hope they will forgive me. I've talked it over with Carrie and Emma, and they see this plan as God opening a window where I only saw a closed door before."

"Going on this medication for MS is not a closed door." Ruth scooped mincemeat out of a bowl on top of the sliced apples she'd laid in the pie shell. "If anything, having medication is your open window, not this harebrained Mexico scheme."

"Mamm, you're the first one to try a new home remedy. I thought you'd be behind me with this."

"My remedies have been used for decades. Generations. They're not some crazy doctor's excuse to take fifty thousand dollars from someone."

"She's not getting the money. The clinic in Mexico is."

"More crazy people." Ruth dropped the pastry lid on the pie and crimped its edges together with energy. "But you're not crazy. You need to be obedient and not do this thing."

That was the crux of the matter. Was she an obedient child of God or was she risking her very life in the church for her own selfish will?

Even now, when she thought she'd made up her mind, Amelia felt at odds with herself.

"I *am* obedient. I accept that the church can't pay for it, even if it means giving up my livelihood. And I truly believe that if I come back well — or at least with the disease stopped or slowed down — I can be a productive part of the Body. Isn't that what God wants?"

"He wants you to submit to the elders, who know better than you what is best for the Body." Daed's voice was firm, though distress and confusion lurked in his eyes. He would never admit to doubt in the church's leadership, though. A man of humble authority himself, he just didn't have it in him to go against those God had chosen to be his spiritual leaders.

Where had this rock in the stream of her obedience come from? Was it fear? Did she not trust God's leading enough?

Elam gripped her bad hand, and a bolt of pain shot up her arm and into the bottom of her skull, rattling her brain. If it hadn't been for iron self-control, she might have leaped off the chair and dumped him on the floor. "Wait, my little man." She eased him off her lap, nearly gasping with the pain, as if she'd laid her palm flat on the hot stove.

"Amelia, are you all right?" Ruth examined her, brows furrowed together. "You're as white as this pastry."

"I — Yes." She rubbed her hand, hiding it in her apron. "It's a little sore today."

This was a new development. The Anabaptist martyrs of old had withstood fire and stoning and all kinds of awful deaths for the sake of their faith, and here she was, flattened by a burst of nerve pain from a system that was slowly going haywire. Had Lila Esch had to deal with this, too? If *she'd* had a chance to go to Mexico, would she have taken it, or continued on the path the

263

church said was the right one?

Amelia would never know now.

While Isaac and Elam tended to the fire, the little boy carefully putting in a small log despite his wariness of the glowing red coals, she got busy washing the baking dishes in the sink as she'd done since she was small. When those were finished, she prepared brussels sprouts with bacon and made gravy for the roast.

By the time they heard the sound of a buggy in the lane, dinner was ready and the smell of baking pies filled the house. Isaac brought the boys out with him to see to Eli's horse, and Amelia took advantage of the quiet to give herself a talking-to.

No blushing, no babbling, and no sneaking peeks at his nice eyes, Amelia Beiler. Keep this friendly but businesslike, and don't lose your composure if he smiles at you.

Not that that was very likely. She'd turned down his offer of help and all that it implied, hadn't she? The man had no reason to waste any smiles on her anymore. Not the kind a man gives a woman he'd like to see in his home anyway.

When everyone came in, she was ready with a company smile and the offer of a cup of coffee while Ruth bustled from stove to table, setting out all the food.

"*Denki,* Amelia. That would be nice — warm these cold fingers right up."

She set the cup and saucer down at her oldest brother's place next to Mamm, then settled on the other side of the table with Matthew and Elam. After they all said a silent grace, she helped Elam to some potatoes and handed them to Matthew. But instead of taking them, Matthew gazed at Eli.

"Are you going to buy our dad's shop?" he asked.

Isaac looked down, smiling into his beard. Ruth said, "Matthew! That's none of your business." And Amelia just stared at her firstborn. What on earth had possessed him to blurt out such a thing?

Eli looked a little startled but covered it with a smile. "Not that I know of. I don't think your *Mamm* is keen on selling right now."

"Matthew, have some potatoes."

He took the bowl and looked up at her. "But, Mamm, you just told Daadi you were going to."

"I know I did. And little pitchers have big ears, it seems."

Eli spooned brussels sprouts onto his plate, not looking at her, giving her a chance to smooth things over.

Well, she had to tie the knot in the bull's tail now. She'd invited him over to talk about this very thing, hadn't she? "I've decided to sell the shop, Eli, as Matthew said." She nudged the boy with her shoulder to show him he wasn't in trouble for poking his nose into adult business. "There's an expensive treatment for my condition —" *Oh, just say it.* "The MS — that won't be funded by the church, so I need to raise the money for it."

He made an encouraging noise, eating Ruth's good roast beef with zest and making it obvious without being rude that he already knew the details. She did like a man who appreciated a woman's cooking — and knew how to consider her feelings.

"The thing is, one of our customers has made me an offer. And since you were interested, too, I thought it only fair that you have a chance to say your piece. If you are still interested, that is."

"I hear you were planning to head back to Lebanon soon," Ruth put in. "Friday?"

"I was." Eli took a sip of coffee, though it must be tepid by now, what with the amount of milk he'd put in it. "I've had a good look around Whinburg, and there are one or two prospects for work."

"There are?" Amelia asked. "From what

Mel— from what some of the other men have said, not too many Amish folks are looking for help. With the economy the way it is, even the *Englisch* are cutting back and not expanding."

"While I was looking around, I noticed that there weren't too many of the men doing electrical conversions — you know, taking *Englisch* washing machines and dairy machinery and suchlike and converting them to run off air pumps or batteries."

"You're right there," Isaac said. "We get that done in Strasburg, or we do it ourselves."

"So I thought I might try my hand at that. I could have a little shop with a wagon and travel around helping the men with their conversions."

"So you're not interested in pallets, then." Amelia wondered why this sudden shaft of disappointment had lodged itself in her middle. She was merely being polite in giving him the chance to offer, wasn't she? She'd practically already decided that Bernard Burke and his hundred thousand were the prime candidates.

"I didn't say that," Eli replied, with a smile across the table at her. "If I were going to settle here, I'd need something useful to do, that's all."

"And are you planning to settle?" Amelia would never have been so forward as to ask, but Ruth had no such qualms. "That's a big decision."

"It is," Eli agreed. "One I've been mulling and praying over for some time. The Lord still hasn't made it clear to me what His will is, though."

And behind the quiet words, Amelia heard: *If I had a chance with you, it would be plenty clear.*

If only things were different! A person could get used to sitting across a table from that smile. Matthew and Elam seemed to like him, too — otherwise Matthew would never have opened up and spoken so boldly to him.

But she just couldn't sentence this kind man to years of caring for an invalid. Oh, life might be very sweet — at first. But they would pay for that sweetness in month after month of the kind of hardship Emma had endured — the kind that had made Lila Esch's husband, Milner, lose forty pounds and put years of pain in his eyes.

No. She must resist the silent wish of a man who would never speak it out loud until he had a sign from her. She must be strong for both their sakes.

And if he moved here and took up a business — any business — and decided to give up and marry someone else . . . well then, she would have to be strong about that, too.

A sinking feeling of cold despair slid down her spine and into her belly.

She would be strong, for the boys' sake. God's will might be her first priority, but He would not have blessed her with them if He had not believed she would put them first, too, would He?

The potatoes and gravy felt like wallpaper paste in her mouth. She drank a little water and said, "So this customer, he offered me a hundred thousand dollars for the shop, based on a forty-thousand-dollar profit last year. That would include the land and equipment, as well as the materials on hand."

Eli raised his brows. "That's a very generous offer."

"It is." Isaac nodded over his roast beef. "But I think Amelia would give a fair chance to an Amish man, even if his offer wasn't quite so high." Her father's gaze held hers.

She almost said, *I would?* — but bit it back just in time.

"The attraction of the *Englisch* man's offer," she began carefully, "is that it would be enough to finance the treatment, but there would be enough left over for me to start again with a smaller shop."

"True," her father said. "But if a good business stayed within the church, then God would bless you with prosperity in another start, even if you didn't have money right away."

Oh, dear. This was not what she had hoped for. But she said nothing, only waited for Eli to speak. This money would be coming out of his pockets, after all.

"I'm not sure I could match such a generous offer as this *Englischer* has made, even if I wanted to," Eli said slowly. "I was thinking more along the lines of seventy or eighty thousand, depending on how friendly the bank manager is feeling on the day I go in." Again that self-deprecating smile turned in her direction, but it didn't warm her the way it had earlier.

Would the church take sides about this, too? Would people judge her for allowing her business to go outside the church, thus depriving an Amish man of a way to make his living? Would everyone see her as greedy and self-serving and proud instead of desperate and trapped in a situation over which she had no control?

Was she flouting God's will in trying to find a way out?

What was she going to do?

Eli's gaze, at first warm and humble, had begun to reflect her alarm — though probably not for the same reasons. "I am sorry it is so little," he said. "I'm not a rich man, just one who knows how to work hard."

"It's not little," she managed, stalling for time. "It's a very nice offer." If she hadn't heard Bernard Burke's first, she probably would have been thrilled.

"Of course you can't decide tonight," he went on. "Why don't I have a talk with the bank, and then, once I know for sure what I can manage, I'll come and talk with you again."

"When will that be?" She wanted to be in Mexico by January, and the wheels of the Amish moved slowly when it came to big decisions. That was often a good thing, but not in her case. With every day that passed, a little more of her myelin got nibbled away. Time was running out.

"I was planning to leave on Friday. I'll be home by Saturday night, and I could go in and have a talk on Monday. So if you'll be in the shop Tuesday morning, I could call then."

She nodded. "That would be fine. I told Mr. Burke I would let him know next week."

"*Gut.*"

"*Ja.*"

There didn't seem much else to do then but finish her dinner. Ruth asked Eli how they were doing up there at the Martin Kings', and the conversation drifted away from Amelia's concerns. But her thoughts ran along the same track, speeding into a future she couldn't yet see.

What should I do, Lord? What is Your will? And, Lord, why did You bring this kind, hard-working man to sit across the table from me if You had no intention of allowing us to be anything to each other?

CHAPTER 14

Isaac took the boys out to the barn to help him move some hay from the loft for the few cows he still kept, though Amelia thought it was a little strange to be doing that after dinner instead of during the day. It wasn't until Ruth vanished, murmuring something about a tisane she had steeping, that Amelia realized something was going on.

"I . . . I suppose I'd best be going," Eli said, turning his black hat around and around in his hands. "Tell your mother *denki* for the dinner. And you, too. *Denki.*"

"You're most welcome. Anna's coleslaw was delicious." Oh, this was so silly. "Eli, I apologize for my parents. I think they think I'm sixteen and my first boy has come calling."

He straightened, and his shoulders seemed to relax with relief. "I didn't know what they thought — or whether I wanted to laugh or run."

What a gift to be able to be as honest with this man as she was with Emma or Carrie. Well, nearly as honest. There were certain topics you would never bring up with a man — and courtship was usually one of them.

"I hope you won't run. I hope you'll feel as comfortable here as you would in your own home."

"You make me feel that way." He paused. "Wherever you are. Even out in a rainy field."

She ducked her head and blushed. "Eli —"

"I know. You've told me where you stand. I know it's only been a year since you lost the one you loved. I can enter into those feelings, too." She looked up, and at the question in her eyes he said, "I lost my wife and son a few years ago. They were making a left turn in the buggy at an intersection, and a truck ran the stop sign."

She drew in a shocked breath. "Oh, Eli. How awful." How strange that they should both lose the ones they loved in nearly the same way. And doubly strange that she had not heard of it, even via Aaron and the Kings.

"It was. For nearly a year, I doubted I would survive. Only the hand of God, the prayers of the church, and the daily care of my family got me through."

Amelia nodded. "I know. God looks after His own." She had wondered about his story, but if she'd asked anyone, they would have thought her interest was personal. She would not give people any more to talk about than they already had. "So you have no other children?"

He shook his head. "Kate had very difficult pregnancies. We lost two before Jonathan came along."

To wait so long for a child and then have him taken away so suddenly and cruelly . . . Amelia laid her hand on his arm without a thought to how it would look. "Eli, I'm so terribly sorry. We know God knows best, but sometimes accepting His will can be a battle in itself."

He nodded, covering her hand with his own. "It has been. I won't be shy about admitting it. Perhaps that's why I like spending time with your boys. It comforts me somehow." He looked down at his hand, as if he'd just now realized what it was up to. "You're a very comfortable family."

"I think you mean comfort*ing*." With a smile she tried to reclaim her hand, but she didn't get far.

"I mean, I'm comfortable with you."

"So . . . so you said."

"Couldn't you tell me why you're pulling away, then?" His voice was so low it was practically a rumble in his chest.

She let him have her hand. It was her left — the one that didn't work. It lay in his, inert, and only the fact that he was squeezing it gently gave it any semblance of life at all.

"I have multiple sclerosis, Eli."

"And so you said. That makes no difference to me."

"It should." Her voice gained a little strength as she realized she would have to get him to understand, once and for all. "It will make a very great difference in ten years, when I won't be able to cook or keep house. When I'll be in a wheelchair, maybe held up by a strap across my chest. When y— When someone would have to care for me instead of having me care for him." She took a shaky breath, and this time when she pulled, he let her go. "I would not wish that on anyone."

"Amelia, you and I have both said the wedding vows. You remember? We promised the ones we married that if they were afflicted with bodily weakness or sickness, we would care for them."

And we said those vows when we were

young and healthy and disease was some-thing that happened to other people. "I remember. But —"

"If someone loved you, he wouldn't mind caring for you. He'd do it gladly."

"But it would be a sacrifice I'm not willing to let someone make."

"You should leave that up to this . . . someone."

"Maybe he doesn't have any idea what he would be getting into." When Eli opened his mouth to speak, she went on before he could get the words out. "And there's another reason. If I sell the shop — no matter who to — and go to Mexico to have this new treatment, the bishop has as much as told me I'll be put under the *Bann* for disobedience."

His eyes widened. "Why on earth?"

"Because they don't believe it's scriptural to put the substance of an animal into the temple of the human body."

The significance of this sank in. "But you believe this treatment will help you?"

"For the boys' sake, I have to do it. If there's even a slim chance that I won't become that person in the wheelchair that my teenage sons will have to look after instead of getting out and leading their own lives, I want to take it."

He nodded slowly. "And that . . . someone who might be there, too? He would not have to do so either, would he?"

Too late she saw where he was going. "I can't ask that of . . . of anyone. To wait and see, I mean. That would not be fair. Even if I did come back better, I would still be facing *die Meinding.*"

This would be the point where he would realize that it was better to court a woman who was not only healthy but unencumbered, too, instead of wasting his time on ifs and maybes.

"You might. Or you could consider another community, one that doesn't hold such a strict line where medical matters are concerned."

"But then I would have to take the boys away from their home and family."

"*Ja,* possibly. But Lebanon County, you know, is not so far away."

He'd put one over on her again. "Eli, it's impossible."

"Maybe. Maybe not. Nothing is impossible if it's within the Lord's will."

"But finding out His will is the hard part." The lump in her throat was so big she couldn't get words past it. How was it possible that this man could hint at a future when she had given him so little encouragement?

Now she knew what it meant to be humbled to the dust. "Eli," she whispered. "You must not say such things to me."

"Telling me what to do already?" he teased, his voice as soft as a touch.

"I can't," she said, half to him and half to herself.

"You think about it. Have your treatment and know that in Lebanon County someone will be waiting and thinking about you."

"Don't. I don't want you to." She was so close to tears she could hardly speak. She could not ask these things of him, no matter how willing he was to do them. Not when she hardly knew her own heart. "Don't waste your life waiting, Eli. How is it that you have never married again? You must go find a girl in Lebanon County who is free to . . . to care for you as . . . as you should be cared for."

"I don't want a girl. I want a woman. A capable, godly woman who has been tried and tested and come out as gold."

Fool's gold. "You may want such a woman, but the one standing here is empty and hurting and frightened."

"But when God heals those hurts, you may think differently. And you will be thinking of your boys as well."

Oh, why did he have to say that? Because she was not the only person she had to think of. The fact was that the boys were her first thought — and they missed having a man to look up to. Daadi was wonderful, but they didn't have him at bedtime when she was fighting them to go upstairs. Or in the middle of the night when Elam woke with his fears of the dark, calling "Daed! Daed!" in such a faint, pitiful voice that she wondered it did not reach Enoch in heaven and break his heart, despite what the Scripture said about there being no grief there.

Her boys would bring comfort to a faithful heart that had lost his family. For those reasons alone — Eli and her sons needed each other — she could be tempted to allow him to court her and see if such a path was really God's will. But for herself? The choice was much more difficult, and selfishness was always the easiest, most joyful path.

At first. But when she had to count the cost, would it be worth it then? Better to count it now and make the decision than have to do it later, when the cost would only increase.

The door to the sunroom opened, and Eli stepped back. Amelia realized just how close they'd been standing — he would merely have had to lift his arms and she would have been in them. And only now, as the gap between them widened to a polite distance and pain and loss rushed in to fill it, did she realize the magnitude of what she was giving up.

"And then, to top it off, he offered me a ride home."

Oblivious to the fact that half the congregation was on the other side of Old Joe's daughter's bedroom door, Emma and Carrie sat next to each other on the bed, hanging on every word. They'd come in to pin up Carrie's hem after she'd accidentally put her heel through it, and Amelia had seized her chance.

"Even Matthew forgot to complain when Eli wouldn't let him drive. He was too busy listening to his stories about the crazy pigs they used to have on his father's farm."

"He shouldn't have let him drive anyway, not at night," Emma put in. "But never mind the pigs. Eli Fischer really asked if he could court you, straight out, in so many words?"

"He did." Amelia sighed. "Right there in Mamm's kitchen, with me standing at the door like I was wishing he would go."

"Which you weren't," Carrie said. It

wasn't a question.

"No," Amelia said slowly. "I was practically in his arms the whole time and didn't even realize it."

"Your mother's going to make hay with that one." Emma tried to smile and failed miserably.

"She didn't see. He stepped away just in time, and that's when he asked to give us a ride home. So Mamm had enough hay to make with that." She put her fingers to her temples, feeling the organdy of her *Kapp* — a soft reminder that prayer should be a constant thing. "I don't know what to do."

"Let the poor man come around." As if just remembering that someone could walk in at any moment, Emma got up and leaned against the door.

"You know why she can't," Carrie told her. She brushed the Ohio Star quilt on the bed with one hand, and in her face Amelia could practically see her own thoughts. What a pity that life wasn't so organized as those straight, orderly seams. Each lay just as it should, and when it didn't, a little pressing of the iron soon convinced it where its duty lay, so that its neighbor could lie flat and show to best advantage, too.

"I know why she *thinks* she can't." Emma wasn't going to give up until she'd said her piece. "If you can do something as daring as travel all the way to Mexico, you can certainly take a chance on a man when he offers himself to you on a plate."

Amelia chewed her bottom lip. Was that bitter tone directed at her or at Emma's own circumstances? Perhaps she was still thinking, *You've had two chances, and I've had none. Don't waste what another woman would treasure.*

"I can't let him go any further — to sacrifice himself for me," she said at last. "He would come to hate me in the end, like —" No, she couldn't say that out loud.

Emma settled herself more firmly against the door. "Were you going to say like I hated my father? I didn't, you know. Being glad he's at peace isn't the same as hating him."

"And being glad there's peace in the house isn't the same as being glad he's dead." Carrie finished the thought.

"But I wouldn't be dead." Amelia struggled to find the right words. "It's not the same. He would come to resent me, I know he would, and wish that the day-in, day-out drudgery of caring for me were over."

"I don't think he's that kind of man," Emma observed. "I don't know him very well, but if there are two kinds of people —

givers and takers — it seems to me he falls in the first category. Love makes it easy to give."

"But givers need to be given to as well."

"And you would. While you could. After that, it's up to the Lord. Who's to say your future is going to look like Lila Esch's anyway? God might have something different in mind for you."

"I can't take the risk. And I can't let him take it either. Or even think about taking it, which is what he's doing now."

"You mean you don't trust God." Emma, drat her, sounded just like Mamm.

"I trust that *He* knows what He's doing. The problem is, *I* don't know what He's doing. All I know is that I have to sell the shop and go to Mexico. I have to do what I can to get well. Everything else is up to Him. Eli said he would wait, but I can't hold him to that."

Emma put her hands behind her and gripped the door handle. "Amelia Beiler, sometimes I just want to spank you. Don't you know I would give ten years off my life for a man who would say such a thing to me?"

Shame washed over her. "I know."

"Then *what* is the problem?"

"I . . . I guess I have a hard time trusting

that it could be so. That it could be real. Because Enoch promised me . . . and then he . . ." She couldn't go on. Instead she pushed away from the dresser and walked over to the window. The sky had begun to clear, just when she would have appreciated a howling gale to match her mood.

"Enoch would have kept his promises if it weren't for that drunk driver," Emma said fiercely. "Don't go losing faith in him because he never got a chance to show it. And don't lose faith in Eli Fischer because you won't give him a chance to show it either."

Amelia blinked, clearing the blur of tears out of her vision. "I wasn't — I didn't . . ."

"You just told us you did. The truth is, if you're going to shortchange a fine man like that, I don't want to hear about it." Emma's mouth trembled, and she carefully released the door handle, as if reminding herself not to give it a good hard slam.

"I'm giving him a chance to have a happy life and forget a woman who may only wind up being an invalid."

"I'm not listening."

She'd known that Emma was stubborn, but she'd never seen her like this. Amelia crossed the room and took Emma's shoulders, as though offering a massage. But even

285

her muscles felt as stiff and unyielding as bone. Amelia squeezed gently with her right hand. "Don't let a man come between us, *Liewi*."

Emma turned away, as if Amelia weren't even there. "He looks at me like I'm one of Mamm's friends — like I'm from another generation, when he can't be any older than I am. How do you think that makes me feel?" She didn't wait for an answer — not that Amelia had one. "All through our *Rumspringe*, I listened to the two of you talk about this boy here and that boy there, and heard all about your dates, and stood up with you and witnessed your vows when you were married. But I am done listening to you talk about Eli Fischer." She slid sideways, out from under Amelia's hands, and went into the bathroom across the hall. Water sloshed into the sink, and they heard her splashing her face.

Carrie and Amelia exchanged a look, and one of Carrie's delicate brows went up. She tilted her head in the direction of the door.

Emma kept her back to her, though she must have heard her feet on the polished planks. Without a word Amelia slipped both arms around her waist and laid her head on Emma's shoulder.

"Forgive me. I was selfish. I know how

much it hurts you." Emma sniffled. Amelia pulled a hand towel off the rack next to the sink and passed it to her. "I get so tangled up in my own problems I forget that you and Carrie have them, too."

"I'm thirty years old and I've never even been kissed," Emma whispered into the towel. "What is wrong with me?"

Amelia squeezed her. "Nothing. God has something else in mind for you. Don't give up hope. He's keeping you separated for someone truly wonderful, that's all."

"I hoped that Eli might be the one." Emma blew her nose as Carrie came in and leaned companionably against the doorjamb. "But when you dumped those beet pickles all over him at Mandy Lapp's wedding and he wore that shirt like Joseph's coat of many colors, I knew there was no chance."

"There will be a chance for you with someone," Carrie said softly. "God is faithful to those who love Him."

"Just as He's faithful to someone out there who will love you," Amelia said. "Keep your heart open."

Emma was still, and Amelia heard herself, as though the words had echoed back from the bathroom walls.

She never had been very good at taking her own advice.

CHAPTER 15

Amelia had no sooner opened the shop and taken off her coat than Brian Steiner from the cabinet shop next door came in. *"Guder Mariye,* Amelia. *Wie geht's?"*

If she told him the truth, they'd be here all morning. "Fine, Brian. Is everyone well? How is your mother?"

"She's good. That tea Ruth sent over settled her stomach, and she's been her usual self ever since."

"Mamm will be glad to hear that. So are you in need of pallets on this chilly morning?"

He laughed, his open, guileless face still reddened from the wind. "If I did, it would be to build a fire in the shop. Guess we all have to work a little faster and get the blood moving."

"At least until the heaters can do their jobs."

Shoving his hands into his coat pockets,

he rocked forward. "So . . . I hear you might be interested in selling the shop."

Had the rumor from a couple of weeks ago finally made it back around to where it had started, or was the one from last week just getting off the ground? She hadn't a doubt that the men would have chewed it over yesterday at church. "I might be. Why?"

"Well, we've been thinking of expanding a little. If we bought the shop, we could keep the pallet business going and use your extra space to store the lumber we use in the cabinets."

She nodded. It was a sensible plan. Small-industry space didn't come up so often in Whinburg — at least not at the prices an everyday person could afford. "Have you talked about an offer with your dad and the other boys?"

"We have. We could give you a down payment of fifty thousand by Christmas and then pay you monthly for the rest, for a total of eighty thousand. Contingent, of course, on seeing the books. Then it might go higher or lower. This is just a starting figure."

"It's a fair figure to start," she acknowledged. It was also in line with what Eli had told her — which made a decision even more impossible. "But I have to tell you that one of my *Englisch* customers has offered a hundred."

Some of the high color left his face, but that could be because he was out of the wind and warming up. "You wouldn't sell out to an *Englischer,* would you?"

"Yours is the third offer I've had, both inside and outside the church. I might have to hold an auction." She tried to lighten both her discomfort and his with a smile.

"Whose is the other? Eli Fischer?" When she nodded, he went on, "And I heard that one of Old Joe Yoder's nephews is thinking of getting married, so he's looking for solid work close by. There's a lot of money in that family. You might get some inquiries from that direction, too."

"Really," Amelia said faintly. The rumors really had feet, then.

"I was talking to Melvin Miller on Friday, while you were out. He said he was going to talk to the bank about selling the farm and getting a smaller place. If he does that, he might have enough for a down payment on the shop — and we were also kicking around an idea or two about buying in together."

Amelia wished she were sitting safely behind her desk instead of standing help-lessly over here by the coat tree. At least then she'd feel a little bit in control. She'd have her invoices and bills to remind her that she had responsibility here. Like it or not, she was more than a housewife who would fade into the kitchen when the men gathered to talk business.

Now they were talking *her* business. She'd been brought up all her life to submit, to obey, to defer. But she couldn't do that now. She had her health to think of — and the boys. If she wasn't going to let Eli court her, she still had to keep working at some kind of salable trade so she could put clothes on their backs and good food on the table. She couldn't afford to be crowded by men from all corners of the community — even if they were anxious to do the right thing for her and keep what Enoch had built in Amish hands and out of Mr. Bernard Burke's.

Poor man. He had no idea what he was up against.

Brian was looking at her as if he expected an answer. What had they been talking about? Ah. Melvin Miller, buying in with them.

That was a new one. Carrie had not said a word about it yesterday. But maybe she hadn't known, if Brian and Melvin had put their heads together once Amelia was out of the shop and on her way home to her boys.

"Melvin has been with me just a couple of

292

weeks," she said, treading carefully. "Do you feel confident in his ability as a partner? It's a big investment, giving up the farm and moving. He wouldn't want to do it on a whim — if he wasn't completely committed to doing this for his trade, I mean."

"Well, you'd have to talk that over with him. But it would lessen our investment and give him a stake. And now would be the time, before planting starts in the spring and he gets caught up in another year on the farm."

Oh, how Carrie's eyes would glow at the prospect of getting away from that farm. She would be so happy with a nice little house on five acres, where she could plant a big garden and worry about nothing more than potato bugs that might spoil one row, instead of some virulent corn infection that could destroy an entire season's worth of income. Carrie would give anything to feel safe and cared for — and if that was off her mind, she might be able to conceive.

And then there was Eli, who wanted to create a life in a new community. And now Brian, wanting to expand a little — not enough to get too big for his britches but enough to serve the customers the Steiners had.

All her friends, people she cared about, all

with good and worthy goals. How on earth was she to make a choice when taking one man's offer meant dashing the dreams and hopes of the others?

Did men think this way when they made their business decisions? Or did they simply total up the columns and may the best number win? How could she live with herself if the farm went under and Carrie and Melvin were left with nothing? How had she once thought life was complicated when her only concern was getting the washing done before she went off to work?

When Brian had gone back to his own shop, Amelia tried to concentrate on the bills. The business was like a child — you had to feed it and keep it healthy, no matter what was going on in the rest of your life. So she got out the checkbook and worked her way through accounts payable. At least with the fifteenth coming up this week, she'd be able to bill a few of the big customers' orders to fill the monetary well again.

The twelfth already. The Sunday after next would be Christmas. Where had the month of November gone? At least she'd been able to sew a pair of pants for both boys, and Emma usually put together a basket of candy and cookies for them to share, since she made one every year for Karen's kids. If

Amelia planned to give anything to her parents on Second Christmas, to her two best friends and her nieces and nephews, she'd better get busy. Hmm. They were all busy making quilt blocks. Maybe she'd make potholders out of some of her other fabric. She could whip one of those together in an hour or so, and goodness knew they were useful. She should check her fabric cupboard when she got home and —

The phone rang, and she realized she'd been staring into space instead of opening envelopes.

"Whinburg Pallet and Crate, this is Amelia."

"Hi, Amelia, it's Darcy from Dr. Brucker's office. You were going to call me and schedule your extraction?"

Oh, dear. As if in answer, the broken tooth throbbed, though she hadn't done anything to bother it. Well, maybe it didn't like the way her jaw had suddenly clenched. Amelia did her best to relax her muscles. "Yes, I was," she said weakly.

"We just had an opening for Monday the nineteenth — a week from today — at nine. I know Dr. Brucker was trying to get you in sooner. How is the tooth?"

"It's been better. It's sore when I chew on that side, and I have to try to remember to

295

keep food out of it."

"Maybe I could shuffle some things around. I have a feeling I'm going to get a cancellation this afternoon. How do you feel about being on standby for four o'clock?"

This afternoon? Get a tooth pulled? Oh, no. "It's not that sore, really. I'll be fine until Monday."

"Are you sure? Because if today doesn't work, I could squeeze you in on Wednesday at lunch."

"No, no. Thank you. Monday will work just fine."

"I don't blame you. I'm not so keen on getting them yanked either. You might consider getting a porcelain crown, you know. It wouldn't be gold, and no one would know it was there." When Amelia didn't answer, she went on, "All right. But if you experience any more pain or swelling, call us, okay? Because we have contingency plans for emergencies, and you'll have been waiting a little longer than we like."

"Thank you. I will."

She hung up, feeling breathless — as if she'd narrowly missed being hit by a car or stepped on a rotten board in the barn loft and jumped aside just before it collapsed.

You're such a baby.

Even Elam was braver when she took him

to the dentist. His little hands would grip the arms of the chair, his gaze resolutely glued to the silly cartoon animals pasted on the ceiling, while the dentist probed and scraped and drilled. Matthew, too. So she had no excuse to put it off when she wouldn't allow that in her own children.

Besides, better to get it done now. Then it would be all healed up by the time she went to Mexico in January.

Maybe she'd better take that Wednesday appointment. Ruth would undoubtedly have some mixture to put on the gap to take the pain away, or a tea that would help her sleep.

Amelia reached out to pick up the phone, and it rang under her fingers. She jumped, then, when it rang a second time, took a deep breath and let it out slowly.

"Whinburg Pallet and Crate, th—"

"Amelia." The smile in his voice stopped her.

"Eli." The syllables lay as smooth as cream on her tongue. *Wie geht's?*

"I'm well. And you?"

"I just hung up from the dentist. Think of me next Monday at nine when I'm having a tooth pulled."

"That shouldn't be too difficult."

"I hope not. But with a broken tooth, you never know if there's going to be enough for them to get a hold of or if they'll have to dig around a bit."

"I meant it shouldn't be difficult to think of you."

Her throat closed up. *Don't say things like that to me. Not when it's impossible.* "Did you have a good journey home?"

"I did. I think I surprised my sister-in-law, though. I found her in the kitchen, measuring for new curtains. Another example of the efficiency of the Amish Internet."

"Oh, dear. What did you do?"

"Well, I was sorry to disappoint her, but the old ones will have to do for a while yet."

"What do you mean?"

"I spoke to my bank manager today, as I told you I would. We had a long talk."

"And what does he say?"

"He has to do the paperwork, but he gave me to understand there would be no problem with a loan, if I wanted one."

A wave of happiness rose up out of nowhere and washed over her. Eli would move to Whinburg. She would get to see him in church every other week. She could still have his friendship, if nothing else. But what did he mean about the old curtains?

"Your poor sister-in-law. It's hardly fair to make her live with old curtains if you're planning to move." She hoped the smile in her voice transmitted itself down this pesky, crackly phone line. Where was he calling from? A phone shanty near his home?

"Well, that's just the thing. I went in to have that talk because I'd told you I would, but I think it would be best if I accepted the fact that my future is here in Lebanon County."

She heard his words — or rather the sound they made crashing up against what she'd expected him to say. She sat silently, trying to make sense of the rubble.

"I'm sorry, Amelia. Truly. But I had a lot of time to think on the bus back here, and it came to me that God is closing doors that I thought might once be open, and I should pay attention to Him before fingers get pinched."

She thought she understood. "I would not want you to have that pain," she said quietly, gripping the receiver with both hands. "But I want you to know your friendship is precious to me."

"And yours is to me," he said gently. "But we must leave it at that, *ja?*"

He was right. She must not say the words fluttering helplessly on her tongue. To speak would be to drag him into her eventual misery, and she would not do that to a friend. She could only say his name, like a plea, or a prayer. "Eli . . ."

"I will say good-bye for now, Amelia. I will pray that you get your health and happiness back again. And I wish you every good thing."

Still she could not force another word out. And he must have taken her silence for dismissal, because a second later the dial tone rang in her ear.

She dropped the receiver into its cradle.

Every good thing.

Right at the moment, she couldn't see a single good thing, anywhere.

On Tuesday afternoon Amelia pasted a smile on her face as the Stolzfus buggy rolled up the lane, and she hugged Emma and Carrie at the door. But as she hung up their coats and black away bonnets, she realized that some hurts went so deep it would be impossible to share them while they were so fresh. So she pretended that everything was all right, even as they caught up on their news and laid out their stitched blocks.

Slowly, the pattern that Carrie had envisioned took shape on the sitting-room floor. It really did look like a sunrise over green fields — using the green instead of black had been the right decision.

What message would the latter have given?

Sunrise over scorched fields? Amelia squelched a bitter smile. If the quilt had been for her, it might have been appropriate. Because that was what her life felt like. Scorched, burned. Used up. Good for nothing but being plowed under until she could find the strength to start over again. Then maybe there would be hope for a few green shoots to show their fragile heads.

On Wednesday, after dinner at her parents', she and Elam walked slowly down their snowy lane so that Matthew could get the mail out of the mailbox and catch up to them. The boys made a game out of walking in her footsteps so that it looked as if only one person had come home. She didn't know whom they hoped to fool, but the laughter of both boys as they tried to match her longer stride comforted her.

She needed to follow their innocent example and find joy in the little things. It was clear that joy in the big things was not part of God's plan for her at this season in her life.

When the boys were settled at the table putting together a puzzle, she finally had a moment to look at the mail. Oh, good, another packet of circle letters from Katie Yoder. She had almost a week, then, to read through them and write her own before she passed it on to Emma on Tuesday. A new issue of *Family Life,* that was *gut.* Several circulars from shops in town. A letter from Lebanon.

Eli.

Her stomach sank while her heart sped up its rhythm. Had their conversation on Monday been as hard for him as it was for her — so hard that he'd changed his mind and was now writing to take everything back?

She ripped open the envelope and pulled out the sheet of foolscap inside.

Dear Amelia,

I hope this finds you as well as can be expected and that you are having a good week. Here in Lebanon we have had snow, which makes it interesting to get to church. There is something to be said for meeting in the barn or the equipment shed. I'm sure the ladies who have to clean up after sixty pairs of muddy feet in their homes think so, too.

But I did not begin this letter to talk about the weather or housework. I don't know why I began it, unless it's to try to explain myself. You probably aren't interested in hearing, because you have made it clear that you don't think a future is possible for us. But I should not have brought it up over the telephone, with cars going past on the highway and the neighbor boy hanging around outside in the cold, waiting to call his girl.

Instead I should have written while sitting in this quiet kitchen that will soon be the domain of my brothers' wives. When I think of what this kitchen used to hold and what it holds now, the silence can be a dreadful thing. But in it at least I can hear myself think. Our conversation was so brief that you would not know I had spent three days working up to it. Or how much of my heart it took to say those words to you. But now that they are said, I must stand by them.

I suppose you think it is unreasonable of me to have these feelings when we hardly know one another. And yet something in your spirit calls to mine, and it seemed like this might be a good foundation for a friendship and maybe more. But despite that, I understand your worries, and I will not burden you with a hope that looks to sustain itself on next to nothing.

Forgive me if my clumsy words have hurt you again. Bringing you yet more pain is the last thing I want to do. I just wanted you to know that with me, hope may be skinny from its diet lately, but it's still there.

I pray I will hear some good news of you when you come back from your adventures in Mexico.

Until then I am

Your friend,
Eli

"Mamm?" Matthew peered into her face. "Who is the letter from? Are you crying?"

Amelia blinked too late — a tear had already escaped. Maybe more than one. Next to her, Elam gazed up into her eyes, his lip wobbling. Any second he would burst into tears, just because something had upset her. She gathered him into a hug and then got up to give Matthew a reassuring squeeze from behind. Surreptitiously, she wiped her eyes on her sleeve.

"It was a sad letter, but I'm better now."

"Did someone die?"

Her heart constricted at the thought that her little boy would connect sadness only with death. Death itself was no mystery. Every Amish child was taught practically from birth that it was a part of life, something that was in God's keeping and not their own and therefore not to be feared. But all the same, it was a heavy stone to lay on a child so young.

"No, not someone. Some*thing*. Something worth grieving for." She cleared the roughness from her throat. "But now who would like some hot chocolate before bed?"

"Christmas chocolate?" Matthew looked hopeful, the letter forgotten.

"No," she said with mock sternness. "I'm sure you were bad sometime today, so it's a powdered packet for you."

"Noooooo!" Matthew put his hands around his throat and pretended to choke. "I'll do anything, but not the powdered stuff! Not when it's nearly Christmas!"

Shaking off the blues for the boys' sake, she put milk on to heat and got the block of chocolate down from the high shelf where she'd put it, out of the reach of eager fingers. She shaved off a quantity and stirred it into the milk. "Mammi made this for me and your aunts and uncles when we were small, as a special treat," she told them. "It —"

"— tastes like Christmas," the boys chorused.

You knew you were getting old when your children could repeat the ends of your stories by heart. But some of her fondest memories were of the whole family gathered around the table eating gingerbread cookies and mincemeat tarts, drinking Christmas chocolate that always tasted richer and more satisfying than any other drink.

She could give her boys the chocolate. But a father? Lots of brothers and sisters to share memories with? A safe haven to come to with a mother in it who had time to bake six different kinds of cookies for occasions like that?

Oh, Eli.

She had chased him away, hadn't she? And with him she'd chased away the possibility of making any kind of memory at all.

CHAPTER 16

The next day dawned bright and crisp — so bright that it hurt Amelia's eyes to look at the snowy fields. Fence posts wore fluffy white hats, and cardinals flitted in and out of the trees, flashing red as they hunted for the last of the berries hanging under crusts of white. The broad sky felt as blue as the ice in the ponds — just as impenetrable, just as cold — but the sun held the promise of warmth in the far-off spring.

If her senses told her true, more snow was on the way and a white Christmas next weekend was guaranteed. The boys would be delighted. The last day of school before the holiday break was next Friday, and already they were planning how they were going to spend Christmas Eve with their cousins, who were arriving from Mount Joy that day in a big van. Amelia would be glad to see her sister and brothers and their families, who would be divided up between the home farm, Christopher and Esther's place, and her own. It would take her out of herself — and Mamm would be so distracted she wouldn't have time to pay too much attention to her.

She would close the shop between Christmas and New Year's, since business slowed more the closer they got to the holidays. How wonderful it would be to immerse herself in her family and forget everything but their fellowship and love.

It would be so busy she would have no time to think, and that would be a Christmas gift in itself. And if she was lucky, the gap left by her broken tooth would have healed enough to allow her to eat some of the good things on the table.

She decided to walk to work. Pulling on her snow boots and wrapping a shawl around herself under her black wool coat, she was as warm as she could be. And the deep brim of her away bonnet had the advantage of cutting down the brilliance of the sun reflecting off the snow as she walked.

What she really needed was a pair of those sunglasses. Wouldn't it be funny to have some like she'd seen on the tourist women? If someone looked into her face under the bonnet brim, all they'd see would be a pair of big black lenses, like a housefly. For the first time in several days, Amelia smiled at herself. How shocked Mamm and Mary Lapp would be at her wayward thinking.

Ach, well. Like starlings, worldly thoughts came and went and did no harm. It was the ones that stayed and roosted in your mind, pulling up the seeds that God had planted, that you needed to look out for. Resolutely, she batted away the thought of Eli Fischer, so persistent it had become more of an ache, and focused on the beauty of the world that God had made.

Behind her she heard the brisk trot of a horse and tramped a little deeper into the snow on the shoulder to give the driver room. When the horse slowed, she turned to see who it was.

Melvin, wrapped in a knitted muffler up to his nose, waved one mittened hand. "Want a ride, boss?"

"*Denki.* It's a surprise to see you out here." She patted the horse's nose as she went around to the passenger side and climbed in.

He waited until she got settled under the buggy blanket, then shook the reins over the horse's back. "I figured with the weather so nice you might be walking, so I came around the long way."

"That's very kind. Your poor horse probably didn't appreciate the extra two miles, though."

"She's a tough old girl. She likes the exercise. Keeps her from getting fat." A quarter of a mile went by in comfortable silence. Then Melvin cleared his throat. "I wanted to talk to you anyway, so it wasn't much of a coincidence. An accidentally-on-purpose one, maybe."

Talk to her, in this much privacy? "If you're wondering what to get Carrie for Christmas, she was looking at flannel sheets in the store a couple of weeks ago. The ones in the display, the five-ounce ones that are really warm."

"That's good to know. But it wasn't what I had in mind."

Oh, dear. His mother was coming for Christmas. Or he was going to make her a firm offer on the shop. Or . . .

Amelia stifled the questions and lifted her eyebrows instead, inviting him to go on.

"It's about your friend Emma."

Amelia blinked. That was the last thing she'd expected him to say. "What about her?"

He seemed to be choosing his words very carefully. "Now, I'm not one to pass on the gossip, so don't take me wrong. But I've

310

heard others talking. I thought you and Carrie might want to drop a hint to her that she's causing speculation and encourage her to walk a little more circumspectly."

Drat this bonnet and its deep brim. Amelia twisted in her seat to stare at Melvin front-on. "What on earth are you talking about? Emma is the most circumspect woman I know." She hardly stirred out of her house, for goodness' sake. What could the gossips possibly do with that?

"It could just be she doesn't have much experience and isn't going about it in the usual way."

"Going about what?" Amelia squashed the temptation to grab him by the shoulders and shake it out of him. "What experience?"

"With courting."

Her mouth dropped open, but no sounds came out. She couldn't think of a single thing to say except a parrotlike, "Who's courting?"

"Emma Stolzfus. And Aaron King. Apparently."

Amelia yanked at the strings of her black bonnet and pulled it off. She couldn't possibly be hearing correctly. "What did you say?"

"The word is that Aaron is courting Emma. And people are talking. So the next time you three get together over your quilt, you might want to hint to her that she should be a little more discreet about it. You have to admit they make an unusual pair."

"They don't make *any* kind of pair! Emma and Aaron are not courting. Good heavens. That's impossible."

Unbidden, her memory flashed to the day Eli Fischer had given her a ride down this very road, the day he'd asked if he could come and help out around her place. Aaron King had been walking out here by himself. She'd thought then that it was a little odd for him to be on foot so far from home, but had dismissed it from her mind in light of the emotional events that had happened afterward.

No. Completely impossible. There had to be another explanation.

"That's what Carrie says, too. If they're not, they're not." Melvin sounded as though the subject was closed, but Amelia hadn't gotten there yet.

"Of course they're not. You should have listened to Carrie and not said another word." Then, in her agitation, she backtracked. "Who on earth would say such a thing? Emma looks after her mother and hardly goes out except to Karen and John's or to pick up medicines or groceries in town. How can that be construed as dating Aaron King?"

"I understand they've been seen together, late at night."

That was courting behavior — if you misunderstood what you were looking at. "By whom?"

But, like gossip, that couldn't be pinned down either. Melvin shrugged and made the turn off Edgeware Road onto the county highway for the half mile into town. "Too bad he doesn't still work for you. We could embarrass the truth out of him."

"Dating Emma Stolzfus would not be cause for embarrassment," Amelia said a little stiffly. "Any man would be lucky to get her." But Aaron was not a man yet. He hadn't even joined church. And therein lay the cause for talk.

With a quick glance, Melvin said, "Of course. That wasn't what I meant. Sorry. But boys that age are easy to tease. That's all."

With the determination of a woman behind a six-mule team, Amelia turned the conversation to their upcoming day of work, but inside, resolve was firming up in her mind. Something was causing people to worry this subject, the way chickens worried a piece of bread when they bit off more than they could swallow. And there was the proof of her own eyes: Aaron King had definitely been leaving the Stolzfus place, a package under his arm. Between her and Carrie, they would pry the truth out of Emma and settle these rumors once and for all.

Emma did not deserve to have people whispering about her and smiling behind their hands at the thought of an old maid and a teenage boy in a courting buggy. No. She and Carrie were her best friends, and they would protect her from that humiliation. They would have to be quick, though. If Amelia's tooth was to come out Monday, it wasn't likely she'd be able for much on Tuesday — including their quilting frolic.

"Melvin, are you and Carrie going to Karen and John's on Friday night for the potluck?"

"I think Carrie mentioned something about it. It's Lena's seventy-fifth or some such?"

"Seventy-eighth. Emma will certainly be there. I'll make sure we get a chance to speak to her before anyone starts asking awkward questions."

Melvin nodded, drawing on the reins to slow for the light at the intersection.

"In the meantime, if anyone says anything

about it, tell them it's not true."

"If it's not true, it might be hard to speak to her," Melvin pointed out.

"If people have seen them together, there's a perfectly logical reason for it," she said. "He might be looking for work. Emma could have hired him to do some painting. It's just a shame that the first conclusion everyone comes to is courtship — and that they don't stop with thinking, like they should."

Melvin glanced at her with a quizzical look as he negotiated the turn into the Steiners' storage yard and his horse headed straight for the stalls. "I'm sorry it upsets you."

"It's not your fault." But it did upset her. Because as soon as she heard about it, the speculation would upset Emma. Amelia could only hope that she wouldn't hear about it from anyone but her best friends, in privacy, the subject broached with love and concern.

Friday evening Elam hung on to her left hand — which couldn't have done much to save him if he had slipped, but she needed her right to hold the box containing the casserole dish of scalloped potatoes for the get-together. Presents were unnecessary, but a potluck where her neighbors could do something concrete for her was both a way of saying happy birthday and providing just a little for the widow. Matthew led the way down the drive, which her brother Christopher had shoveled after he'd done Mamm and Daed's. Normally they'd go over the fields to the Stolzfus home place, but Elam would never be able to fight his way through the unblemished drifts. And if he did, he'd arrive soaked to his chest, and she might as well hang a sign on him inviting every cold germ in the county to come and visit.

The distance was too short to bother with hitching up the horse, and anyway, the exercise was good for them.

As long as she didn't drop the casserole.

When they arrived at the big farm, Karen met them at the door. "*Willkumm,* Amelia. Hallo, you big boys. You grow two inches every time I see you. Here, let me take that box. Oh, scalloped potatoes. Mamm loves those. Let's put them in the oven to stay warm."

Amelia nodded over her shoulder, undoing Elam's coat buttons and toeing off her boots at the same time. She ran her shawl through the sleeves of her coat and handed it and the boys' coats to one of Karen's girls. That way she'd be able to tell which was hers when it came time to go. Every woman knitted or crocheted her shawl with a pattern as individual as she was — all plain, of course, but some did a nice bit of openwork trim above the fringe, and some knitted and purled in a certain way. Their coats were pretty similar, but a woman could pick her own shawl out of a heap on the bed without too much difficulty.

In some congregations the *Ordnung* was so strict that it regulated the width of the pleats in a woman's sleeve caps and where the brim of her *Kapp* could fall on her ears, not to mention how deep the hem could be on her skirt. The knitting pattern a woman used in her shawl was probably a matter of equal obedience in those places. But not, fortunately, in Whinburg, where Bishop Daniel and the elders had more important things to think about.

Matthew disappeared upstairs to the room of Karen's youngest boy, who was also eight, allowing Elam to tag along. Amelia made her way into the living room, where a small crowd was gathered around Lena.

"*Hallich Geburtsdaag,*" she called from the edge of the group, earning a smile from the little lady.

"*Denki,* Amelia. If you're looking for her, Emma went back to the *Daadi Haus* to get my six-o'clock medicine."

Perfect. She looked around for Carrie but couldn't see her in the crowded room. "Are Melvin and Carrie here?" she asked Erica, the wife of one of Old Joe Yoder's many nephews, who cradled a baby in her arms.

"Haven't seen them, but it's early yet."

Hmm. Melvin and David had left the shop at three, when she had locked up and gone over to wish the Steiner boys a merry Christmas. Had they dropped in to visit someone on the way over? Or had something awful happened, like maybe they'd hit a patch of ice and the buggy had gone into the ditch?

No. She couldn't think that way. As Erica had said, it was early yet.

As she visited and laughed with the other well-wishers, she kept an eagle eye out for Emma's return, but she was certainly taking her time. Young Erica slipped out onto the back porch, where some of the men were, and when she reappeared in the kitchen, she had her husband, Josh, in tow.

Suddenly Amelia remembered what Brian Steiner had said about one of Old Joe's nephews being interested in the shop. Oh, dear. She needed to talk to Emma, not fend off questions about property values and annual income. But she was trapped against the bookcase by a cluster of older ladies who were determined to give their best wishes to Lena on her birthday and who were as immovable as so many rocks.

"Amelia," Josh Yoder greeted her. "*Wie geht's* on this snowy evening?"

"*Gut, denki.*" There was no escaping now. Well, Carrie wasn't here yet anyway. Amelia would wait until she could grab her, and then they'd corner Emma together. "And you? You're brave, bringing the little one out so young."

"He was so bundled up we could hardly find him to show him to Lena," Erica said shyly. "Amelia, we wanted to ask you — I mean, we heard that —"

"We heard that your shop was coming up for sale," Josh said, to his wife's evident relief. "If so, I'd be interested. Have you got a solid offer?"

Half a dozen people stood within arm's reach, all of them with ears. "*Ja,*" she said slowly. "Perhaps we could talk about this another time? It's Lena's day, and —"

"You do have a solid offer?" Josh's gaze held hers, intent. "What range are you thinking?"

"Josh, maybe Amelia isn't comfortable talking business among all these people." Erica touched his arm, and Josh took a step forward. Amelia fell back. "Let's go into the kitchen."

Before she could think of a polite way to refuse, she found herself cut out of the group and herded across the kitchen to the back door as though she were a heifer and the Yoders a pair of blue heelers.

It looked as if she was going to talk business whether it was appropriate or not. Fine, then. At least she had a direct view of the front door. *Please,* dummle sich, *Carrie.* When she finally arrived, Amelia would go and greet her, even if she had to leave Josh in midsentence.

"I've had three solid offers," she said, "in a range between seventy and a hundred thousand dollars."

Erica sucked in a soft breath, then laid the baby against her shoulder and patted its back, hiding her face in its soft warmth. "So much?" Josh looked stricken, as if she'd set the price high on purpose to cut him out. "A hundred thousand? Who has that kind of money?"

"One of my customers."

"I heard that an *Englischer* was interested. Is that him?" When she nodded, his cheeks, already ruddy from the warmth in the house, flushed dark. "But you're not going to consider it."

"I'm considering them all."

Behind her the door opened and Brian Steiner stepped in, his brother Boyd on his heels. A blast of cold air broadsided them, and Erica turned her body to shelter the baby until they got the door shut. Brian raised an eyebrow as he looked from Josh to Amelia.

"Nice to see you, Josh. Having a nice visit?"

Josh straightened, as if to make himself as tall as Brian. "Just talking business with Amelia, here."

"*Ja?* Interested in pallets?"

"Maybe. And you?"

"Maybe. I got my licks in earlier in the week."

Josh turned to Amelia. "You didn't tell me that."

"I said I was entertaining other offers."

"You did. So . . . Brian, this *Englischer,* who else?"

"Melvin Miller," Amelia said reluctantly.

"I heard that Eli Fischer was one of them," Erica offered softly. "But maybe that's not true anymore? Since he has gone away?"

Amelia set her teeth. She would not talk about Eli. "I would not say so."

"So that's four of you, then," Boyd said. "Pretty hard decision there."

"Only three." Joshua gazed at her. "Because you can't really be serious about the *Englisch* man's offer if you're thinking about the good of the Kingdom."

Why shouldn't she be? If you left the good of the Kingdom out of it, Bernard Burke was the obvious choice. And therein lay the rub. Who could leave the good of the Kingdom out of any decision?

"Are you serious about that one, Amelia?" Brian asked. "You'd give some thought to letting a profitable business go to the *Englisch?*"

"Have you been talking with my parents?" A question of her own would be useful while she tried to think whether it would cause less offense to answer truthfully or simply to decide now was the time to fetch Emma from the *Daadi Haus,* with or without Carrie.

"Ja." She raised her eyebrows, and Brian went on, "You obviously have, too, if you know your father's feelings about it. I think you should take Isaac's counsel. He's a wise man and has given this some thought."

"I've given it thought, too." She did little else, it seemed. "But there are circumstances that make it necessary for me to get the best price I can."

"As a friend, let me caution you," Erica

said, her voice soft and earnest. "Don't let human nature get the better of you. Greed can come disguised as many things, even 'circumstances.' "

Wrestling with a spurt of temper, Amelia swallowed the hot words that flooded her mouth. Erica was only doing what she herself planned to do for Emma — give her good advice. She must not speak sharply to a woman who was trying to help.

"It's not a question of greed," she said at last, her voice as steady as she could manage. "I have to have some medical treatment. It's expensive. That's why I'm selling."

No one reacted.

Of course not. Because they already knew. The whole settlement probably did.

"I understand," Joshua said.

Do you really? Amelia wanted to ask. His hands could save a child from falling in the snow. Hers could not. If he couldn't do that, would he be standing here asking all these questions?

But Joshua wasn't finished. "I just think you should take the needs of others into consideration as well as your own, that's all."

"I am. I'm considering them very carefully."

"And the needs of your brothers and sisters would come before this *Englisch* man's." That was hardly fair. He'd never even met Bernard Burke. She said nothing, and Joshua persisted, "Because to do otherwise would be to put the world first, before the church. You wouldn't want to do that."

He had backed her into a corner. If she said no, she would be obliged to cut poor Mr. Burke out of the running. If she said yes, she would be condemned in their eyes for doing the very thing the preachers talked about on Sundays. Drat Joshua Yoder anyway. If he hadn't been born into an Amish family, he would certainly have been a fancy lawyer by now.

Brian Steiner looked as though he was thinking the same thing. "*Ach,* now, don't be too hard on her, Joshua. It's not as if she would be put in the *Bann* if she sold to this *Englisch* man and not one of us."

"Wouldn't she? But if it hurt our ability to make a living, we might think of going to the bishop and asking him to intervene."

Erica paled, but Amelia had had enough. More words burned their way to her lips, icy as wind chill. But before they could fly out to do their damage, Matthew and Elam and two other little boys rattled down the staircase, coats on, and dashed out the front

324

door, nearly knocking over Melvin and Carrie as they came up the steps.

So instead of blistering them with her opinion, she stretched her mouth into a smile. "I need to make sure my boys haven't done any damage to that box Carrie has in her hands. Excuse me."

With the skill of a skater, she wove between them and intercepted Carrie in time to take the box from her. "Keep your coat on and go over and wish Lena happy birthday," she whispered, the words running together in her haste to say them. "Then meet me at the *Daadi Haus.* I have to get out of here."

CHAPTER 17

It took only moments to consign the box to the women in the kitchen, rescue her coat and shawl, and slip out the front door into the cold darkness of the yard. Past the garden and down the path, both frozen into crunchiness, she walked as fast as she could until she reached the line of poplars. There she waited in her black coat and dress, a shadow as dark as any cast on the snow by the skeletons of the trees.

Tiny shivers were just beginning to coast up her back when she heard boots squeaking in the snow. "Carrie?"

"*Ja,* it's me. What's going on? Joshua Yoder practically jumped on Melvin, and now they're all talking a mile a minute in one of the downstairs bedrooms."

"Joshua's angry with me because Bernard Burke has more money than he does."

Carrie fell into step beside her. "That's a funny thing to be mad at *you* about."

Lamplight from the *Daadi Haus* shone across the snow. Emma was still there, then. She seemed to be having a hard time locating that medicine.

"He's afraid I'm going to sell to an *Englisch* man and do him out of a way to make a living."

Carrie sniffed. "He may as well be mad at Melvin, then. Or Brian Steiner. Or Eli." She sneaked a sideways glance at Amelia, who chose not to see it.

"He said he might even go to Daniel Lapp and ask him to have a little visit with me."

Carrie clutched at her scarf, her hand twisting in it convulsively. "He said that? To you? Right out loud?"

"*Ja* to all three."

"Said what out loud?" And there was Emma, standing in the open door. "I could hear you two talking all the way from the windbreak."

A little breathlessly, Carrie told her as they crowded inside after knocking the snow off their shoes. "That Joshua." Emma shook her head. "Even when we were scholars, it took so little to set him off. He'd turn all red and bluster and bellow, and if you didn't know better, you'd think he meant it."

"I think he meant it." Amelia unbuttoned her coat for the second time in half an hour.

"I thought I had a battle with my temper. Maybe I should be thanking God for His good work. Especially when Joshua took care to counsel me that I would be putting the world ahead of the church if I sold to Bernard Burke, and wouldn't that be a sin."

"That's not fair," Emma said. "He should mind his own business."

"I think he's trying to," Carrie pointed out. "He's just a little ahead of himself."

They didn't have much time, if Lena was to get her medicine anywhere near six o'clock. Amelia would be just as happy to change this subject anyhow. "Speaking of folks minding their business, I heard something that you should know about, Emma."

Carrie shot her a look, and Amelia met it steadily.

Emma didn't seem to notice as she waved them to a seat on the couch. "And what is that?"

"A while back I saw Aaron King walking down the road here. It's miles from their place, and yours is the only drive besides mine on this side."

"So he must have come from here, is that what you're saying?" Amelia nodded, and Emma rolled her eyes. "Let me guess. Folks are talking, aren't they? What are they saying now?"

"Some seem to think that . . . I mean, obviously it's not true, but . . ." Carrie floundered to a stop. "He was really here?"

"He could have been visiting over at the big house," Amelia said. "Is Karen's John taking on some help?"

"No." Emma sighed and seemed to come to a decision. "If I can't tell you two, then I can't tell anyone. Yes, Aaron King has been here. Late at night, after Mamm went to bed. Several times, in fact."

Amelia goggled at her, and then she and Carrie turned simultaneously to gape at each other. "Are . . . are you — It's true, then?"

"Is what true? That he was here? *Ja,* I just told you so."

"No, not that. They're saying that the two of you are . . . courting." Amelia almost couldn't get the word out. It couldn't be. Emma wouldn't. Aaron King? With the *Englisch* haircut and the custom speakers and the colored reflectors plastered all over his buggy?

Now it was Emma's mouth that hung open. Then it snapped shut. "Is that so? I suppose they think that's hilarious, do they?"

"I . . . I don't know." So it wasn't true. Emma was too incredulously angry for that

329

to be the case. What a relief. "But there has been talk. Emma, you must be more careful. It wouldn't do to stir up any more."

But Emma had recovered herself. "Well, I suppose I'd rather they thought that." She smiled, a wicked smile. "Maybe we should play it up a little more, he and I. Build a — What do the *Englisch* call it? A smoke screen."

"A smoke screen for what?" Carrie demanded. "Emma Stolzfus, what are you and that boy up to?"

"Not just him. I don't suppose you heard any whispers about me and Alvin Esch, too?"

Alvin Esch, the great-nephew of poor Lila, had just turned sixteen. Amelia had seen him across the field last Sunday, showing off his brand-new buggy.

At their blank faces, Emma grinned. "I can see what you're thinking, and you're wrong. They haven't suddenly developed a thing for older women, and both of them are little brothers to me. Don't you remember I looked after Alvin and his tribe of brothers and sisters back when I'd finished school?"

"Then what . . . ?" Amelia couldn't even think how to finish her sentence.

The self-mockery faded from Emma's

eyes. "We're writing. That's all. Me, Aaron, Alvin. Writing. It's like a club. We meet here after Mamm goes to sleep, and we read one another's papers."

Silence fell in the sitting room. Emma reached over to pat their knees, as if giving them comfort.

"Don't look at me as though we're all going straight to a lost eternity. It's harmless. Aaron is working on a short story, and Alvin is . . ." She paused. "Well, promise it won't go any further than this room." She looked at Amelia until she was forced to nod. "He wants to go to college in Lancaster, so he's working on his high-school diploma by correspondence. The packets come here, and he does his homework assignments while Aaron and I write."

"And his parents don't know?" Carrie breathed. "Oh, Emma."

"I'm not deceiving anyone," she retorted. "If his father asked me, I would tell him. But Alvin isn't a church member, so there's nothing to stop him."

"But how can you encourage him to leave the church?" Amelia asked softly. Because of course he would have to. Hardly anyone went past eighth grade to high school, and by the time you were of age to go to college, you were also of age to join church. It

331

boiled down to a choice of one over the other, and once they chose an education, very few ever came back. "This will break Will and Kathryn Esch's hearts."

"It's not my choice to do so, Amelia. It's his."

"But you're making it possible."

"Maybe I am. Maybe I . . ." Her throat seemed to close up, and she cleared it. "Maybe I want to see him do what I could not, because of Mamm and Pap."

"Emma, you would never leave the church," Carrie said stoutly.

"Not now, but there was a time when I thought about it."

"We all think about it. That's what *Rumspringe* is for. And then you make the right choice and give your life to God."

"But Alvin isn't in that place yet," Emma said. "So he comes here, where no one is going to judge him or force him to make a choice before he's ready."

Again silence fell as Amelia tried to take it in. She'd always known that Emma had a rebellious streak hidden deep under her dutiful exterior. Who wouldn't whose choices had all been sacrificed for love? But it was one thing to rebel on your own. It was quite another to involve other people — and even to aid and abet them in their disobedience.

"How long do you plan to let this go on?" Amelia asked.

"Until the boys get tired of it, I suppose," Emma said. "But that doesn't seem likely. Alvin has at least another year of correspondence courses left. And Aaron . . . well, once he got bit by the writing bug, there was no holding him back. One of his letters to the editor was published in the *Whinburg Weekly,* did you know?"

Carrie shook her head.

Amelia said, "I see it in the newsstands in town, but I never pick it up. The pictures on the front aren't what I want Matthew and Elam looking at."

"Maybe not, but it was Aaron's first published piece." Emma moved the balls of wool in her knitting basket to one side and took out a folded-up paper. "Page three."

And there it was. Amelia read it quickly and lifted her head. "He wants the school basketball courts to be left unlocked for public use?"

Emma shrugged. "He has a right to his opinion. Whether anyone listens is another thing. But that's not the point. The point is, he got to speak, and people will hear him. It doesn't actually matter if anything comes of it or not."

Amelia could only imagine what Martin and Anna King would think. Amish folk did write letters to the editor, of course. Emma certainly did — there was her ancient manual Smith-Corona right there under the window. They wrote about worthy things, though — traffic safety and privacy from the tourists and the importance of family life. Things that might affect the whole *Gmee.* They did not write to urge the use of the basketball courts for frivolous play. Only Aaron would think of such a thing.

She couldn't understand why Emma supported it, but obviously there was nothing more to be said. "I hope you know what you're doing."

Emma nodded. "I know what you're thinking. You think I'm encouraging them to sin. But I disagree."

"I'll pray that God changes your mind," Carrie said gently. "Because if their families find out, there will be trouble, and you know it."

"How will they find out? Everyone is too busy laughing about Aaron courting me. If that keeps everyone distracted, then I'll bear it gladly."

If she was so blind to good sense, there was no reasoning with her. Maybe later, when she'd had some time to think it over, they'd bring it up again. "Emma, your mother will need her six-o'clock medicine."

Emma nodded. "I know. But I needed a few moments of peace by myself." Then, at their distressed faces, she added, "Not that I'm not glad to see you. I am. But you know me. I like the quiet much more than I ever get to enjoy it."

She would have more quiet if she weren't helping teenage boys to disobey their parents. But Amelia merely put her coat back on, let herself out into the snow, and kept her mouth shut.

It wasn't until after a lovely sheet cake had been cut and passed around that Amelia noticed with some relief that Josh and Erica Yoder were missing. Even if they planned to leave early, surely they wouldn't have taken the baby out to the barn while Joshua hitched up their buggy? *It's none of your business.* This was evidently the lesson the good Lord wanted her to learn this winter. She had enough troubles of her own to deal with, so what was she doing looking around for the young mother? Checking to make sure she was doing the right things for her newborn?

You'd do better to go and find your own boys and make sure they're not up to something.

335

As a matter of fact, that was a very good idea, seeing as they'd run out an hour ago and not come back.

"Karen," she said when she found her in the kitchen, "did your David come in? My boys were with him."

Karen turned from the sink, where she was up to her elbows in dishes, scrubbing the plates and bowls people had brought so they could take them home clean. Two of her sisters-in-law were wiping them dry as fast as they came out. "I think he took a bunch of the boys up the hill behind the barn to go sledding. They tried to take my cookie sheets to use, but luckily I caught them just in time. I told them they'd better find something in the barn to put dents in."

Amelia shook her head. "Next they'll be tying butter knives to their boots to go skating."

"Shh!" one of the other women said. "Don't give anyone ideas."

"I'd better go out and have a look. I don't want Elam to get warm and take off his coat. Not in this weather."

Out of the blue, Emma appeared at her elbow. "I'll show you where they are."

Amelia had been coming to this farm her whole life — had gone sledding herself on the back hill with Emma and her siblings

336

when they were all children. But she said nothing, only nodded and got ready to brave the cold yet again.

"Thanks for giving me an excuse," Emma said as they went down the back steps. "Mamm would notice if I went back to the *Daadi Haus.*"

"Are you all right?" Amelia gave her the once-over, but she looked just the same despite being muffled up to the nose in a scarf. "I don't remember you being this antisocial before."

"I'm not antisocial. I guess I should thank you for warning me earlier. Now I know why everyone is looking at me as though I've just told a big joke."

"They'd better not say anything to you." Though Amelia didn't know what she'd do if people did rib poor Emma about her new beau. Give them a talking-to?

In the distance, behind the barn, Amelia heard the shrieks and calls of the children as they coasted down the hill on whatever bits of flat material they'd been able to find. With the moonlight reflecting off the snow, there was plenty of light to see by. When the barn door swung open, Amelia actually had to blink and wait for her eyes to adjust to the brightness of the Coleman pole lamps inside. The man who had come out closed the door, and it took a moment before she saw who it was.

"Bishop," she greeted him, and beside her, Emma murmured a greeting as well.

Daniel Lapp blinked at them both. He could obviously see a pair of women, but it took him a couple of seconds to identify them under their wrappings. "Amelia? Who's that with you?"

"Emma Stolzfus. We're going up to make sure my boys aren't killing themselves on the hill."

"Emma." He smiled. "I'm afraid Aaron King isn't out here. Most of the *Youngie* are at Mandy and Philip's new house."

Amelia heard Emma's slow, controlled intake of breath. "I'm a little past those kinds of gatherings. It's my mother's birthday, so my place is here."

But he didn't seem to hear her. "I have to say, I think you might look for someone older. Aaron hasn't joined church, and it's not fitting for you to be seeing him."

Emma had her hands jammed into the pockets of her coat. Amelia took her arm, gripping her elbow in a silent warning to hold her tongue.

"Emma and Aaron aren't dating, Bishop," she said clearly, as though he were deaf. "Whatever you've heard, it's a silly rumor."

"Too many people are talking, and when that happens, there is usually a basis for it."

"Well, there isn't in this case."

"Don't be too sure of that, Amelia." Emma stepped away, so that Amelia was forced to let her go.

While Amelia shook her head, trying to keep her friend from this foolishness, Daniel Lapp's brows drew together, white under the black brim of his hat. "So the talk is more right than these things usually are?"

"I'm saying people shouldn't be so quick to judge," Emma replied lightly, as if it didn't matter in the least that the news would be confirmed and all over the settlement before breakfast. "Amelia, if you want to visit with the bishop, feel free. I'll just run up and make sure Elam and Matthew aren't turning into snowballs."

Amelia hadn't yet recovered her powers of speech. But she didn't need them. Daniel Lapp was already focusing his frowning gaze on her. "The two of you are a pair," he said. "One in a courtship unbecoming to a spinster in her middle age and one in a business unbecoming to a widow."

"Emma isn't middle-aged," Amelia managed. "She's only thirty."

"Don't quibble. I want to know why you are going against the advice of those who seek to help you and pursuing this Mexico scheme."

"I —"

"I just spoke with Joshua Yoder, and he tells me that you are entertaining offers for your shop because you need the money for a medical matter."

"Y—"

"Moses Yoder and I have diligently sought the will of the Lord in this matter, and it has come to us that you should not do this. You are not the only one of us who has been stricken with this disease, Amelia. Be content with the medicines that were good enough for others. Don't make yourself of more importance than they."

Her very insides rebelled against the unfairness of his thinking. But an Amish woman would never argue with a man set in authority over her, never mind the bishop. There was only one thing she could say — and it was the truth. "I have to think of my boys."

"Then think of them. Think of them without a mother while you go off spending their future in a foreign country. Think of the example you set for them in taking your own course instead of listening to those who would guide you. Think how they will feel when you come home, poorer in every way except your own self-will."

Dismay and rebellion rose up in her throat and choked her, forcing her to bow her head. She could say nothing. Because in the eyes of the church, he was right.

But did it make her wrong to want to be healed? How could that be?

"It is causing a rift among our menfolk, the sale of your shop," Daniel Lapp said, more gently. "If you do not go for this treatment, you will not need to sell your business, and our men can turn their minds to the work of their own hands. We will have peace in our barns again and talk about the weather forecast and what kind of seed we'll plant in the spring, instead of whether or not Amelia Beiler will sell her husband's shop to an *Englisch* or an Amish man."

It was her fault that the Whinburg men hadn't the sense of a goose? That they were squabbling among themselves like children instead of acting like sensible adults?

Unbidden, a picture of Carrie on her knees in front of her mother-in-law's bare feet flashed into Amelia's memory. Carrie had humbled herself before the whole church in order to be obedient to the will of God. To do the right thing for peace in her household.

Could Amelia live with that example set

for her and not be encouraged to do the same? Did she have the strength to bend so that there would be peace in the *Gmee?*

Daniel Lapp nodded at her and took a step in the direction of the house. "You think it over. On your knees. I know you will do the right thing."

He was correct about that at least.

She'd be happy to do the right thing — if her heart would only tell her what it was.

CHAPTER 18

She was not under the *Bann* yet, but if she willfully disobeyed the guidance of the ones God had chosen to lead their community, she soon would be.

Bishop Daniel had shone the light on her path.

And yet Amelia could not walk in it.

She and the boys trudged home from a family dinner at Chris's, the snow squeaky clean as soap powder under their boots. There would be more snow by morning — which meant Amelia would be walking with the boys to Mamm and Daed's for dinner tomorrow night. At least tomorrow was an off Sunday, so she would not have to navigate drifted roads in the buggy with a horse who had been cooped up too long without exercise. Once in the house, she stripped the wet clothes off them and hustled them into the washroom for a hot bath, and when their skin glowed pink with cleanliness, she could only hope there would be no runny noses and coughs at this time next week.

Elam may have been willing for a bath, but when he got to the bottom of the stairs and looked up into the dark stairwell where his brother had run up moments before, his little body stiffened with resistance. "Mamm, can't I sleep with you?"

Instead of hauling him up the stairs by one arm as her own mother might have done, Amelia put the lamp on the floor, sat on the bottom tread, and pulled him into her lap. "You're a big boy. You haven't done such a thing since you were a baby. Why would you want to now?"

Elam looked up again, as if Matthew might come jumping out from around the corner, ridicule in his voice. "I'm afraid," he whispered.

"Of the dark?"

He nodded. The lamplight limned the rounded curve of his cheek and shone on blond hair that would darken as he got older. Her *Bobbel,* so small and so afraid.

"It's only dark, my little one. It's so weak that the lamplight chases it away. It can't touch you or hurt you."

"But it comes back. And Daed isn't here to protect us."

And suddenly she understood with heart-

344

breaking clarity what was really going on. Why hadn't she seen it? Because she'd been so concerned with herself that she hadn't spared enough time or thought for her children, that was why. *Father, forgive me. And give me words that will comfort him.*

"But there is One who is, Elam. And Daed is with Him right now, whispering in His mighty ear, asking Him to watch over us and protect us."

She waited a moment in silence. Matthew was the one who acted first and thought later, when he got into trouble. Elam was slower, more careful, thinking things out before he did them. Maybe that was the problem; as she knew herself, lying in the dark gave you far too much time to think.

"How do you know?" Elam whispered.

"Because I have prayed for that very thing, too, Daed and I together. And I know God has heard us, because I feel peace in my heart. He has taken away the scary things in the dark, and I'm able to close my eyes."

"If you close your eyes, the bad things will come."

"If I close my eyes," she contradicted him gently, "I can see God's great hand cup itself around our house and barn and everyone in it, keeping us safe until morning. No bad things will get past that hand, Elam."

"None?" His voice was stronger, and she took heart.

"Well, maybe a mosquito in the summertime."

His body shook in a silent giggle. "And He protects us all? Even the cat?"

She held him away a little. "What cat?"

"The one that comes at night." His cheeks reddened. "Sometimes I feed her."

Enoch had been allergic to fur, so the boys had never had a pet, making do instead with the barn cats at Maami's house. "Is this cat wild?"

"Maybe she was, but now mostly she's just hungry. I'm sorry, Mamm. I hear her outside, and I come down in the night to give her something to eat."

"Elam Beiler. I thought you were afraid of the dark, and here all the time it's been a delaying tactic."

"*Nei*, Mamm, honest. I was afraid, but . . ." A little moment of growing up seemed to happen, right before her eyes. "I guess I'm not, am I, if I can come down and feed her?"

"See? You're protecting this cat the same way the good *Gott* protects us."

He smiled, and his shoulders straightened, as if a load had been removed. "Can I feed

346

her now?"

"You can give her some of the scrapple we had for breakfast. And see if she'll spend the night in the mudroom. It's too cold out there for cats."

Elam slid off her lap and went into the kitchen, where she heard the clinking of a spoon on a saucer. She must be sleeping better than she thought if she hadn't heard those sounds late at night. She hadn't even realized that food was missing. When the kitchen door opened, she leaned on the jamb of the mudroom to see a little gray cat not much older than a kitten slip inside and welcome the food with feline joy. Elam was careful to shut the outside door, and she drew him into the kitchen, closing the mudroom door behind them.

"Can we keep her, Mamm?"

"Is she a good mouser?"

"I think she is. You can't see her bones."

"If she will earn her keep, she can stay." Elam hugged her, and she held him close, her little boy whose kindness had overcome his fear. "And now upstairs with you. It's way past time for bed."

"Mamm, why don't you sing with us anymore?" Elam wanted to know after prayers, as she tucked him into bed next to Matthew.

She sank into the low chair beside the bed. Another delaying tactic. "I sing with you." Why, it had only been . . . *ach*. Just how long had it been?

"Not in days, you haven't."

"Weeks." Matthew turned over and propped himself up on one elbow. "I want to sing the golden song."

Two weeks — maybe longer. Had she been so self-centered that she hadn't given her boys the minute it took to sing a verse — a little ritual they'd been keeping since babyhood — in that long?

"Then we'll sing it," she said. "*Denkes* for reminding me. How does it go?"

Each day I'll do a golden deed . . .

They knew the simple tune by heart, so she took the bass line and sang the responses, playing a different character — a fat man, a crotchety old lady, an angel — with each repetition. By the time they got to the end, the boys were giggling so hard they couldn't get the words out. Even when she'd kissed them good night and turned out the lamp, she heard Elam muffle a snort under the quilt. That made Matthew jostle him, which made Elam squeak and snuffle with the effort to be quiet.

But she pretended not to hear it as she went downstairs. An opportunity for a good laugh was all too rare these days. Who was she to shush one into silence?

As she cracked the mudroom door, she saw that the saucer was empty and the cat had curled up on a discarded jacket. Even the smallest members of the household were safe. Through the window she could see the snow falling faster, growing thicker by the minute. *It's going to be a wild one tonight — please, Lord, keep every last one of our folk safe as they make their way home.* Thank goodness the boys had brought in lots of wood earlier in the afternoon. With her good hand, she maneuvered two more logs onto the fire and thanked *Gott* for small blessings like a stove that could heat a whole house and keep them cozy on a night like tonight.

Why are you not content with the small blessings?

Mamm might as well have been in the room with her.

I am *content with them. I am even content with an unexpected pet. And isn't my health a blessing? Shouldn't I do everything I can to preserve what God has given me?*

Was she really putting herself above Lila Esch — thinking herself so much more valuable than any other sister in the faith?

I don't think that. I just want to be a mother to my boys. Why is that so bad?

Lila had probably wanted the same. And there was Victor Stolzfus, too — God had seen fit to take his mind and leave his body hale and strong. Had Victor struggled against His will and cried out in his most private thoughts, *Why me, Lord?*

Time and chance happened to all men. Maybe God wasn't in this at all. Maybe viruses and bad cells just were, and God allowed them to run amok in people, not because He had a plan but because humans were frail and that's just the way life was.

Amelia looked down at Matthew's pants in her lap, wondering how the mending had gotten there. She didn't remember sitting down and getting out her sewing box. It wasn't like her to lose track of herself — or to think rebellious thoughts such as these. Of course God had a plan. If He didn't, life would be too frightening, wouldn't it? She couldn't imagine going through the days without the knowledge that the Lord of the universe kept her in the palm of His hand, safe and warm, just the way she had explained it to Elam.

What she needed to do was get down on her knees for some serious prayer. Seek His face. Find out His will for her. Not sit here speculating about why viruses attacked one person and not another when both were in the same house — in the same room, even.

She set the mending aside and slid to her knees in front of the chair.

Lord, please help me to know Your will. Am I to go ahead and sell the shop and travel to Mexico for the treatment? Or is it Your plan that I stay here and do as Lila did, taking medicine each day and trying to keep up hope? If that's so, Lord, I will have to move back to Mamm and Daed's. Do You want them to bring up my sons in their old age?

An idea bounded into her head like a deer into the garden.

When her brother Mark moved here in the spring, the solution was not to live here while he and his family moved in with Mamm and Daed. No. She could deed this house over to him and take the boys back to the farm. It would be a trial to her soul to live under Mamm's thumb again, but at least the boys would not be forced to give up their prospects to nurse her. Mark would be close enough to walk over for the day's work, and Mamm would have guinea pigs in the house for her remedies. And Amelia would have somewhere to live until . . . until a wheelchair was not needed anymore.

She shut her eyes more tightly, hands clasped under her chin and feeling the prick of the scratchy carpet under her knees. How could she not have thought of this before? She'd been so worried about the boys and living arrangements and the details of life that she'd left the Lord out of the equation. And suddenly He'd sent the solution to her like a gift.

A solution that would wither her heart to dust even as her body withered to uselessness.

Behind her closed eyelids, darkness whirled, shot with erratic light that showed nothing. *Is this truly Your will, Lord? That I give up hope of health and bow to the will of those You've chosen to be my shepherds?*

She waited, the house silent and still save for the crackle of the fire, muffled behind the window in the door of the stove.

Thump. *Thump.*

Something heavy crashed against the front door.

Amelia's heart kicked in her chest, and she leaped practically out of her skin. She scrambled to her feet and staggered to the window, willing blood back into her tingling legs. She could see part of the front porch from here.

Daed? Emma?

Some trouble from the road? Maybe an *Englisch* driver had gone into the ditch and had walked down here looking for help. And

352

here she was, a woman alone except for two little boys and a cat, with not so much as a rolling pin to hand for protection.

The person thumped on the door with a fist and made a sound, but whether it was a cry for help or not, she couldn't tell.

Lord, protect me.

If anyone was in trouble on a cold, snowy night like tonight, she had to help.

She grasped the door handle and pulled it open, and Aaron King fell onto the mat in a whirl of snow.

Luckily, there was still some coffee left in the pot from this afternoon. Amelia heated it, poured in some cream, and handed it to the lanky boy in the chair in front of the stove, along with a big slice of pumpkin cake. He reached out of the blanket she'd bundled him in and took cake and mug cautiously, his feet as close to the stove as he could get them. The legs of his worldly jeans began to steam as he wolfed down the cake.

"Don't sit so close — when the fabric gets too hot, it will burn your legs."

"That would feel *gut*," he mumbled, his teeth clinking against the china mug. "I never was so cold in my life."

He'd had on a fancy denim jacket lined with fleece that now hung over the back of a chair, facing the stove. "That's because you're not wearing a proper coat. What were you thinking?" *And why are you here?*

"Honest?" He glanced up at her. "When I walk, I get too warm, so I didn't bother with the coat."

"I'm thinking you won't do that again." He shook his head. "You could have gotten disoriented and frozen without a soul knowing about it until your father missed you in the morning."

"It wasn't that bad," he muttered, but he hitched his chair a little closer to the warmth.

"What are you doing out this way?" She already knew, of course. But she wanted to see if he would tell her on his own.

His glance was sharp and wary, his answer not so. "It's a whiteout out there. I got all *verhuddelt* and turned in at the wrong lane. Sorry to bust in on you like this."

"I'm glad you did bust in. From the shape of you, you might not have made it over to the Stolzfus *Daadi Haus.*"

Silence.

"I know why you go there, Aaron. Emma told me."

"There's nothing wrong with it," he said into his mug. She could see he was trying to recover from the shock. "Lots of men date girls older than they are."

Oh, so brave, to risk his reputation like this in order to protect his secret. She got him another piece of cake. "Nothing wrong with it at all," she agreed quietly. "If that's what you were really doing. The wrong is in deceiving your parents."

"I'm not deceiving them. Nobody tells their folks who they're seeing."

She waited for him to listen to himself. After a moment she said, "I'm sure they've heard. But that's not the real reason, is it?"

More silence. He was probably stewing under that blanket, wondering what she was getting at and not daring to tell her. But she wasn't a mother for nothing, with a little experience at encouraging boys to tell the truth.

"I know about the writing, Aaron."

He sucked in a breath through his nose, and some cake crumbs went down the wrong pipe. "Who told you?" he said when he could speak.

"Emma herself. You and she and Alvin Esch, apparently, all in a club together."

"It's not like that. It's a safe place. My dad would never —"

"That's just the point. He would never allow it. You mustn't deceive him — it's not fitting, and it would grieve him."

"Amelia, he wouldn't grieve for one second. All he cares about is having another hand around the place. It never even occurs to him one of us might have a brain and want to use it."

"Maybe you should talk with him about it. He might surprise you." Martin King let Aaron drive around the countryside in that outrageous buggy, after all. How much worse could a silly letter to the editor be?

Aaron only shook his head. "Nothing I do makes him happy, so what difference does it make?"

"It's our place to obey our parents while we're under their roof," she said gently. "When you have your own place, then you can write as many letters to the editor as you want."

"Did you read it?" The slouch disappeared. The only time the boy came alive was when he talked about writing. The rest of the time, he behaved as if he didn't have a spine and depended on the chair to hold him up. "What did you think?"

"I thought it was nonsense." He flinched, as if she'd hit him. "Oh, not that you published a letter — that was very brave. But, Aaron, the basketball courts? If you're going to do something that will anger your father, at least you could write to urge a stop sign down at the corner where Victor was killed, or some other useful thing. Not about opening the basketball courts."

"I thought it would be fun for us to be able to play volleyball inside in the winter."

"You are the only one who thinks so, then. Who's going to go into town to play when there are warm barns all over the settlement?"

"I suppose you've never done something that everyone else thinks is nonsense." He slumped again, sulking.

She reached over and squeezed his hand. "I'm sorry I called your work nonsense. It was the subject I meant, not the act of it. And you're wrong. People have been telling me I'm doing something nonsensical for days."

"What — the Mexico trip? For your MS?"

If even oblivious Aaron had heard about it, it must be the subject of some pretty spirited discussion at Martin King's table. "Yes."

"Don't let what everybody else thinks stop you."

"But I'm not seventeen. I'm a widow with two youngsters who has to put them first. And I'm a member of the church, unlike some people I could mention. I have to obey Bishop Daniel if I want to be right."

"Emma thinks you should go."

She saw that his mug was empty, so she took it from him and put it in the sink. "Emma shouldn't talk about me with you."

"Oh, she wasn't. But from some things she said, I got the message."

"Well, what either of you thinks isn't important. It's what God thinks that matters." Even as she said the words, she felt a sinking in her soul. *Lord, I hope You will give me the strength to go through with it. Because right now I don't have any.*

"How do you know that what Bishop Daniel says is what God thinks? He could be speaking through Emma instead."

"I know because of a message to my heart, Aaron." She felt a bit strange saying such a thing to him. In the whole time she'd known him, they'd never discussed anything deeper than the length of a pallet nail.

"And I write because of a message to my heart. Because I have to. How come nobody says that's God's will for me?"

"Because nobody knows what you're doing, you rascal," she said crisply. "You can't take what you want to do and call it God's will. You have to pray about it."

He got up and shook out his wet pant legs. "Oh, I have. A lot. And the answer is always the same." He handed her the blanket. "Can

358

I borrow a coat? It's too late to go to Emma's, so I'll just head home."

She shook her head. "You're wet, and that wind would whistle through you like you were a chain-link fence. I'll get some more blankets, and you can bunk on the couch."

"Lucky thing there's no church in the morning."

"You'd have to go like that." Which would be impossible. Jeans and a worldly shirt in the holy place where God was? His mother would never recover. "Or borrow some of Enoch's clothes."

But, fortunately, they didn't have to deal with that. She got some blankets out of the linen cupboard, and when she returned to the front room, she found him gazing at her curiously. "What is it?"

"I always thought you didn't like me."

She straightened in surprise. "Whatever gave you that idea? I hope I didn't treat you badly." She tried to remember, but nothing came to mind other than perpetual exasperation at his slouching. "If I did, I'm sorry for it."

"No, nothing like that. It was more how you looked at me. Like you were mad at me for something, and I could never figure out what."

"Oh, Aaron." She put the blankets down

next to him and a pillow on top of the pile. "I ask your forgiveness. It wasn't you. Maybe I'm just . . ." She took a breath. "Just mad at my own situation. Mad at the way things are."

There. She'd admitted it — that this lump of anger lay inside her like a rock under a smooth-running stream. She was angry and afraid and hated the fact that she couldn't do what she felt was right for her boys. That she wasn't even allowed to try. That the good of the church was more important than the good of Amelia Beiler.

Ach, there it was. She was as much a rebel as Emma and Aaron, wasn't she? Only she hid her selfishness and unwillingness better — from the church and from herself.

"You could always write a letter." His voice was filled with kindness and sympathy, and in the lines of his face in the lamplight she got a glimpse of the man he might be someday.

She smiled, because he was trying to cheer her up. "Maybe I will," she said.

But the only place she'd want to send such a letter would be to Lebanon, Pennsylvania, and she'd made that impossible all by herself.

Next Sunday would be the Christmas ser-

360

vice, and early in the week Amelia's family began to roll in. Her aunt and uncle and several cousins in the New Hope connection were expected tomorrow and the next day. Christopher and Esther lived just over the hill, where Esther's kitchen was no doubt as busy as Ruth's while they prepared food days in advance. Their brother Saul and his wife, Connie, would come from Intercourse on Christmas Eve, as they always did, and at some point during the week Mark and his family would arrive in Lancaster on the big Amtrak train from Greensburg, the nearest station to their home outside Smicksburg.

She couldn't wait to see Mark and Adah and the children, including Emily and her new husband, but if she were to share her thoughts about Mark's taking over her mortgage, she would have to make up her mind once and for all before everyone got there.

Ruth kept a sharp eye on her at dinner. She didn't say anything, but when Amelia passed a dish of pickles to her cousin on her left with both hands — in case one of them failed and they had a repeat of the infamous beet-pickle-flinging incident — Ruth's lips folded together in a way that meant she was bottling her words, saving them up for later.

Sure enough, as Amelia and her sister Lavinia and the latter's thirteen-year-old twins helped clean off the huge table after dinner and got the desserts and coffee ready, Ruth pounced.

"How are your hands? Do you see any improvement?"

"How can I, Mamm? I'm not on any medication yet."

"Well, when are you going to start? And please don't tell me 'After I come back from Mexico.' You're not still planning to do that, are you?"

And here it was, days before she was ready to say the words. "I . . . I'm not sure."

"How can you not be sure? I heard that Daniel Lapp was forced to speak to you on Friday night."

"I don't know if he was *forced* to —"

"You've shamed us, Amelia. Your unwillingness to listen to the ones in authority forced him. Honestly, what does it say about you that you disobeyed your parents to the point that the bishop finally had to step in?"

Amelia's good dinner rolled uneasily in her stomach. She hated fighting with Mamm, and yet with a woman so outspoken it happened nearly every time they were together. "I'm trying the spirits. Trying to decide what's best for the boys and for myself."

"Folks older and wiser than you have already done so and given you their thoughts. You would do well to listen."

She would do well to go out to the woodshed and scream. But she merely said, "*Ja, Mamm*. And when do we expect Mark and Adah?"

She didn't have much of a hope that this would distract her mother, but for once Ruth allowed the conversation to veer from the course she'd charted for it. "They'll be here Thursday. How are you set for beds? I'm thinking their boys should stay with you."

"We'd love that. I'll find a mattress for young Ryan, since he's twelve and probably won't want to share a bed with the smaller ones. Or he and Matthew can bunk together in the second bedroom, since they're closer in age and Matthew worships him."

Lavinia chimed in, and they spent the rest of the evening visiting and making arrangements for everyone. Amelia sometimes wondered if her father thought these things just happened by magic. The men seemed so unaware of what went on behind the scenes, the careful logistics and planning that had to be in place before people came, so that everyone could focus on the joy of being together.

Christmas, after all, was the season for children, first and foremost for the Child whose birth they celebrated. But it was the women who made it happen with a thousand daily details, creating the atmosphere of happiness and homeliness that made such gatherings so special. Even Mary, so long ago, had probably done her best to make her little family comfortable in that faraway stable under the guiding star.

How many more Christmases did Amelia have before she could no longer manage mixing bowls and serving spoons? And now her left leg seemed to be acting up. Since Friday night the tingling in it had not gone away, and a chill of fear had lodged itself in her stomach. It hadn't even been two months since the first of the symptoms had appeared. Was the disease progressing fast? Was this normal? How was she to know?

She had no one to ask unless she called Dr. Hunter and told him she was ready to begin his standard course of medicine.

Lord, You've shown me a course to take. Could You please give me the strength to take it?

CHAPTER 19

Before the sun came up on Monday morning, while it was still just a gray promise in the east over the frozen fields, Amelia fed the little cat — who to Elam's delight had somehow moved into the house when nobody was looking — closed her eyes to the laundry waiting to be done, and loaded the boys into the buggy.

"They'll be fine here for the day," her sister Lavinia assured her when she got to the home farm. "You'll be feeling poorly after getting that tooth out, so maybe we'll just keep them for the night as well. After chores are done, there's fresh snow on our hill for sledding, and the twins have a new board game that they're dying to play."

Amelia hugged her in gratitude. Truth be told, she was feeling pretty sorry for herself right now, and she wasn't even in the dentist's chair yet. The trip into Whinburg went far too quickly, despite the fact that the roads were snowy because the plows hadn't made it out this far. Fortunately, the heavy trucks of the *Englisch* had packed it down as they came and went, and Daisy had careful feet.

She tied the horse to the hitching rail in front of the little complex housing Dr. Brucker's offices and threw a heavy blanket over her back to cut the wind. "You'll be all right here, girl. I shouldn't be more than an hour, and then you'll have to put up with me whining and crying all the way home."

Daisy snorted, as if to say she'd believe it when she saw it, and Amelia found herself smiling despite the butterflies in her stomach. She climbed the steps, picking her way carefully though someone had shoveled them off not very long ago. Maybe she was the first patient of the day, though at eight forty-five it already felt as if the day were half over.

She had no sooner opened the door with the brass plate on it and taken a step inside when her left leg went numb to the hip. It crumpled under her, and she fell through the doorway, still hanging on to the door handle for dear life. If she hadn't been, she'd have measured her length on the damp carpet before anyone could make a move to catch her.

"Ma'am, are you all right?" A young man, wearing what looked like a silver fastening bolt through his eyebrow and a couple of rings in his lip, grabbed her by the elbow. "Let me help you up."

He might be strange enough to willingly disfigure himself, but she couldn't fault his kindness or the strength in his arms as he set her on her feet the way Enoch used to stand up the bags of feed in the barn.

"Th-thank you." She brushed the snow off her skirts and tentatively put her weight on her right leg. Was this to be the way of it? The leg tingling in warning, then giving out completely whenever it felt like it? Just as her hands did. Was the wheelchair much closer than she'd feared even in the blackest hours of the night?

"You sure you're okay?" The young man peered into her face, then all at once seemed to realize he still had hold of her arm. "Excuse me."

"You're very kind, and I'm very clumsy. Thank you."

"Hey, no problem. It's kinda slippery out there, isn't it?"

Slippery was the least of her difficulties. But someone had raised him to care about other people, and the pierced lips had a nice smile. His teeth, certainly, were perfect. She smiled back, touched her *Kapp* to make sure it hadn't come unmoored in all the excitement, and turned to the receptionist, who was half out of her seat behind the counter, looking alarmed.

"I *told* them to shovel and sweep out there. Is that why you fell? Do you think we need to salt it, too?"

"No, no. It was my own clumsiness. I have a bad leg."

The receptionist — Darcy, that was her name — sank back in relief. "I'm sorry about that. Both the steps and your leg. Old football injury, huh?"

Amelia stared at her, lost. What on earth did she mean? The girl colored. "Never mind. Cultural reference. Dr. Brucker is snowed in this morning, so Dr. Sweeney is going to get you prepped for surgery, and by the time he's done, Dr. B should be here. Is that okay with you?"

"Dr. Sweeney is new?"

"He's been here awhile, but you haven't been coming in all that regularly for your checkups."

"It's difficult to get away," Amelia said lamely. Her teeth were not exactly number one on her list of things to worry about. As long as they kept chewing, she was satisfied. "I floss, though, as you told me last time, and I make the boys do it, too."

"That's good. Here we are. Just make yourself comfortable, and Dr. Sweeney will be back in a shake."

When the young man with the lip rings — now wearing a white dentist's coat — opened the connecting door and called her name a few minutes later, she stared at him in confusion. "I was expecting Dr. Sweeney."

"That's me." He smiled at her as if they were old friends and led her to the exam room. "Sorry, I should have introduced myself in the waiting room. I also should have realized that my first patient was Amish. Maybe I wouldn't have been so familiar."

Amelia shook her head while he maneuvered the chair so that she was lying nearly prone. Her bob, braided at the nape of her neck, forced her head too far forward, so she wriggled until it fit into a crease in the headrest a little better. "You were not too familiar. You were kind."

He adjusted a light on a plastic band on his head and turned on another light to shine in her mouth. "Open wide. I fall up steps all the time. My mom tells me it's because I have so much data in my head that sensory information doesn't have any room to get in."

" 'At's not 'y problem," she said around the pick. " 'Ine is MS."

He stopped probing. "MS? Yeah? Were you diagnosed recently? It doesn't say anything about that in your chart."

"Six or eight weeks ago," she said. "First it was my hands, then my arms. Now, this morning, my leg decided to go out on me."

"Tingling, numbness, even pain in the extremities? Burning?"

She nodded. Goodness. He was a dentist. How did he know about things outside the mouth?

"And you've had a positive diagnosis of MS, with MRIs and everything."

Hesitating now, she nodded again. "The doctor looked at the pictures, and he said he was nearly positive he saw lesions. Those combined with my symptoms made him sure."

"So the pictures didn't show lesions absolutely?"

"Not absolutely, but — Why are you asking me these questions?"

"Open."

She did, obediently. He probed around for a minute, his pick gentle on her gums, before he spoke again. "Amelia — can I call you that?"

"Uh-huh."

"You've got an awful lot of metal in here."

"Uh-huh." The results of a good twenty years' worth of trips to see Dr. Brucker. " 'At's why I'm here. Lost one."

"Okay, you can close. Yeah, I see that. Nothing a crown won't fix, and it will be much cheaper than an extraction. But what I'm concerned about is the number of fillings. See, there's been a lot of research lately on the subject, and we're finding out that people can have the symptoms you're describing and not have MS, or even fibromyalgia, at all."

Amelia went absolutely still, as motionless as a deer sensing something unfamiliar in the woods.

Dr. Sweeney didn't seem to notice. "These fillings you have here? They're old. We're encouraging people to have them taken out and replaced by a composite — you know, that white stuff that matches your teeth. Because one of the ingredients they use in the amalgam is mercury, and sometimes the heavy metals build up so much in a person's body that they start affecting the nervous system. So that would give you shooting pains, numbness, lack of responsiveness in the limbs, that kind of thing. Are you following me?"

She couldn't have taken her gaze from his face if the end of the world had happened then and there.

Or maybe it had, and he was the only one holding out a lifeline.

"Not MS?" she whispered.

"You'd have to get it checked out with blood tests and stuff, but it's worth it, don't you think? It's another road to try."

"What would I have to do? If it's true?"

"Well, first we'd replace all these bad boys so they quit leaching mercury into your system. That's a bunch of hours in the chair. Either you get crowns and fillings or we pull them all and give you false teeth. Your choice." Amelia shuddered. "Yeah, I'd go with the crowns myself. Then you go see a doc who puts you through detox — chelation, they call it. Diet, pills, supplements. Then, hopefully, things return to normal and you go on your way rejoicing."

"No wheelchair," she whispered.

"No wheelchair. If it turns out to be this and not MS for real."

Please, God. Let it be this. Is that why You didn't want me to go rushing off to Mexico? So I would stay long enough to go to the dentist and learn this?

Mercury poisoning. Of all the things she might have dreamed in her wildest imaginings, this was the absolute last she would have expected.

Dr. Sweeney muttered something about not needing surgical prep and left the room. Amelia lay there while the horizons of her world rolled back and the sun of hope burst over the rim, dazzling her with its brightness. If she had not been lying flat out with a tray full of instruments suspended over her chest, she would have fallen to her knees, praising God.

Who could imagine praising Him for being poisoned?

But compared to all the things she had feared, being poisoned was a blessing. It was curable. There was hope.

She could hardly wait to get out of here and have a blood test. How fast could Daisy cover the distance between this office and Dr. Stewart's?

Even when Dr. Sweeney brought out his big needle and drill and began to work on her tooth, she hardly felt it. Because try as she might not to let hope blossom in case it was cruelly crushed, she couldn't stop her mind from winging its way over fields and hills, imagining how she would tell her family and Carrie and Emma that she would not have to leave but that God had provided a way of escape and she might be cured.

And if it wanted to wing a little farther, say, in the direction of Lebanon . . . No. She reined in her unruly, impossible thoughts and focused on Dr. Sweeney's hands instead.

If all this turned out to be true, she was going to write the dentist's mother a thank-you letter.

The next day Amelia left the shop in David's and Melvin's hands and got to the bus stop just in time for the Number 46 bus that would take her out along Edgeware Road. At home half the laundry still waited for her, but she was going to close the washroom door and not think about it. Nothing was going to keep her from the quilting frolic with Emma and Carrie there today.

The boys had stayed overnight at Lavinia's and would come back to her at dinnertime, so she soaked in the strange sensation of being alone in the house while she made coffee and set the meat pies she'd put together last night in the oven to bake for lunch. When she went to the side window to look out across Moses Yoder's field for the fourth time, she saw a tall figure swathed in black making its way toward the house. A few minutes later, coming from the other direction, Carrie walked down the lane.

Amelia flung open the door, and the cat scooted in. "Hello, *Liewi*. What have you done with your buggy?"

Carrie removed her black bonnet and untied the knitted scarf under it, finally revealing her golden head and its slightly flattened *Kapp*. "I caught a ride with Erica and Joshua Yoder. Melvin is going to come and pick me up later. I hope you don't mind company for the whole afternoon."

"As if I could mind." Amelia hugged her tightly. Goodness, but Carrie was thin under her clothes. "Are you eating properly?"

"*Ja,* Mammi." Carrie made a face at her. "Better now that Melvin has steady work, thanks to you."

"Lucky for you my sister sent over a bag of jelly doughnuts. You're going to eat one right now, as soon as I pour the coffee."

"What's got you all in a buzz today? And where did that cat come from?" Out on the back porch, they heard feet stamping off snow, and then the kitchen door opened, preventing Amelia's reply.

"Let me take your coat."

Emma divested herself of all her wrappings, one by one, handing them to Amelia to make a big pile in her arms. "Mamm gave me new gums for Christmas, and am I ever grateful. They're higher than my old ones, so my feet are actually dry even after walking the field. Hullo, who are you?" She bent to pet the little cat as it wound around her ankles.

"That's Elam's cat," Amelia called from the closet, where she was hanging up their coats. "He calls it Smokey because it's gray."

"I didn't think you liked animals around the house," Carrie said. "You don't even like my chickens on the porch."

"Chickens belong in the barnyard — except at your house, where they're members of the family and have their own chairs at dinner." A woman's maternal instincts cropped out in the strangest places — in the summer you were as likely to find a chicken in Carrie's lap as you were a cat in any other household. "And the only reason we never had pets is that Enoch was allergic to them. But Elam befriended this one. I didn't have the heart to refuse him — he asks for so little."

Carrie had poured the coffee and set out the jelly doughnuts. "Aren't these supposed to come out later?" Emma wanted to know. "I smell something in the oven."

"We're going to live dangerously and eat our dessert before our dinner." Amelia grinned at her.

"Since when do you live dangerously?" Emma gave her the once-over from *Kapp* to shoes, the way the old ladies used to when the three of them were *Rumspring*ing and testing the limits of hem heights and hairdos. "Something's different. What are you up to?"

"Oh, about five foot seven." Emma rolled her eyes, and Amelia felt a laugh bubble up in her throat. "I have such good news — at least I hope it will be good — that I hardly know what to think or do or say."

"You'd better say something quick, or I'm going to shake you," Carrie told her. "Did Eli Fischer write again?"

"No. This has nothing to do with him."

Carrie looked a little disappointed.

"At least not . . . No. Nothing to do with men of any description. Well, one man, maybe."

"Amelia . . ." Emma's tone sounded a warning. "If you have good news, please tell us, because heaven knows you need some, and we want to share it."

Unable to keep it in any longer, Amelia plunged into the story of her visit to the dentist, watching their expressions go from concern to horror to astonishment to joy. With a shriek, Carrie threw her arms around her, and Emma hugged them both at once.

How long had it been since they'd celebrated something in such a childlike, uninhibited way? Carrie's engagement? The morning Amelia found out she was pregnant with Matthew? It felt like fresh, cold water in the desert after many miles of trudging under the hot sun, battling the mirages of the devil.

"So I went rattling over to the doctor's office after Dr. Sweeney did my crown and replaced two other fillings on that side, and I told her all about it," Amelia finished over her shoulder as she took the pies out of the oven. "She did a whole bunch of blood tests and promised that she'd get the results to me as fast as she could, even if she had to drive them out here herself."

"That would be the best kind of house call," Carrie said, her eyes glowing. "Oh, I hope it's true. I mean — I'm not glad that you have this poison in your blood, but that it's not MS."

"I'd welcome it," Amelia told them bluntly. "Anything is better than losing a limb at a time until I'm as useless as a tree after the ax is finished with it."

"You would never be useless, even if your arms and legs didn't work," Emma said. "Your spirit would have been an encouragement to everyone in the house."

"Maybe on the outside. But on the inside I would be in a screaming rage the whole time. So what good would the outside appearance be? The Lord would know, and eventually everyone else would, too."

"You never accepted your diagnosis, did you?" Carrie asked softly, obediently biting into a jelly doughnut between forkfuls of meat pie thick with mushrooms and onions and hot, buttered, mashed squash. "Did you plan to go to Mexico after all, despite what the men would say — and what Bishop Daniel would do?"

Amelia hesitated. They knew her too well. "I thought the Lord had shown me clearly that I should abandon Mexico and resign myself to the treatment that had been good enough for Lila Esch." They might as well know this, too. "That night Daniel spoke to me was the longest of my life — longer even than the first one I spent without Enoch, which I thought I would never survive. And long as it was, I never did come to the place of peace."

Carrie reached over and covered her hand. "I know you would have been willing to submit."

"It's one thing to know man's will, but it's terrible to have no clear picture of God's will. That is a very unhappy place to be. For every sign saying yes, there was another saying no." She glanced into the sitting room at the couch, where there was no evidence that Aaron had ever been there, much less spent the night. He'd been one of the signs saying no. "Now I wonder if all of it was meant to stall me just long enough to get to the dentist, where I could find out the real reason all this was happening to me. *If* this is what's happening. We don't know yet, and we won't until those results come back."

"They'll say you don't have MS," Emma told her firmly. "God would not have gone to so much trouble just to leave you in the same place. You'll see. It will all turn out well."

Amelia began to stack their plates. "It's in God's hands. Let's think about something else and make the time go faster. Where are we on our quilt?"

While she made short work of the cleanup, Carrie and Emma spread their squares on point on the sitting-room floor. When they had them all laid out, the three of them stood in the dining-room archway and gazed at the pattern. Emma took their hands and squeezed. "It really does look like a sunrise over green fields, doesn't it?"

The colors shifted and changed from cool to warm, moving through the shades of the rainbow and the flowers of summer.

"I've gone without hope ever since I saw that first doctor," Amelia said softly, "and here it was all the time, dawning over the fields we were making. I insisted on seeing just the fabric, not the meaning we were putting into it."

"That'll teach you." Carrie bumped her with one shoulder. "Never give up hope."

"That goes for more than quilts," Emma said quietly. "Amelia, I have to ask. . . . If your diagnosis turns out to be different, why did you say it would still have nothing to do with Eli Fischer?"

Amelia kept her gaze on the field of triangles and squares. "Because it doesn't. I made my choice, and now I can't unmake it."

"Who says?" Carrie asked. "If your circumstances change, there's no reason your answer couldn't, too."

"I'm not going to chase him." The edges of the pieces were beginning to look a little blurry.

"I wouldn't say it was *chasing* a man to tell him you no longer have a life-threatening disease," Emma said. "Eli is a good man. He would rejoice with you."

"I know he would. But he'd also think I was hinting that he should maybe come

381

around again, and I can't do that." Amelia took a breath and let it out slowly. "I've learned my lesson. I'm too independent and too proud — too inclined to think like some of those tourist kids do, that it's all about me."

"I think that in Eli's mind it *is* all about you." Carrie grinned, but neither Amelia nor Emma smiled back. Instead Emma's brows drew together a little.

"You would not even write to him as a friend, to tell him your good news?" she asked. "You would let him hear it through Martin and Anna King?"

Amelia shrugged. "I can't control what people write about in their letters. Anyway, if it turns out that it isn't MS, then I'll still have a long row to hoe. I'll have dental work, chelation — whatever that involves — and who knows how long for recovery. I need to concentrate on getting well for the boys' sake. I can't think of anything else right now."

Emma didn't press her further but shot Carrie a glance that Amelia couldn't read. It was just too bad if the girls didn't like her answer. And if Emma was so eager for romance and courtship, she should try being a tiny bit more forward and see if she couldn't start her own.

Amelia ignored the little pang in the most secret part of her heart, protesting at every word. She'd meant it. She had learned her lesson. Galloping off to share her news in Lebanon was something the old Amelia might have considered. This Amelia knew better. When you took things into your own hands, it only led to trouble and gossip and the possibility of being separated from God's people. She couldn't go through that again.

"Shall we get to work?" Emma moved from between them and opened the sewing cabinet, changing the subject once and for all. "The rows will go together fast on the diagonal, even if I couldn't bring my machine today."

"I'll sew the seams if you two will pin and match them," Amelia said. "It's all I can do to get the pins in my *Kapp* and apron these days. I even had to wear one of my snap dresses to church last week because I couldn't get my fingers to work well enough to pin the front of my good dress."

Carrie and Emma each took a pincushion full of straight pins and knelt at opposite corners of the piecework. "Folks who are looking at the front of your dress hard enough to see whether it's snapped or pinned should be ashamed of themselves,"

Emma said. "No one will judge you for that."

"Maybe a month from now you'll be able to," Carrie said with as much of a smile as she could manage given the pins between her lips.

Maybe. Please, liewe Gott, *let that be so.*

Carrie brought her the first corner, and she bent her attention to her sewing. The afternoon measured itself out in squares and rows, and the sun had just dipped below the dark tracery of the hawthorn trees that lined the road when Amelia clipped the last thread and pushed back her chair. She shook out the pieced top, and the girls laid it on the floor once more.

"We've done good work," Carrie said.

"No pride there," Emma teased her.

"I can tell the truth without pride," Carrie retorted. "Facts are facts, and it's a fact that we work well together."

"*That* is a gift from God," Amelia told them. "Imagine trying to make a quilt with Mary Lapp."

"Or Mary Lapp and my mother-in-law," Carrie added. "Imagine what that would look like."

"A crazy quilt?" Emma suggested.

Amelia choked down a giggle. Carrie tried to stifle one, too, but the harder she tried not to laugh, the worse it got, until finally the two of them gave up entirely and just let go.

"Good thing the boys aren't here," Amelia gasped, wiping her eyes on her sleeve. "They would be correcting us for our disrespectful ways."

"It wouldn't be so —" Carrie stopped when Emma lifted her head, listening. *"Was isht?"*

"There's a car coming up the lane."

Amelia flew to the front window to see a small blue car nosing its way up a lane that was four inches deep in snow. Her heart seemed to stop in her chest.

A woman was at the wheel. A woman with red hair who clearly hadn't been exaggerating — who had meant it when she'd said she'd drive the results over personally if she had to.

"It's Dr. Stewart!"

She wrenched open the front door and would have run down the steps if Carrie hadn't grabbed her arm. "Amelia, you have no shoes on!"

So she was forced to wait behind the screen door until Dr. Stewart climbed out and waved a brown envelope. "Hi, Amelia. I have your results here."

She could not ask. If the news was bad —

if she still had to face the years with MS —
she could not bear it. Suspended between
hope and despair, she watched the doctor
pick her way across the snowy yard and up
the porch steps.

"Well, aren't you going to ask me?" Dr.
Stewart prompted.

Amelia opened her mouth, and no words
came out. A huge lump had formed in her
throat, and she couldn't force a single sound
around it.

"I will ask for her," Emma said, reaching
out to take the envelope. "I am Emma
Stolzfus, her friend from the farm next
door. What did the tests say?"

"Your blood is *full* of heavy metals." Dr.
Stewart's gaze locked with Amelia's. "You
don't have MS," she said clearly, slowly, as
if she wanted to make sure there would be
no misunderstanding. "You have mercury
poisoning, and starting today we're going to
do something about it."

Amelia's legs gave out, and she fell to her
knees on the cold boards of the porch floor.

But it had nothing to do with nerve damage — and everything to do with an over-
whelming surge of gratitude that lifted her
soul into the sky.

CHAPTER 20

Dear Eli,

Merry Christmas. I hope this letter finds you well. We are all well here, except that my two youngest brothers and my second-youngest sister tried to go ice-skating on the pond. It would have been fine except none of them know how to skate, so my sister is upstairs with a sprained ankle and my brothers have extra chores to do as punishment for not taking care of her.

I don't know if you heard, but I got a letter to the editor published in the *Whinburg Weekly.* People think it's foolishness, but I'm happy about it. Emma Stolzfus writes letters to *Family Life* all the time, but she doesn't use her name. I don't think people realize how many opinions of hers they've read or whose advice they're taking. Maybe if they knew, they'd think different about her.

I suppose you've heard we're courting. Me and Emma, I mean. People can say what they want, I guess, whether it's true or not. She's a smart woman. My old man says I'm not very smart, and maybe that's true. But at least I got a letter published and he hasn't.

Let's see, other news. We have about a hundred relatives here for *der Grischdaag.* And Amelia Beiler hasn't sold her shop yet. She got spoken to by the bishop and told to stay put. Mamm says she has lead poisoning and has to have all her teeth pulled, so I guess she'll be staying put for sure. My dad says if people would obey God and not get big ideas about going to Mexico, things like this wouldn't happen. I don't know about that. Last I heard, going to Mexico wasn't a sin. I'd sure like to go there someday.

I'd settle for Lebanon, though. Any sign of folks needing a hand up your way? If I don't get out of Whinburg, I'm liable to go crazy. All the girls here are too old, too young, or related to me. I'm strong, and I have my own buggy. Let me know.

It was nice to have you visit. Mamm

says to come back anytime.

Your cousin,
Aaron King

That winter, the old-timers said, brought the most snow any of them had seen since the 1950s. The days were dark with lowering cloud, and when it wasn't snowing, people emerged to dig themselves out with gradually decreasing patience. Even Bishop Daniel was heard to say that surely God Himself must be tired of snow. But the gloominess of storm following storm only made the rare sunny day more precious, the way a jewel in a tarnished setting shines more brightly for its surroundings. Then the boys were able to go outside, and even through the kitchen window Amelia could hear their shouts of laughter as they rode pieces of cardboard down the hill.

Her days were not easy.

After she'd made several visits to the dentist that seemed to take hours apiece, Amelia's mouth was finally rid of all the metal that had been working its damage. Then it was time for the cleansing process: vitamins, supplements, and strange new routines to help her body purify itself.

"For your personal hygiene, don't use things that contain petroleum," Dr. Stewart advised her, which meant she had to go to Karen Stolzfus for a beeswax lip balm instead of the store-bought one she'd been using since she was a teenager, and she had to change to a natural shampoo and homemade hand cream. "And eat lots of raw honey and olive oils." The first was easy — Karen bottled honey for the tourists in the summer from the bee boxes in the orchards. The second meant a trip to the fancy grocery in Strasburg and a little change in the flavor of her cooking.

The boys never noticed. And no matter how strange it sounded, Amelia followed the doctor's instructions to the letter. She was well schooled in obedience and taking no chances.

When the snow finally showed signs of easing up and the snowdrops on the south side of the house raised their shy heads to look about them, Amelia put on her prayer covering one morning and pinned it to her hair. It wasn't until she was halfway down the stairs to make breakfast that she realized she'd done it without thinking — without that fierce concentration that made mechanical movements as laborious as threading a needle with mittens on.

She paused on the stairs, hand over her pounding heart. Her range of motion was coming back.

It was working.

She tried to tamp down her excitement, to think practically and not get caught up in a tiny bit of progress and imagine herself cured. When they'd manifested, the symptoms had always come and gone like clouds in April. They would likely come and go for a while yet on their way out.

That's what her rational side said. The rest of her rejoiced at every molecule of change. Even a tiny step — the merest twitch of a muscle — was reason for celebration.

She was so focused on the climb out of the pit of despair that she had a hard time following the snowdrops' example and lifting her head to look about her. As a result, when Aaron King dropped into the shop one afternoon at the slushy end of January, for a split second she wondered why on earth he was so late for work.

No, no. What's the matter with you? He hasn't worked here in months. The mind was a funny thing. Maybe hers was so determined to block out that terrible time that it had skipped right over it and brought two separate days together the way she brought the two corners of a sheet together to fold it.

"Hello, Aaron. *Wie geht's?*"

"Hey, Amelia." For once he was dressed Amish, with broadfall pants and a plain shirt under his sack coat. His broad-brimmed black hat was pulled low over his forehead, as if he were trying to keep his ears warm. "I didn't expect you to be here."

She raised her brows. "Why not? Did you think I'd sold it?"

"No, I knew that Bishop Daniel told you not to. I just thought that with lead poisoning, you know, you wouldn't be up for it. Where'd you get that, by the way? I read on the Net that these kids in South America got it by chewing on the windowsills and eating the paint. Is that why you had to have all your teeth pulled?"

Was the boy crazy? *"Was in der Himmelswelt sagst du?"*

At her tone of astonishment, he looked nettled. "That's what Mamm said you had."

Amelia recovered herself. The grapevine did not have its facts in order, as usual. "I don't have lead poisoning, Aaron. It's mercury poisoning. From the fillings in my teeth. I had them taken out and replaced with composite. See?" She opened her mouth, and he peered inside. "No lead, no metal, just my own teeth. You shouldn't listen to gossip. It's a bad habit and just gets us all in *Druwwel.*"

392

With every word she spoke, he hunched his shoulders a little more. "Uh-oh. I guess I'm in it deep with Eli, then."

"Eli who?"

Now it was his turn to raise his brows at her. "Eli Fischer. Who else?"

Her heart jerked in her chest, and she took several deep breaths, reaching for calm. "Oh?"

"He's at our place. We were talking at supper last night, and he asked about you. About whether you had false teeth." He peered at her, and she stifled the urge to bare her teeth like a horse to show him again. "Guess not."

Eli. Well. The man had a perfect right to visit his relatives whenever he wanted. She had to stop thinking she might be a reason for anyone to do anything at all. That was vain and arrogant, and after all she'd been through, she should know better.

"I hope he's enjoying his visit," she managed to say in a normal tone.

"I don't think he is. So you haven't seen him?" He looked around the office as if the man might be hiding behind a cabinet, then strolled to the door to look in the back. But there was no one there except David and Melvin, hard at work on an order that Melvin had brought in after he'd talked the ear off some poor *Englischer* at a machine shop in Lancaster.

"I'd have told you if I had," she said. "If I'm not selling the shop, as you say, then he has no reason to come down here, does he?"

"Whatever. Guess I'll be on my way, then. I'll probably see him at dinner."

"Good-bye, Aaron."

When the door closed behind him, Amelia collapsed in her chair. *Breathe. In. Out. This means nothing to you. Whether he's been in town for a week or a day, it doesn't matter. And yes, you will see him on Sunday, and you will treat him as you would any friend. Nothing more.*

It wasn't as if they'd been corresponding, after all. She had not answered his impassioned letter, nor did she believe he expected her to. He had asked to court her on the spur of the moment, out of pity. At best it had been a burst of manly protective instincts. It didn't mean he'd been carrying unwanted feelings in his heart all this time and come dashing fifty miles or more when he heard news of her.

That was like something out of one of those novels Emma used to read when she was younger. Such things didn't happen in real life. Sensible plain people depended on the Lord to reveal His choice of partner, not their own flawed desires and impulses.

But her heart was not listening to this bracing lecture. Instead she felt a squeezing in her chest, as if two hands had taken her heart between them. *How long has he been in town? He hasn't come to see me. He took me at my word and has learned not to care. And I am a fool for wishing he hadn't.*

She must not let this grieve her. She had work to do — good work that provided for her boys and made her useful. She picked up her pencil and prepared to do battle with the accounts payable once more, when the phone rang and made her jump.

It won't be Eli. Control yourself. "Whinburg Pallet and Crate, this is Amelia Beiler speaking."

"Hey, Mrs. Beiler, remember me?"

She smiled, and it spread into her voice. "Mr. Burke, of course I remember you. You're one of my best customers. How are you?"

"I'm well. Better than well. I'm the happiest man in the world, and you're the woman I hold responsible for it."

Good heavens. Had he forgotten she'd told him weeks ago that the sale of her shop was off? "And why is that?"

"Remember that lunch we never had? And you told me the cook at the Dutch Deli was a widow?"

"Yes." That conversation belonged to another life, to a woman who seemed much younger and more innocent.

"Well, that cook's name is Liza Nielsen, soon to be Liza Burke! I proposed yesterday, and she said yes, and it's all your fault."

Amelia laughed. "I'd say you had something to do with it, too. I'm very happy for you. She's a lucky woman."

"I'm the lucky one. Would you be able to come to a garden party we're having by way of reception in the spring? Not the ceremony, because we're just going to a JP, but a little do afterward at our new place?"

By April she ought to be able to manage a knife and fork in public, one in each hand. "I would be honored. Thank you for thinking of me, Mr. Burke."

"Bernard. If you're going to eat canapés in my backyard, the least you can do is call me by my name. Liza would say the same."

What was a "can of pay"? Never mind. "Bernard, then."

"I'll send you an invitation with all the details as soon as we work them out."

"I'll look forward to it. Thank you."

"No, thank *you*. If not for you, I'd still be grouchy and single and wondering what to do with myself. Now I'll be grouchy and married and helping to run a fine little restaurant. You'll have to come by. I still owe you lunch."

"You don't owe me a thing, but I will come by sometime soon. Good-bye, Mist— Bernard."

She hung up the phone, still smiling. How kind people could be. She'd never been to a worldly wedding reception, but maybe it was time to learn a new thing or two. She couldn't picture Bernard Burke in anything but his baggy overalls and a trucker's cap. Maybe he would change clothes for his wedding.

Maybe Eli Fischer is here to find a different woman to drive home from church.

Angrily, Amelia chased the thought out of her mind, and it flapped off to sit in the distance, waiting for her next unguarded moment.

And there would be one. Of that she was sure.

Such a moment came that very evening. Amelia had just kissed Matthew and Elam good night — smiling because they could barely keep their eyes open long enough to say their prayers and sing a little verse after all their exercise in the snow — when she heard a knock on the kitchen door.

He's come. Her heart jumped into a gallop the way Daisy did when she got spooked by a gopher at the side of the road.

Nei. Schtobbe dich. It was probably Mamm, plowing over here in her rubber boots to give her the homemade hand cream she'd asked for or the shampoo she'd already gently refused because it smelled worse than any amount of dirty hair.

She forced herself to cross the kitchen at a walk, and when she pulled open the door, Emma blew in on a whirl of snowflakes.

"Oh, no, has it started snowing again?"

"*Ja,* just now. I can't stay long — I want to get home before Mamm goes to bed. She mustn't try to manage both the kerosene lamp and her oxygen tank."

Amelia kissed Emma on her red and chilly cheek and took her coat while the latter unwrapped her knitted kerchief. *See? Emma. Stop longing for what you can't have and be grateful for the gifts that come unannounced.* "I'm glad to see you. Please don't tell me you're here to say we can't come over tomorrow." It was Emma's turn to host the quilting frolic. How was she going to manage to avoid the subject of Eli Fischer for two hours? Maybe she should read the paper so she had plenty of other subjects to talk about.

"No, everything is fine." Emma took the iced cookie Amelia offered her and bent to pet Smokey. "I wanted to know if you'd heard."

"Heard what?" There could be any number of things to hear. Emma could be engaged to Aaron King, for all she knew.

Emma straightened, and Smokey vanished upstairs. "That Eli Fischer is back and staying with the Martin Kings."

"Aaron was by the shop today. He told me."

Emma's eyes narrowed. "Why would he do that? It's one thing for me or Carrie to say such a thing to you. Aaron has no business —"

"It's just as well. Apparently the word among the King connection is that I've got lead poisoning because I've been chewing on windowsills. No wonder I had to have all my teeth out and get false ones."

Emma practically spat cookie crumbs, and Amelia handed her a napkin along with a cup of *Kamilletee* — one of the things that Ruth was skilled at compounding. When she could speak, Emma said, "Well, that does beat all. Even the *Youngie* couldn't come up with that one in their games of Telephone."

"What it tells me is that Eli hasn't come back because there's . . . anything to attract him in Whinburg. Who would drive fifty miles because of a story like that? There must be some other reason." *And I don't want to know what it is.*

"The mud sales don't start until the end of February, so it can't be that. Another wedding, maybe."

"It's awfully late for a wedding."

"There's still lots of time." Emma twinkled across the table at her. "Stop playing like you don't know what he's here for."

"It's not me. If it were, he'd have come calling already."

"Maybe he's working up the courage to try again."

"Maybe you're imagining things."

"I don't think —"

Amelia held up a hand. "Emma. Much as I love you, you have to stop." Her voice wobbled, and all the humor drained out of Emma's face. "I have no hopes in that area, and it just hurts me when you talk as though I should. I told him no when he asked to come around. He's not going to ask again."

"But your situation is different now."

"Maybe. But it could be years before I'm better. I need to submit to those that have the rule over me and not try to manage everything by myself. Look what happened when I tried that."

"So you're just going to sit here and let life happen to you?" Emma's eyebrows rose. "You, the woman with an opinion about everything?"

"Too many opinions. Too much pride. Too much independence. I've learned my lessons, Emma, all too well." At least her voice sounded firm, no matter how much she wanted to bury her head in her arms and cry.

Emma gazed at her across the kitchen table, her eyes filling with her own pain. "But, Amelia . . . if it's true — if he really is here for you — what would you tell him?"

They needed more hot tea. Amelia got up to fetch the teapot from the counter. "There's no point in imagining such things."

"Just tell me."

Hands wrapped around the warm body of the pot, Amelia stared down at it. "I couldn't be so lucky a second time. I can't think about it, Emma. Please don't make me."

"All right, *Liewi*." Emma pushed her mug away and got up. "No more for me. I have to get home."

She pulled on all her layers again — shawl, coat, scarf, mittens — and went out, her tall, dear form disappearing into the dark as soon as she was out of the bar of light from the door. Amelia sighed and picked up the teapot. Her mother always said chamomile calmed the spirit as well as the stomach.

She poured a second cup, all the way to the top.

CHAPTER 21

Dear Eli,

If you were to tell me your life was none of my business, you would be right. But Amelia Beiler's life is my business, so for her sake I'm going to stick my neck out.

She is determined to walk the narrow path of obedience. She says she's too independent and proud, and God and the Gmee have conspired to show her the error of her ways. I don't agree. I bet if you were to talk to her, you could convince her that trying to get well isn't pride and looking for a cure isn't independence.

And shutting herself off from the chance of happiness isn't obedience.

Try again.

I want to plant celery in the spring. It will give people something to talk about.

Sincerely,
A friend

■ ■ ■ ■

At the quilting frolic the next day, Amelia was quite happy to let Carrie dominate the conversation as they shook out the pieced quilt top on the boys' bed and talked over all the different kinds of borders they could put on it. Carrie wanted to do a border of small squares set on point to make diamonds, but Emma disagreed. "It will be too busy. Besides, what will it say that will add to the message in the piecing? That our hope is surrounded by little bits of noise?"

Since the quilt was to be Emma's someday, Carrie deferred to her opinion, and the planning turned to how many borders and how wide they should be in order to accommodate the feather pattern Emma wanted.

Emma, Amelia noticed, was just as happy as she was to keep the attention away from herself, and when the conversation made a dangerous turn in the direction of men, she leaped to the switch and was happy to support Amelia in discussing Melvin and his odd knack for talking to people and bringing in business.

"I'm glad there's something he can contribute to the shop." Carrie's eyes glowed with pride and happiness — an expression they had seen all too rarely in the years she'd been married. "God does seem to have blessed him with a gift. I'm just glad it's one that can help you."

Carrie took the pieced top home with her, since they'd agreed on her house for next week. When she'd gotten her wraps on, Amelia stepped outside and automatically looked up to check the weather.

Clearing. What a miracle.

The sun had already put itself to bed in a bank of clouds close to the horizon, but at nearly four o'clock on a late January afternoon, that wasn't surprising. She'd better hurry, though, and get over to Mamm's for dinner and to collect the boys before it got really dark.

The fastest way there was by Edgeware Road, but even then, walking the half mile in the ruts in the snow made by passing vehicles was going to take longer than the ten minutes it took in summer. Thank goodness she could count on Daed or Chris to take them all home in the buggy after supper.

When she heard the rattle of a buggy coming along behind her at a decent pace, she had to abandon the nice hard track she'd been walking in and stamp a hole in the drift by the side of the road to wait until it passed.

But it didn't pass. Instead it slowed to a stop.

"May I offer you a lift?" The voice was pleasant, the voice of a good neighbor or a considerate driver.

The voice of Eli Fischer.

She lifted her head, and recognition flashed in his eyes.

He didn't realize it was me. Would he have stopped if he had?

"Amelia," he said on a long breath. "Please. Get in and let me take you wherever you're going."

She shook her head. *Please let me sound normal. Please don't let him know my heart is pounding fit to jump out of my chest.* "I don't want to give you any trouble. You were on your way somewhere at a pretty healthy clip, so it must be important."

"Was I? I was thinking, I guess, and didn't notice that Caesar here had picked up his feet. I mean it. Get in or I'll climb out and get you."

It was only a quarter of a mile. What harm could being in such close quarters do now? She could put on a pleasant, good-neighbor voice, too, and he would never know that her knees were shaking to the point she might stagger like a chicken getting up from a dust bath.

She settled into the left side of the buggy, reaching for calm. "*Denki,* Eli. It's very kind of you."

"It saves me from lying, it does."

She raised her brows in his direction as he shook the reins over the horse's back. "Lying?"

"I've been driving in circles, trying to come up with a story that would explain my turning up on your porch. And now, see? The Lord has saved me from myself."

He was going to turn up on my porch! Feeling a little giddy from adrenaline and hardly daring to believe he might mean what she thought he meant, she gave a shaky laugh. "You didn't need a story. You could just have come over, as friends do."

"Yes, but I wouldn't be coming as a friend. I mean, I would . . . but not entirely. I mean, there would be more to it than that."

They sat in a moving buggy. Her senses told her that the fields scrolled away on either side, white and punctuated by the cross-stitch of fences. But she felt as though she were in a bubble, as though her world had contracted to these few feet of space between storm front and rear wall, and outside there was nothing but silence.

Waiting.

The way the fields waited for spring.

She was supposed to say something. "Oh?" she managed.

The horse had slowed. Presently he stopped, waiting for direction from the driver. But the driver had turned sideways in his seat and was gazing at her with all the hope of harvest in his face.

"Amelia, I have been told a number of strange stories during the last few days, so I must hear the truth from you. You no longer have this MS? You have something else?"

She nodded. "I never had MS. The whole time it was mercury poisoning from my fillings. The dentist took them all out and put in white stuff that looks like my teeth. And now the doctor has me on a program to clean the metals out of my system. It's working, too." She smiled, dropping her gaze to her mittened hands. "I pinned on my *Kapp* without even thinking about it yesterday. I haven't been able to do that in weeks and weeks."

"So you are going to be well." The relief in his tone was palpable.

"*Ja*," she said softly. "I'm going to be well."

He came for you. What if he asks again? What are you going to say, after all your brave

408

words to your friends?

"I am glad to hear it. It pained me very much to see you suffer." He swallowed. Amelia held her breath.

An eternity burned itself out in a couple of seconds.

"Look at this horse, standing in the road." He shook the reins, and the buggy lurched into motion. Amelia's breath went out of her in a whoosh, and tears pricked her eyes.

Fool! He wasn't going to ask you . . . anything important. He's just a friend who is concerned for your well-being, like Moses Yoder or Mary Lapp or anyone in the Gmee. *There you go again, thinking you're the be-all and end-all. Shame on you.*

The last hundred yards progressed in silence until Amelia said, "My parents' lane is just there. I was going to get the boys, and we usually stay for supper."

Banal words. Words you could say to a neighbor. Words no one could find fault with.

And oh, how her treacherous heart longed for more!

This is a fine situation. You had your chance. There's no use crying over spilled milk, Amelia Beiler. Best to just pick up the bucket and move on.

The branches of the trees, weighed down

with snow, leaned into the lane and brushed the sides of the buggy. The lane had a single bend in it, and for a moment they lost sight of the house, now glowing in the twilight as though Mamm had just lit the lamps.

With a tightening of his hands, Eli pulled up the horse. "Amelia, there is something I must say, and you must stop me if you don't wish to hear it."

Her breath backed up in her throat. "What could a friend say that I wouldn't want to hear?"

"Simply that I don't want to be friends. I want to be more to you. I want it settled between us. Amelia, I told you my feelings months ago, and I wonder if today you might give me the same answer or a different one?"

She couldn't speak. She would weep if she did.

"I've heard you're too independent. Well, so am I. But we could learn to depend on each other, and on God."

"He . . . He has told me I'm too proud. You don't want that, Eli."

"No, I don't. But I have a little struggle with that, too. We could keep each other humble." He smiled. "I bet you're a much better pallet maker than I am."

"It's an easy skill to learn," she whispered.

"Will you teach me? Just in case I might ever have to know such a thing?"

For a split second, she teetered on the edge of two choices. But, really, there was no choice. Or rather her heart had made it long ago, and her mind had just caught up sometime during the last half mile. "Yes."

"Will you let me come and help you and get acquainted with your boys?"

"Yes." Like a newly opened spring, joy began to bubble up in her heart.

"I can't be Enoch," he said in a low tone. "Even if we decide to look into the future together, I can't ever replace the one you loved first. Nor would I want to."

His humility humbled her. "And I would never want to take the place of your Kate. Besides, you are Eli, and you can't be replaced."

"Would you be willing to think of the future someday, Amelia?"

The fields themselves gave her the only answer possible, as they waited for the warmth of the sun to soften them into usable, good soil once again.

"I already have," she whispered.

Something moved in the gray light — two somethings that called her in high voices that would deepen into the voices of men before she knew it, and before she was ready. She put a hand on the reins. "Come," she said. "Put the horse away and then come in for dinner. My family is waiting for us."

But before he could reply, Matthew and Elam had opened the driver's door and flung themselves, snowy boots and all, onto Eli's lap, shouting their greetings.

And somehow, when she moved even closer, his arms were long enough to fit around them all.

GLOSSARY

Spelling and definitions from Eugene S. Stine, *Pennsylvania German Dictionary* (Birdboro, PA: Pennsylvania German Society, 1996).

Bann: ban, state of being shunned
batzich: proud
bitte: please
Bobbel: baby
Daadi: Granddad
Daadi Haus: grandfather house
Daed: Dad; Father
Deitch: Pennsylvania Dutch language
denki: thank you; thanks
Dokterfraa: woman who dispenses home remedies
Druwwel: trouble
dummle sich: Hurry up
Eck: corner; tables where the bridal party sits
Es ist zu kalt fer dich.: It's too cold for you.

gakutz: throw up, vomit
genunk: enough
Gmee: congregation; community
Grischdaag, der: Christmas
grossmeenich: proud
Guder Mariye: Good morning
gut: good
Hallich Geburtsdaag: Happy birthday
Haus: house
Hochmut: haughtiness; pride
Isht gut: It's good
ja: yes
Kaffi: coffee
Kamille; Kamilletee: chamomile; chamomile
tea
Kapp: woman's prayer covering
leddich: single
Liewi: dear; darling
Mamm: Mom, Mother
Mammi: Grandma
Maad: maid
Meinding, die: shunning, the
meine Freundin: my friends
mupsich: ugly
nei: no
Ordnung: discipline; order
Plappermaul: blabbermouth; chatterbox
plotz: to fall
Rumspringe: running around
Schatzi: little treasure

Schtobbe dich: You stop it
schee Meedel: pretty girl
Ungeheier, es: the monster
verhuddelt: confused
Was isht?: What is it?
Was machst?: What's happening?
Was in der Himmelswelt sagst du?: What in heaven's name are you saying?
Was sagst du?: What did you say?
Was tut Sie hier?: What are you doing here?
Wie geht's?: How's it going?
Willkumm: Welcome
Youngie: young people
Zucker: sugar

CROSSES AND LOSSES QUILT INSTRUCTIONS

In the Amish Quilt trilogy, the characters make a quilt they call "Sunrise Over Green Fields," signifying the hope of the Cross rising over our lives and work. I hope you'll join me in making it as well, so I've divided the instructions into three parts to go with the three books in the series. In *The Wounded Heart,* we'll begin by piecing the quilt blocks. In Emma's book, *The Hidden Life,* coming in June 2012, we'll assemble the blocks together with background blocks and triangles, then sew the borders. Then, in Carrie's book, *The Tempted Soul,* coming in 2013, we'll choose quilting patterns, mark them on the fabric, and quilt. Lastly we'll bind the edges, and our quilts will be finished!

I pieced the top using 25 solid and patterned fabrics, with the piecing in each row in a different shade (from the bottom: blue, green, lavender, pink, peach). If you're like me and you have a drawerful of scraps from dresses and craft projects, this is a good way to use some of it. After all, Amish women use what's on hand. But if you want to use only two colors for the contrast piecing, or use only traditional Amish colors (black, blue, green, sage, lavender, burgundy, purple), or really get creative and make each piece a different color, go ahead. It's your quilt!

I based this project on a quilt dated 1898 in the collection of Faith and Stephen Brown. These instructions are for a twin-size bed quilt. Use fewer blocks for a crib quilt, a table runner, or a beautiful wall hanging. Alternatively, you can shrink each piece by 1/2 inch for the crib quilt; the finished block size will then be 7 1/2 inches.

Size (pieced area, no borders): approximately 38 × 65 inches
Block size: 9 1/2 inches
Number of pieced blocks: 15

EQUIPMENT:

Rotary cutter, mat, and lip-edge 5-inch-wide ruler (I use Olfa/Olipfa)
Thread to match background color

Scissors
Sewing machine

Yardage for pieced area only:

Background fabric: 3 yards of 45-inch wide
Dark contrast: 1 yard of 45-inch wide
Light contrast: 1 yard of 45-inch wide

For simplicity we'll measure yardage as though we're making a three-color quilt: one color for the background and a light and a dark for the contrast piecing. If you're using lots of different fabrics, or using fat quarters, make sure you have enough to make up the total contrast measurement.

Piecing the Blocks

Preshrink all fabrics. If you're using cottons or cotton blends, you want the fabric to shrink before you cut it, not after it's sewn into your quilt. Dry in a hot dryer to shrink fabrics as far as they'll go, and press everything smooth so it's easy to cut.

The Crosses and Losses block appears complicated, but if you look closely, it's just a square divided into four smaller squares. Those in turn are divided into four even smaller squares, making 16 total squares in the block, some of which are formed by two triangles joined together. We're going to piece the smaller squares first, then sew them together in rows.

For the most part, we don't cut individual squares and triangles. We cut strips, cut them across, rearrange colors, and sew those pieces together. All pieces are sewn with a 1/4-inch seam allowance.

Follow these steps for each block in the quilt.

Step 1: Background Triangles

a. Fold your background fabric right sides together, selvedges together.

b. Using the rotary cutter, ruler, and mat, and cutting across the grain (ninety degrees from the selvedge), cut a strip 3 inches wide.

c. Cut five 3-inch squares across the strip (remembering that you have to cut only once because there are two layers of fabric).

d. Cut each square from corner to corner to form 2 triangles, giving you 20 triangles total. You'll have some triangles left over; use them in the next block.

Step 2: Dark Triangles

a. Fold your dark contrast fabric right sides together, selvedges together.

b. Again, cutting across the grain, cut a strip 3 inches wide.

c. Cut one 3-inch square across the strip (remembering that you have to cut only once because there are two layers of fabric).

d. Cut each square from corner to corner to form 2 triangles, giving you 4 triangles total.

Step 3: Light Triangles

a. Fold your light contrast fabric right sides together, selvedges together.

b. Again, cutting across the grain, cut a strip 3 inches wide.

c. Cut three 3-inch squares across the strip (remembering that you have to cut only once because there are two layers of fabric).

d. Cut each square from corner to corner to form 2 triangles, giving you 12 triangles total. You'll have some triangles left over; use them in the next block.

Step 4: Squares

    a. Cut a 2 3/4-inch strip from each of your background and dark contrast fabrics.

    b. Cut two 2 3/4-inch squares across the strip of background fabric to make 4 squares total.

    c. Cut one 2 3/4-inch square across the strip of dark contrast fabric to make 2 squares total.

Step 5: Bicolor Light Squares

    a. Matching the long sides, with right sides together, pin the 6 light triangles to 6 of the background triangles.

    b. Sew the triangles together along the long side in a continuous chain (meaning sew the triangles one after the other in a sort of kite string, not cutting the threads in between) to make a chain of 6 bicolored squares. Be careful that you don't actually stitch the squares to each other.

    c. Cut the threads and press the seams toward the darker fabric. You should have 6 bicolor light squares.

Step 6: Bicolor Dark Squares

a. Matching the long sides, with right sides together, pin the 4 dark triangles to the remaining 4 background triangles.

b. Sew the triangles together along the long side in a continuous chain (meaning sew the triangles one after the other, not cutting the threads in between) to make a chain of 4 bicolored squares. Again, be careful that you don't actually stitch the squares to each other.

c. Cut the threads and press the seams toward the darker fabric. You should have 4 bicolor dark squares.

Step 7: Row 1

a. Sew one background square to the light triangle side of one bicolor light square, as shown.

b. Sew the background fabric side of a bicolor dark square to the light triangle side of a bicolor light square, as shown.

c. Press seams toward the darker color.

d. Sew the background triangle side of the first pair to the dark triangle side of the second pair, as shown, and press.

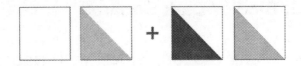

Step 8: Row 2

    a. Sew the light triangle side of a bicolor light square to a background square, as shown.

    b. Sew the dark triangle side of a bicolor dark square to a dark square, as shown.

    c. Press seams toward the darker color.

    d. Sew the light square side of the first square to the dark square side of the second pair, as shown, and press.

Step 9: Row 3

    a. Sew the dark triangle side of a bicolor dark square to a dark square, as shown.

    b. Sew the light triangle side of a bicolor light square to a background square, as shown.

    c. Press seams toward the darker color.

    d. Sew the dark square side of the first pair to the background square side of the second pair, as shown, and press.

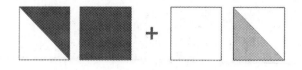

Step 10: Row 4

    a. Sew the light triangle side of a bicolor light square to the background side of a bicolor dark square.

    b. Sew the light triangle side of a bicolor light square to a background square.

    c. Press seams toward the darker color.

    d. Sew the dark triangle side of the first pair to the background triangle side of the second pair, as shown, and press.

Step 11: Assemble the Block

    a. Press the seams of each row in opposite directions so they lie flat when sewn together. (i.e., for Row 1 press right, left, right; for Row 2 press left, right, left; etc.)

    b. Sew your rows together, as shown.

Match your seams as closely as you can.

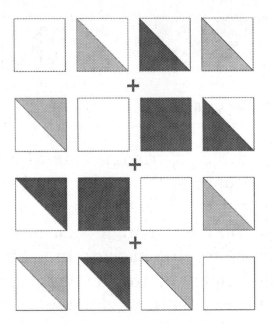

Step 12: *Isht Gut!*

a. Admire your work (without indulging in *Hochmut,* of course).
b. Make 14 more blocks.

READING GROUP GUIDE

a. Amelia, Emma, and Carrie have been best friends since childhood and talk everything out with one another. Do you have relationships like this in your life?

b. What kinds of things do you talk about with your closest friends? What do you keep to yourself?

c. Amelia's parents, Isaac and Ruth Lehman, keep strictly to the old ways. Do you think it was difficult for them to advise Amelia to stick to the tried and true in her treatment?

d. The bishop advises Amelia to stay home for traditional treatment and not to try anything new, even though it might have helped her. If you had been in Amelia's position, what might you have done?

e. Amelia's greatest struggle is with independent thinking in a community that values humility of mind and obedience. Was she successful in curbing her independence?

f. The Amish believe that the woman's place is in the home. What did you think of the way Amelia ran both her husband's shop and her home?

g. Why did Amelia turn down Eli Fischer's offer of help?

h. The Amish put greater value on what people do than what they say. Are you someone who talks things out, or do you tend to go straight into action?

i. Emma struggles with being single, and Carrie struggles with being childless. If you have experienced either of these struggles, how did you handle it?

j. If you had a chance to live as the Amish do for one week, without electricity or cars and always in submission to authority, would you do it? Why or why not?